Whispered MUSIC

by

Rachel Van Dyken

Whispered Music
London Fairy Tales, Book 2
by Rachel Van Dyken
Blue Tulip Publishing

Second Edition

ISBN 13 978-1502321978
ISBN 1502321971
Cover art designed by P.S. Cover Design

It's impossible to thank all the many people that helped make this story what it is. But I'd like to give a special thanks to Laura Heritage. You kept me sane during the times when I would argue with my own characters! Thank you so much for your friendship and tireless hours helping and supporting me! Love you!

PROLOGUE

"HANDS AT THIS ANGLE, young master." Mr. Field was always careful in his scoldings, and for that young Dominique was grateful. He had heard whisperings that not all music teachers were as kind as Mr. Field.

A prodigy—the name hovered over him like a blazing sign. At eleven, even his boyish mind knew that life would never be simple. When other little boys were outside running and playing in the streams, Dominique was in the great practice room tapping away at the ivory.

Music was to Dominique what breathing was to everyone else. He wasn't able to quit the melodies pounding through his head—through his dreams. Often, he would sneak down to the practice room in the middle of the night because his fingers itched so heavily to touch the keys of his favorite instrument. If the music was not played, sleep would not come.

The crescendos, the notes—everything had always existed in his mind. The major scale of beautiful notes descended upon him in times of great happiness, the minor scales—the scales of sharps and flats—often during times of danger. His teacher, Mr. Field, said it was a gift, that all prodigies had a sixth sense. Dominique, however, felt different, too different to play with others his own age. So he poured himself into music as much as he could to his mother's utter delight, for she was always doting on him, telling him that one day he would be a great master and that people from all over the world would pay to hear his gift.

His father, the Royal Prince Maksylov, thought music was only for the weak-minded, and often told young Dominique that unless he grew strong in physical build and learned how to play with others, nobody would ever follow him. That he, as a musician, could never lead.

And so Dominique led the life of being pulled by two parents: one in the direction of the piano room, and the other to the outside light. Both directions held certain feelings of excitement and fear, for Dominique hated to fail at anything and often found it frustrating to have to concentrate on more than one task at a time.

A certain evening, after his parents had gotten in another fight over his musical education, Dominique had snuck into bed careful not to let any of the servants see the pooling of tears around his eyes. He cried, not for himself, but the love lost, for it seemed both parents never saw him as the boy he was, only what they wanted him to be.

After the servants had gone to bed, a slow haunting melody began burning in the back of Dominique's mind. Closing his eyes against the onslaught of music, he put the pillow over his head. But the music would not quit. Minor chords filled with dread and pain drifted in and out of his mind until he thought he would go mad. Finally, unable to keep his body from moving, his fingers carefully started playing the melody in the air, imagining the pianos keys underneath his finger tips as he played the song that would not leave him.

The song progressed; it became more and more angry. The hair on Dominique's arms stood on end. Surely he would die this way! The music was finally coming for him! There was no other option in his mind. He had always thought about how he would die. There was nothing simple about dying for any prodigy. For a musician, there was always music. Always a benediction telling the sad tale of a person's life that had gone unlived.

With a squeal, Dominique ran downstairs to the practice room. If he was to die, he needed to be next to the music; the only hope, it seemed, was to play that song and pray it never return to his head.

He threw open the doors to the practice room just in time to see his father pull back the trigger of a pistol and his mother fall to the ground in a bloody heap. Then, his father turned hate-filled eyes toward Dominique. With sickening fear, he noticed his teacher, Mr. Field, also lying on the floor, dead, just behind the couch. His soulless stare went right past him and his coloring was a grayish white.

"What are you about, boy?"

"Papa!" Dominique froze in place. "Papa, you hurt Mama! What have you done? You—you beast!"

"Beast?" His father laughed, madness etched across his face. He took a stumble to the side-board and poured himself more brandy, not sure at all on his feet as he took a seat on the sofa, his booted foot only inches from Mr. Field's outstretched hand. "I give your mother everything! I give you everything and she repays me with betrayal!"

His voice shook the walls in the room and suddenly Dominique knew where the music had come from. Just as his teacher had said, it had come from within. He had sensed the danger, and the music once silent as he entered the room came back full force as his father trained his eyes on him.

Blood still dripped from the prince's hands as he smiled

and threw the glass of brandy on the floor, shattering it into pieces.

"So you think me a beast, boy?"

Dominique slowly backed away toward the door. It seemed his only hope was to somehow escape the nightmare he had walked into.

"Answer me!" His father wailed, throwing another glass to the floor. "Answer me now, boy!"

"No. No, Papa, you are no b-beast." Tears fell from Dominique's eyes of their own accord, streaking his face with the salty wetness of death.

In a flash, his father was behind him, locking the doors. The music crescendoed again. The finale—he could hear it; he could see it in his mind's eye.

"Well, boy. Why don't you go ahead and play. Play for me, play for your dead mother, and your wicked teacher. Play for us all!" His shout vibrated off Dominique's ears like he'd been shot himself. His father thrust his hands into the air as if directing some invisible choir.

He was mad! The teacher's body lay ever so lightly across his mother's; he needed to step over them in order to get to the piano. In that moment, Dominique knew he would die, knew that he would never get to play with other little boys. The cold stream by his house wouldn't get any use, for he would be dead, and dead little boys did not swim in cold streams.

With a deep breath, Dominique sat at the piano and began to play the melody.

His funeral march.

His benediction.

"Ah, such music is so pleasing. It is so sweet, Dominique, it nearly makes me ache with want, which is apparently what your witch of a mother was aching with. Don't you agree?"

Dominique continued to play, tears blurring his vision. Perhaps a servant would hear the music and think it odd? His mind rejected the notion. It was impossible, for he was often playing music through the night. But this night was unlike any other.

As he finished the song, his father yelled, "Keep playing!"

So Dominique continued to play and shook as he did so. He repeated the same song, for there was no other melody in his head he could find. His father came up behind him, casting a shadow in the candlelight.

"For your sins, for the sins of your mother, I will punish you, once and for all! May you never play again."

With a curse, his father snatched the candelabra from its perch on the piano and poured hot wax and fire onto Dominique's hands. When Dominique screamed in anguish and tried to pull away, his father merely held his hands next to Dominique's, taking the punishment with him, Dominique's struggles nothing for the giant man. His hatred was so deep that he would rather hurt himself and his son than not give any punishment whatsoever.

With a curse, his father threw him to the ground and marched over to the fireplace, taking Dominique's sheets of music with him.

"No! Papa, no!" Dominique wailed, for he had worked his entire existence on those songs. They were his everything. With a sneer his father threw them into the fire.

"Follow them into the fires of Perdition for all I care."

With a scream, Dominique charged his father, his blistered hands reached into the flames, grasping at the remnants of the music. It wasn't until his hands hit the scorching heat that he noticed his father was holding them there as well.

A scream would not come, though Dominique tried. The blackness enveloped him, and he felt once and for all, he had truly died.

15 years later

The carriage dipped, jolting Dominique from his nightmare. Always the same. Always that cursed song. Why was he never given respite? He looked down at his hands, covered by his gloves and never to be seen by the outside world. For their hideous scars were the stuff of legends and dark fairy tales. Surely the girl sitting across from him would expire on the spot if she saw what gruesome brutalities lay beneath his tortured gloves.

With a sigh, he leaned his head back against the leather of the seat. Had he done the right thing in taking her? Now he wasn't so sure.

He looked across the carriage. His gaze rested on the young girl. Isabelle was her name. Or, in his mind, Belle, for the music surrounding her was true beauty, nothing he had ever seen in his lifetime.

The carriage dipped again and the young beauty opened her eyes. "Are we there yet, my lord?"

"No." Dominique despised conversation of any type, especially with a woman. He hadn't any experience with the lot of them unless he needed to satisfy his beastly needs and even then, he never looked at their faces, never kissed them, and never took off his gloves. Women were good for only one thing. Besides that, they could not be trusted. They were full of betrayal and lies.

The young maiden licked her rose-colored lips and pushed her lustrous brown hair away from her face. "Are we close then?"

"Why?" he asked, irritated with her questions. Was she to plague him the entire trip?

"I'm thirsty." She looked embarrassed; her hands were

shaking just slightly. Blast, the girl was probably cold too. What did she think he was about? Being her nursemaid?

"We'll arrive soon enough." He cut off the conversation by looking out the window, so desperate was he to get the girl to stop talking, or at least stop staring at him the way she was, with such curiosity and contempt.

"Why did you take me?"

Dominique took a deep breath then turned his gaze back to the girl. Her piercing blue eyes made him desperate for her to stop looking at him. If there was one trait he was always constant on, it was his honesty. So he told her the truth, not because he was being kind, but because it was the only positive characteristic he had. After all, his mother had lied, his father had betrayed him and his music hadn't saved him at all. Honesty, it seemed, was his only mistress.

With a deep breath, he answered, "Because the minute I gazed upon you, the music changed."

CHAPTER ONE

It is imperative that while writing music, you allow yourself to be lost to it, for those who listen will be the ones who find it, and in that moment a masterpiece will be created.

~The Diary of Dominique Maksylov

ISABELLE BLINKED SEVERAL TIMES. She told herself to take a breath, or speak, or acknowledge that she had in fact heard what the man had just spoken to her, but she seemed paralyzed.

The music.

He'd said the music changed. What the devil did that mean? And why did his eyes close so often as if he was trying to shut out the world? Pain etched in his brow each time he wrung his hands together and try as she might, she could not figure out the man sitting across from her.

She had heard that Dominique Maksylov was eccentric, a beast, in fact, for he bore some sort of bodily scar given to him by his late father, the royal prince. But everything about the man sitting across from her screamed beauty more than beast.

Oh, with his hair unfashionably long and the overgrowth of beard across his face, he looked like a savage from a foreign land, but he was tall, graceful. Every movement he made seemed as if he was conducting some sort of invisible symphony, even when he lifted his hand to push back the curtains of the carriage. She found her eyes positively transfixed—bewitched by such a simple movement.

It made her wonder what else the man did besides play the piano and write terribly tragic music. There had to be some other purpose for this perfect specimen sitting opposite her. Perhaps she was guilty of reading too many gothic novels, but the way his full lips pursed together, how his hair managed to look wild yet purposefully so, well, he appeared like some fallen angel or a werewolf searching the countryside for his long lost love. Isabelle suppressed a giggle; obviously she was left alone too often. For those were nothing but stories, and her reality sat stone-faced across from her; emptiness and longing was etched on his every feature.

It was said that the Queen cried for two days after one of the court musicians played one of Dominique's songs. That she, in such a fit of sadness, refused drink and food. Finally, the King himself ordered the doors to her room to be broken down so he could attend to her.

Isabelle had thought it a lovely story, for it showed how moved the woman had been by Dominique's music, though she had to admit, only someone truly obsessed would go to such extremes. And as much as she loved music, she couldn't fathom being so moved by it. It was difficult for her to understand how the man across from her could make anything beautiful, haunting. Absolutely.

The carriage jolted.

Isabelle pretended not to watch as Dominique clenched his gloved hands in his lap again, and a scowl of pain stretched across his face.

"Are you well?" she asked before she could guard her tongue from being so impertinent.

His cold blue eyes pierced the air between them. She would not look away, could not back down from such a frigid stare even though it gave her chills down to her toes.

"My health is none of your concern. Believe me, if I desire for a nursemaid, I would have married one, instead of you."

"Married?" Isabelle nearly choked on the word. The man was mad! He had kidnapped her! The thought had occurred to her that she would be well and ruined, but never did she think she would be saddled to such a man as this! "What do you mean, 'married'?"

Dominique's head tilted, like that of a feral cat inspecting its meal. "I mean to make you my wife."

"Wife?" Isabelle repeated slowly.

"Yes, you do understand the meaning of the word, don't you? Or are you so young and innocent that I'm going to have to explain every little thing to you? Where we are, why we are going in that direction. Why the trees grow so tall, what is expected of the marriage bed. Truly if you mean to torture me, ask questions now so I can relax in the silence once your speech tires."

Isabelle's eyes widened until she was convinced all he could see was white peering back at him. Her fingers reached to grip the seat and she scolded her lip inwardly for trembling so. Yes, her feelings were hurt. So abrupt was he in his manners and temper! He needed a good lesson, or a paddling, or a mother! Truly, to speak to her in such a manner was beastly, and it was in that moment she decided it was no outward scar that marred him. The scars were on his heart, etched with darkness and bitterness. And even though she was sure he had meant to push her away, he did nothing but convince her all the more to play right into his hurtful words.

He had no reason to lie to her, and she did have all her

trunks, but her own mother hadn't even said goodbye to her! Why was she taken away so abruptly?

She told her lip to stop trembling again, carefully folded her hands in her lap and managed a tiny smile as she leaned forward. "It pleases me to no end to discover your ability to read minds, my lord! To think, I was pondering on every one of those questions and was so fearful to ask them. That is, until you so graciously offered your assistance. So tell me, why do the trees grow so tall?"

Dominique flinched as if someone had hit him and, with a scowl, looked out the window as he answered her. "You mock me? Do you truly wish to vex me this entire trip? I save your life and the thanks I get is a nattering woman who wishes to know why trees grow so tall. Lovely. Although I'm quite surprised your virgin mind didn't first venture to ask the most important question of all."

"And what is that, my lord?" Isabelle leaned even closer, only a breath away from his face. She meant to challenge him, to notify him of her strength so he wouldn't focus on her weakness.

"The marriage bed. After all, we shall be sharing it as soon as we get to my estate, and perhaps earlier if fortune smiles upon you."

He was bluffing. For the first time since their journey she saw doubt in his eyes; either he wasn't used to talking of such things and therefore was not as wicked as he wanted her to believe, or he in his own way was afraid of marriage and the love that came with it.

"Then tell me—" she challenged—"After all, I am such a curious sort. Innocent of the ways of the world. Regale me with stories, my lord. I wait with bated breath. After all, I grow bored and you won't even tell me how far we are in our trip to your estates."

Dominique kept his face impassive as he watched the whirlwind of emotions cross the beautiful Isabelle's features. The minx was bluffing, but he hadn't the heart to be so cruel to her in such short time. Granted, he wasn't sure he had a heart to begin with, but for some reason she tugged at him, which truthfully irritated him all the more.

And the blasted music rolling off of her was the most soothing sound he had heard in years. The chit would probably think him unhinged if she knew that every time she smiled he heard the trickling melody played in the key of G.

Swallowing, he slowly scanned her face, taking in every plane of her soft features. One such as he should not be rewarded with the perfection sitting across from him. Not after doing what he did.

"We, of course, need to cross the channel, then it is only a days' ride to my estate. I imagine we have at least a few days worth of travel with one another."

"You ignored my other question."

"What other question?" He lifted his eyebrow trying not to be amused at her bravery, stupid as it was.

"About the marriage bed." Her blush was becoming and he found a smile trying to crack through his stony features. Blast, it had been years since he felt a genuine smile.

All it took was reminding himself of women's deceit, folly, and finally, of his mother and the worst betrayal of all. It was as if a bucket of cold seawater had been thrown over his head. With a grimace he answered, "Ah yes, the marriage bed. I've half a mind to show you rather than tell, after all, you will soon be my wife, and if anyone needs a lesson in silence, it is you, my dear."

"I dare you."

"Pardon?" Was the woman mad? Did she not know who

he was? What he could do to her? The absolute power he had over her tiny, insignificant life? "You dare me?" At that, he did laugh, good and hard.

Isabelle's chin tilted up, her eyes challenging his.

He must be cursed, or mad, or dreaming, for he had never met a woman who would willingly dare him to do anything, especially when it included ruining her so thoroughly.

Before she could change her mind, he slipped his hands behind her head, jerking her closer. Warm, innocent lips met his with confusion, and then fear as they trembled under his touch. And he meant to make it worse, to make her loathe him, for it was the only way to keep himself safe.

He plundered her hair, wildly pulling the lush golden-brown strands as his mouth accosted hers. However, when she gasped against his lips, his blood roared, and he found that he couldn't stop the challenge even if he wanted to. With what felt much like a grunt or beastly roar, he drove his tongue into the ecstasy of her mouth. Desire shot through him at alarming speed when her tongue met his, carefully at first and then as wrapped up in passion as he. Her hands went to cup his face, softly rubbing his beard, his jaw, not once repaying his savagery with scorn of her own, but tenderness.

Enough to shatter the walls around his heart.

Her taste was sweet, but the need to protect himself was survival, so with great force he pushed her back against her seat and left her.

Her cherry-red lips stood out in contrast to her bright blue eyes as she stared back at him. Her hair was undone to her waist, wavy and thick, glistening in the carriage as if it was merely reflecting off her glowing face.

"I imagine that was your first kiss," he said.

"You imagine correctly." Her voice was slightly shaky. Dominique refused to feel guilty.

With a mocking laugh he tilted his head, trying to appear patronizing and cruel. "I could tell that it was your first kiss and I no longer feel guilty."

"Guilty? I'm surprised a man of your reputation even understands the word." Isabelle's scowl deepened.

"And to think, this whole time I was feeling guilty that I had stolen a London treasure and was being beastly in coveting you for myself, but now I see the truth. You're just like every other debutante—a cold English fish with no ability to drive a man wild with lust. Take your form..." He lifted a gloved hand with a flick of his wrist and shook his head. "You've no beautiful curves to speak of, plain brown hair, and frankly, the skill of the worst of courtesans. So, you see, I don't feel guilty. If anything I should be commended for taking you off their hands."

CHAPTER TWO

Music feeds the soul much like food feeds the body; starve your body of food and it will surely die. Starve your soul of music and I fear the ending would be catastrophic.

~The Diary of Dominique Maksylov

HIS RIDICULOUS SPEECH WAS met with a slap so hard he could do nothing save curse for several minutes as the stinging continued to throb across his face. The chit had attacked him! Surprisingly, he hadn't seen it coming, though he deserved it and more.

When he opened his eyes, the look on Isabelle's face haunted him, for it was the exact look he'd seen daily on his own mother's face after she'd fought with his father.

Memories came flooding back though he fought to keep them tucked away and, in that instant, he wanted nothing more than to be shot.

He deserved worse.

Perhaps to be trampled by the horses drawing his carriage.

Or poisoned by the woman sitting across from him.

But apologies were foreign words on Dominique's lips; they sounded gruff and awkward and, well, if he were being honest with himself, it would only be half-hearted. Yes, he had hurt her feelings, perhaps crossed a line. He grimaced as her face flushed a deeper hue of red. Perhaps he crossed several lines, but the truth of the matter was, by hurting her, he was doing her a favor. By causing her a short amount of pain he was keeping her from a lifetime of agony, for no woman would ever desire to be given false hope.

He could not love.

Would not love.

Had nothing to offer save his title and wealth and even that came at a great cost.

In an epic battle of right and wrong, he decided to change the subject. "We should be arriving at the ship within the hour. You should rest."

Isabelle glared, but did as she was told.

Dominique thanked God, for if the woman found this particular time to fight him at every turn, he would be half-tempted to give in to her. And that would prove dangerous for everyone, especially her. She had no idea the monster she was riding with, the sins he had committed, nor the blood that stained his hands.

Stains that refused to wash away.

Because they were scarred onto his very person.

With a scowl, he turned to look out the window, all the while convincing himself he'd done the right thing. His soul was still as black as ever, but at least he'd saved one woman. One innocent creature from certain Hell. Though one good deed was hardly enough to cover the darkness that consumed him.

Isabelle lurched awake as the carriage came to a stop.

"Out you go," Dominique, said as the door opened. The nighttime air was crisp and damp. Would winter never end? Perhaps it was the cold that made her shiver, surely it wasn't the fact that Dominique's touch still lingered on the small of her back as he helped her out of the carriage.

Abruptly, he removed his hand, and her body gave another involuntary shiver. Mortified, she looked away from his piercing gaze.

"Are you chilled?" he asked, though it would be a stretch to say any hint of concern laced his deep timbre. Icy blue eyes studied her boldly.

"No, merely repulsed," she answered, sweetly refusing to give into the treacherous feelings his touch gave her. Her once-innocent lips burned with the memory of his scorching kiss. Again, she turned away and began walking.

"Where are you going?" he asked, behind her.

"To the—" Isabelle looked around her. Where the devil was she?

Dominique chuckled. "I believe, my lady, that the ocean is in the opposite direction. That is, unless you plan on walking all the way back to London? I know I may be beastly, but believe me when I say there are wolves about. I daresay I'm not the most dangerous creature here."

Another shudder overtook her. "Wolves?"

"Oh yes." Dominique's white teeth glowed in the night. "Don't tell me you haven't heard the tale of the wretched wolf that hunts innocent women with his charm and manages to lull them into a deep sleep before killing them?"

"Ah, so the wolf is you? Self-fulfilling prophecy, my lord?" She stomped by him, hating that he was bringing out the worst in her with every turn. Isabelle had never spoken in such a way to any person and it broke her to do so, but how else was she to keep her wits about her?

"Self-fulfilling prophecy?" Dominique fell into step beside her. An amused smile broke across his face.

Heavens, he was beautiful when he smiled.

"No, my little Belle, it is merely an old tale told by fishermen's wives and those who are too ignorant to know the truth. The Wolf is, after all, a close companion to the Beast, didn't you know? Of course you didn't," he mocked. "At any rate, I'll protect you as much as I'm able."

"What are you going to do, growl at him?"

Dominique stopped in his tracks and with the ease and skill of the most cunning of predators, pulled her flush against his body. "If I have to. Though it seems my growl doesn't even scare you, does it, my lady?"

"I believe the *growl* you're referring to, and the purr that escaped your lips earlier when kissing me are one and the same." She pushed at his chest and stumbled over her own feet as she made her way toward the boat.

"I assure you it was a purr of disgust." Dominique sneered as he caught her arm before she truly did topple over, head first.

"So you say." With a jerk she pulled her arm away and continued to march toward the boat.

"Your Highness." A tall broad man with a Russian accent saluted Dominique and ordered the rest of the deckhands to grab their luggage.

Well, that was odd. He was an earl, not a prince. The idea that this man, this *beast* standing next to her was anything related to royalty was almost laughable.

Unfortunately, she choked on her laugh the minute she stepped onto the most beautiful ship she had ever seen, one of ten that her new husband owned. The *Lullaby* boasted of beautiful intricately carved wood that took her breath away. She barely had time to register her surroundings before Dominique roughly grabbed her arm and escorted her below deck, pushing her into the first room they came to.

"You will join me for dinner," he said, slamming the door in her face and leaving her no option in the matter.

Isabelle wasn't sure if she wanted to stick out her tongue or have a good cry. Wouldn't her sisters be worried about her? And her own mother? What had happened to everyone? Before Dominique had taken her, the family had been in an absolute uproar. Her mother had said that if her sister, Rosalind, didn't marry the Duke of Montmouth, people would begin dying in both of their families. It was believed that a gypsy had cursed them, making it impossible to marry outside the boundaries of both powerful families. The night she met Dominique for the first time, he had been arriving to take his rightful place as the only heir to the Hariss Earldom. Little did she know that the same night she met the beast, would also decide her fate for eternity. For the following morning she found herself in his carriage being escorted out of London, away from her home, her family, and everything she had ever known.

She only hoped that whatever hazards had befallen her two sisters and her mother—that Montmouth had still married Rosalind, and things were as they should be. One of them deserved the fairy tale ending, and since she knew it would never be her, Rosalind was the only logical choice.

Would Dominique even let her contact her family? Isabelle may have been a dreamer, but she wasn't stupid. There was no way this man could have taken her without her family's knowledge. Perhaps that was what hurt the most.

That she'd been sold off to the highest bidder.

One only had to look around to see the obvious wealth of the man, regardless of the money and title he inherited from her father's estate. The Russian beast had no need for an alliance of any kind. Besides, she had no dowry, nothing to offer the man save herself, and he had made it perfectly clear what he thought of her.

A cold English fish.

And although his music was quite famous, she had no idea it could bring the obvious profit she was seeing around her.

Sighing, she took a seat on the bed and looked around the dimly lit cabin. Gold casing covered the wardrobe in the corner. A small writing desk was nailed to the middle of the floor but it was adorned with gold plating on the front. A beast was carved out of the gold and would have normally given her a fright to look at it, but she had just spent hours in the carriage with one.

A mere portrait of one did nothing to her nerves.

A soft knock sounded at the door. Obviously it wasn't the brute coming back to order her around.

"Who is it?"

"Miss Ward." The reply was soft.

"Who are you?"

"I'm to help you ready yourself after such a long journey. Would you prefer me to come back later, my lady?"

Isabelle looked down at her wrinkled dress. It probably would be best for her to be more presentable, not that she was entertaining the thought of dining with that horrible man. But still.

"You may enter." She rose from the bed to greet the lady. Her eyes nearly fell out of her head when a short, plump woman of at least sixty and five bounced into the room.

"Thank you ever so much, my lady. I despise being out near all those scoundrels. To think! Having me travel this whole way by myself, without a chaperone!" The elderly lady patted her coiffure. "I could have been accosted! Or ruined! They stare at me with heat in their eyes. And I do not care for it at all! I cannot stand it!"

"Right." Isabelle tried not to smile, failing miserably. The woman was old enough to be a grandmother. To think that a man would willingly ruin her was the most amusing thing she had heard all day.

"What are you smiling about?" Miss Ward put her hands on generous hips and tilted her head. "Has the master put that lovely smile on your face then?"

Isabelle scowled. "The master, as you so lovingly call him, has locked me in my room and demanded I join him for dinner."

"He's used to people following his orders, my lady." Miss Ward made quick work as she lit candles, making the room immediately feel warmer and more inviting.

Isabelle snorted. "I'm sure he's used to a lot of things. But I am not one of his servants to be ordered about."

Miss Ward smiled. "No, my dear, you're to be his wife, and as his wife you are to mind him regardless of how beastly he can be."

Isabelle exhaled and punched the pillow next to her.

"There, there." Miss Ward took a seat on the bed. "Why don't I help you dress into a new gown, and we'll see about joining the master for dinner?"

"I'm not hungry," Isabelle argued, though her stomach chose that exact moment to growl. What was wrong with her? Never had she acted the part of a spoiled child, but the man had to understand. She had no idea how her family was faring and no way of communicating with them. And to make it worse, she was traveling with strangers to some unknown land.

Miss Ward raised a plump hand to Isabelle's face. "Things always seem easier to handle when you have a warm meal inside you."

Shoulders slumped in defeat, Isabelle nodded.

"Oh, I'm so glad you've agreed! I have the perfect dress! I sewed it myself, I've just been in absolute rapture these past few weeks, in hopes that a lady as beautiful as you would be the one to wear it!"

"I would be honored." Isabelle gave Miss Ward a hug and began peeling off her gloves.

CHAPTER THREE

In my darkest times, music has been my lover, and for that I owe music all of my devotion, for when it counted, music lifted me up, whereas women let me down.

~The Diary of Dominique Maksylov

"WHERE IS SHE?" DOMINIQUE paced the creaky floorboards of the captain's room for the hundredth time. Didn't she know that punctuality was next to godliness? To keep him, of all people, waiting? Did she think she was the Queen?

A throat cleared.

He turned, nearly tripping over his own feet.

"Oh…it's you." Cursing, he merely waved his friend off to the nearest seat and continued his pacing.

"Apologies. By the look on your face, I can only imagine you hoped I'd be wearing a skirt that you could later lift with those gloved hands." Hunter Wolfbane, Royal Duke of Haverstone, smiled and took a seat, plopping his Hessians onto the chair in front of him. "I have to admit I'm used to more swooning when I enter a room."

"Yes, but the rooms you often enter are filled with women."

"Can't you at least pretend to swoon?"

"No."

"Mayhap you'll stumble a bit? It's so dreadfully hard on my ego when I'm not given the praise due to my infamous name."

Dominique let out a hearty laugh. His friend was as mad as ever. "You're nicknamed 'the wolf' for more than just your ability to sniff around women's skirts at court."

Hunter smiled. "Yes, that's true."

Dominique rolled his eyes. To think that the man sitting across from him was none other than the most feared spy in all of England. The smile on Hunter's face seemed careless and simple, yet Dominique knew the horrors that his good friend had seen over the years.

It irked Dominique that the man could be at such ease when seeing pain and death all around him. But he was the best money could afford. A more trustworthy man Dominique had never come across, which is why he needed him here, now.

"By your scowl, I take it I'm not here for a social visit?" Hunter asked, dropping his feet on the planked floor and leaning forward, all traces of a smile gone. His dark features gave him the obvious look of danger when he wasn't smiling. He stared at Dominique with his amber-colored eyes.

"Those blasted eyes could make a man confess a multitude of sins." Dominique swore.

Hunter laughed. "Or a woman confess a night full of pleasure."

"I'll take your word for it." Dominique gave a hollow laugh. The idea that he'd soon have his bride in his bed to confess her pleasure passed through his mind and darkened his thoughts. "I seem to have bought myself a bride."

"Well, leave it to you to just come out and say it. Never were one to mince words, eh, old friend? So, what do you need me to do? Kill her? Find her long lost family? Seduce her dress right off her curvaceous body and—"

"No," Dominique said tersely. "I need you to help me… er... That is..." *Blast.* Why was it so difficult to ask for help? "As you know, I'm not currently in a position to… ahem."

Hunter burst out laughing, "Devil take it! You want help with the chit! Don't even try denying it! You're blushing!"

"I am not—" Dominique roared and ceased his pacing at once. Desperation had made him send ahead for his good friend, but he hadn't thought asking for help would be so blasted difficult. He just wasn't sure how to treat a lady, and not just any lady, but one that represented so much goodness that he could hardly look into her eyes without drowning in the essence of her music. It was the first time in so many years, perhaps his entire existence that he felt at peace. She was the cause, and he could not help but think that perhaps he would be her downfall.

Dominique cleared his throat. "I figured of all my friends, you being the dearest—Cease puffing your chest before I throw you into the sea! As I was saying, you being the most honest, would be able to help me in my pursuit."

"Of what?"

"Getting her to marry me, of course."

Laughter was not the response he expected, though he should have. He had nothing to offer her save money, a title, and a royal lineage that could be traced back to the Czar himself.

But women didn't want such things. After all, his mother had been given everything. And look what happened? Still, it wasn't enough. He could offer her nothing of value, nothing that a girl with such presence could possibly crave.

She would desire children, and a warm bed filled with a

man who could bring her pleasure beyond her wildest imaginations.

What pleasure could he possibly bring with hands such as his? At first glance, Isabelle would despise his deformity, and if she truly knew the reason for it, she would flee.

And no matter how dangerous having her near was…He desired her more than he'd desired anything in his entire existence. But she could never know that. No one could ever know.

"Curious." Hunter cleared his throat. "Why would you obtain a wife in the first place? Don't take me wrong. I've always been a firm believer in using the fairer sex to get through lonely cold nights, but you've never shared that same sentiment."

Dominique wasn't sure how much he wanted to reveal to his friend; then again, perhaps if he knew the reasons it would help his cause.

"She was in danger."

Hunter leaned forward. "How so?"

"I don't know."

Hunter paused, his face a mix of confusion and calculation. "Care to explain?"

"I heard it."

"Insanity calling your name?"

Dominique itched to punch his very smug friend but tempered his irritation. "No, the music, the same music I heard the night my mother died. It followed the girl around the ballroom, and when she looked at me, I knew."

"That you were insane?" Hunter suggested cheerfully.

"No," Dominique growled. "That she was in danger."

"So you took her?"

"Bought her is more like it."

"From?" Hunter examined his nails and waited.

"You see, this is where the part turns into some sort of

gothic horror story. Her father died, or at least the man she had known as her father all her life. But, he was truthfully never her blood relation. The man who sold her to me, the valet to be exact, had an affair with her mother. So you see, it was legal."

"I was worried you were going to say you killed him."

Dominique gave a humorless laugh. "Yes well, too many loose ends and all that. Regardless, I saved her from a fate worse than death, and she should be thankful."

"Yes, I'm sure she's this very moment tracing your name with her hand and imagining what your children will look like," Hunter said dryly.

Dominique cursed and ran his hand through his hair. "It does not matter! I have her, and she is mine!" His fist pounded the table in front of them. "Will you help me or not?"

"I'll help you," came Hunters swift reply.

"Truly?" Dominique jerked his head up. "How?"

"Lie, of course," Hunter answered, examining his hand as he slowly withdrew one of his expensive gloves.

Dominique growled.

"Easy. It was a joke." Both gloves fully removed, Hunter swiftly took off his cloak and popped his knuckles before he pulled the dagger from the sheath strapped around his waist and stabbed it into the table.

"You have more than your music to offer the world, Dominique."

"Are you getting sentimental in your old age?"

"No." Hunter shrugged and flashed a smile. "Just telling you the truth. You do value honesty above all things and I value being honest to a man who I would rather die for than see hurt. If the woman cannot see what value you hold, then I pity her lack of heart."

Dominique shifted nervously on his feet not sure what to say after his friend's bold outburst.

A soft knock came at the door. It was her!

"Yes?" He cleared his throat and tried to force his face into a smile.

The door opened, slowly at first, then burst forth so hard he thought it would come off the hinges.

Miss Ward had her hand pressed over Isabelle's. It wasn't difficult to deduce that Isabelle had been too slow in opening the door and Miss Ward found it irritating. The blasted woman always did treat him like a child, poking her nose in his business when he could take care of things on his own.

"I believe you asked for the lady?" Miss Ward cleared her throat and shot him one of her looks that he imagined was supposed to cause his feet to shake within his Hessians.

"That will be all, Miss Ward. If you'll excuse us then?" He lifted an eyebrow, waiting for her to object, but instead she gave Isabelle's arm a little pat and closed the door behind her.

CHAPTER FOUR

One cannot simply learn music. For a state of being cannot simply be taught. One must feel music, one must breathe music, and in the end, one must be willing to die for it.

~The Diary of Dominique Maksylov

ISABELLE WATCHED DOMINIQUE'S MOUTH twitch, but wasn't sure if he was attempting to keep himself from growling or if that was his idea of a smile.

Either way, it was frightening. It would be so much easier to be unafraid if he would simply do something about his state of dress.

His face was now almost covered with a short beard, and his hair was falling into his eyes and down his shoulders. Yet, she could still see his piercing eyes, and for that reason alone, she remembered his handsomeness. Well, that and his blinding smile. But it wasn't often that he chose to offer one.

"My, my, you didn't tell me how attractive she would be," a male voice said from behind her.

With a gasp, she turned and nearly fainted when the man

set his eyes on her.

Truly, it was as if her lot in life was to be surrounded by men with eyes that seemed to pierce a person's soul.

Liquid-golden brown eyes glowed back at her. The man's face was undeniably handsome and strong. Thick black hair cascaded into a messy heap on his forehead; the man smiled revealing perfectly white teeth that much reminded her of a hungry wolf.

"Forgive my friend, Isabelle, he seems to have forgotten how to behave in front of a lady."

Isabelle snorted. "Yes well, that would put you in good company, wouldn't it, my lord?"

"Bravo!" The other man clapped. "And she packs such a bite too! Tell me, my dear, have you any interest in leaving him for me? I daresay I'd have you forgetting this beast's name after a few minutes in my company." He winked and folded his thick arms across his broad chest.

Isabelle instantly backed away.

"Sure, scare her more while you're at it, Hunter." Dominique's voice held somewhat of a cheerful humor, giving Isabelle pause. She whipped around to look at her captor's face.

A weight seemed to have momentarily lifted, and she wondered if possibly it was because of the other rude man in the room.

"This—" Dominique held out his hand and pointed at the other man—"Is my good friend, Hunter Wolfbane, Duke of Haverstone."

Isabelle gasped. "The Wolf?"

"Ah, my reputation precedes me. I always feel so jolly when others know of my certain skill set." His golden eyes blazed a hot trail from her head straight down to her toes.

And because she was exhausted, angry, and possibly a bit insane, Isabelle marched toward him and poked him in the chest. "Now see here! I may know who you are, but I also know you wouldn't hurt a hair on my head, not with bigger beast a few feet away from me! Whoever taught you manners anyway? Gypsies?"

"I think I'm in love." Hunter tilted his head and sighed.

Isabelle rolled her eyes. "I'm sick of being threatened." She turned her fury onto Dominique, who had the good sense to back up as she marched toward him. "You demanded I eat with you, so let us eat. Otherwise, I'm leaving."

Dominique's mouth opened then snapped shut. All the while Hunter clapped and howled with laughter.

"After you." Dominique pointed to the table on the far end of the room where a dinner lay in wait.

"Thank you," she huffed, still inwardly shaking over her outburst. Since being polite hadn't worked, she thought of a new tactic. If Dominique was going to be such a beast, perhaps he only responded well when people poked at him.

Which is exactly what she intended to do.

Poke him until he relented and let her go home, or at least learned manners.

All three of them sat at the table.

Both men reached for the meat but paused their hands mid-air when she cleared her throat.

"Gentlemen? We have not yet said grace. Now, please bow your heads." She cleared her throat. "Merciful God in Heaven, we beseech thee…" Was beseech an actual word? She continued, "We thank you for this lovely meal, though I apologize in advance for the men disgracing your holy table." A cough erupted, and then a foot began to tap on the floor. Isabelle was never one for church, and truthfully she hadn't a clue what else to say, but in that moment, knowing she was irritating the very man she wanted to irritate the most, a wicked thought took root. She was going to recite the longest prayer known to mankind, even if her stomach growled in protest. And so she continued for ten long minutes. "…Thank you, Lord. Amen."

At the ending both men cursed, which she was certain meant they were going straight to Perdition, considering she had just been talking to God, and they grabbed at the meat, proving their nicknames to be correct.

Beast and Wolf.

They ate in relative silence, except for the loud chewing and smacking of their lips. Good gracious, she thought, they were even more like their nicknames than she realized. They even ate like absolute animals! Isabelle wasn't sure which unnerved her more. The fact that neither man was speaking to her, or that the ship began to heave as it pushed away from the dock.

Getting sicker by the minute, she managed to steal a look at Dominique across the table.

"Did you know—" Hunter tore a piece of meat from the platter "—that Dominique enjoys long walks around his estate?"

"Hunter."

"He also enjoys furry animals, you know the ones. They live in the forest that surrounds his estate. I've heard he even has a squirrel as a friend."

"Hunter!" Dominique barked.

"He's a passionate lover as well. No lady leaves his bed without—"

Why wouldn't he stop talking? She felt slick with sweat and then the contents of Isabelle's stomach heaved onto the floor.

"Throwing up one's countenance," Hunter finished.

Isabelle moaned, too sick to feel mortified that she had just retched in front of two infuriatingly attractive men.

Half-expecting them to shy away from her in outrage, she was stunned to find Dominique immediately at her side.

"Can you walk? Here, just lean on me." He felt her forehead and mumbled something to Hunter, but she was barely listening. Her stomach did more flops.

Dominique led her out of the captain's quarters onto the deck of the large ship. They were already far away from shore, or at least it seemed that way. Everything was pitch black.

"The horizon. You need to look at the horizon," Dominique urged.

"There's nothing to look at. It's all black," she mumbled into his chest.

"Try," he demanded.

Nodding her head, she looked out at the horizon and still saw black but felt immensely better being on the deck rather than cooped up with the two men.

"You'll get your sea legs soon enough." Dominique sighed.

"Mayhap it was your presence that caused me to become ill."

"Wouldn't be the first time."

Isabelle's shoulders slumped. "I'm sorry. That was terribly rude of me. I don't mean to constantly be on the attack, it's just that…"

"It's better this way," Dominique growled. "This way I know exactly where you stand. Far, far away from myself, on the opposite end of what I could never hope to deserve or earn. Truly, if you were kind to me I may just have to like you, and as it so happens, we aren't in any danger of that happening—not now, not ever."

The man's mood swings were making her just as ill as the rocking boat. Shaking her head, she could only look at his stone cold face, the same face that minutes ago held compassion and tenderness. He either needed to visit Bedlam, or he truly was the type of man that would stop at nothing to push those away from him. Including her.

"I say, are you all right?" Hunter came up behind them. "Miss Ward says you should return to your room for a spell."

"No!" she blurted. "I mean, that is, may I stay out on the deck for a while? I'm not used to being in such close quarters."

Hunter studied her for a minute. "As long as you promise not to throw yourself overboard. I'm a dreadful swimmer and this one over here—" he pointed at Dominique "—would surely drown with all that facial hair."

Dominique's answer was to glare, but he didn't deny the truth.

Hunter was obviously trying to cheer her up, but the man was just as much a devil as Dominique was. Only more cunning in the way he minced words. Almost as if he was waiting for the right time for her weakness to consume her, before he devoured her. But then again, that could just be the sickness and imagination playing tricks on her.

"I'll try to restrain myself from such a calming idea," Isabelle retorted, then walked away from both men.

"Well, I believe that went swimmingly." Hunter clapped his hands together then pulled a cheroot out of his jacket and lit it. The winter air was crisp which was exactly what Dominique needed if his blood was to cool from being in such close proximity to Isabelle.

Her soft body smelled of lavender, and he found himself more than once breathing in the scent of her hair as he held her close to his body. For a moment he had forgotten who he was; his concern for her muddied his thoughts. That was until she stiffened beneath his touch.

How could he forget? He was the beast, and would always be such.

"Yes, well, I don't believe I'll be able to obtain her

matrimonial yes on a night such as this."

Hunter shook his head. "I wouldn't be so sure."

"What the devil are you talking about? She's ill! Even if she were healthy she still wouldn't be in agreeable mood."

His friend blew out a puff of smoke. "She doesn't have to be agreeable, she just has to agree, correct?"

"She'll agree. I own her." Dominique reminded him.

"Yes, but it seems to me she needs a little coaxing or reminding of that simple fact. She's strutting all over the deck like a peacock, perhaps she should be reminded why they call you the beast, and me the wolf?"

The last thing he wanted to do was threaten her, but he wasn't the most dangerous man in the vicinity. They could easily protect her between the two of them, but he would feel better if she was staying with him in the captain's quarters rather than on an entirely different part of the ship. And although he owned her, he still couldn't bring himself to completely ruin her further by forcing her to share a bed with him overnight in such a small area without first saying the vows.

And ship captains could perform ceremonies.

There would be no reason to wait.

Making his decision, he turned toward his friend. "How do we go about it?"

"Simple." Hunter shrugged. "Make her believe there can be an unhappy ending to this little fairy tale."

"Make her believe the nightmare," Dominique finished.

"Precisely, where men beat women, and women obey. We both know you wouldn't raise a hand to her, but she doesn't know that, nor does she know what secrets you hide, or the rage within you, or that you feel guilty when you accidently step on an ant. All she needs to know is that you'd be upset with her if she gave you reason to think she would not accept in front of the captain."

When Dominique didn't respond, Hunter continued, "You hired me for a reason. I can be your greatest ally or strongest enemy. I'm good at reading people. She's scared. She's trying to provoke you and see how far she can push you. In order to provide her the protection of your name as well as your bed—you must give her a true reason to fear the Beast. If you cannot do it, I will."

"Fine." Dominique bit out. "And if she never forgives me?"

"Then you've kept your feelings and your heart intact, then you wouldn't have throw yourself over a cliff for some simpering female. And we both know how disgusted you would be with yourself if you actually became vulnerable to the one person who had the power to break you with a single word or look."

Dominique felt uneasy about how well his friend knew him and how well he read Isabelle. Part of him knew that behind all of Hunter's cross words lay a hidden agenda, a purpose. Nothing Hunter did was without reason. He was the most brilliant man Dominique knew and had constantly badgered him about getting a wife and writing music that didn't provoke people to fall on their own swords.

The idea that he was now opposing the notion with such vehemence meant that he was likely using Dominique's greatest fears against him in order to get him to marry the girl quickly.

And for some reason, Dominique didn't care. Because he knew that Hunter was right about one thing. The girl was scared and her fear was what was protecting her from crumbling. If he fed the fear, he would have her in the palm of his hand.

His prize? Knowing she was safe from men like her father and men on this ship. It was all he could offer, and all he was willing to give.

With a curse he strolled toward where she stood on the opposite end of the boat.

Needing courage, he stole a glance at Hunter who had an amused smile on his face and was watching him from afar. A pox on him for making Dominique play the role of such a cad and tormentor!

"Isabelle?"

"Yes?" She turned around. Her blue eyes nearly made him forget the threat he was supposed to give her, but he stood strong. There were more dangerous men out there than him, and he would die before letting anyone touch what was his.

"You have two choices." He circled her slowly as he pulled a dagger out of his jacket and began to play with it.

"And if I don't care for either choice?" Her nostrils flared.

"Then I'll kill you." He said it simply, without emotion, and flicked the edge of the knife so it gleamed in the moonlight. "I would gut you from head to toe in front of the entire crew and throw your body overboard for the fish to consume. I'd cut out your heart and send it to your sisters, and then I would hunt both of them down until I did the same to them as well as the rest of your family."

"You're—you're bluffing!" Her eyes welled with tears.

He tilted his head and paused directly in front of her. "Care to try me?"

Her lower lip trembled as Dominique inwardly cursed again. He had to give her credit where it was due; she was stronger than any woman he had ever come across.

So lost was he in admiring her spunk that he almost didn't hear her answer.

"Do it," she whispered.

"Pardon?"

"I said, *do it*. You wouldn't touch me, not when you worked so hard to steal me away from everything I've known.

I'm not stupid. You wouldn't touch me."

Alarmed, Dominique struggled to hold firm to his threat. The cold blade touched her neck. Her sharp intake of breath gave him pause.

"Oh, believe me. I may not kill you now, but I'll touch you." He growled into her ear as he slowly traced the knife down her cheek. "I'll touch everything. I own you, body and soul, love. And I'll have it tonight or you'll see why they truly call me the beast."

Her bosom rose and fell so rapidly he was afraid she would pass out. Saints alive, he was an absolute cad! The most horrible of men! Whatever happened to asking politely? Or courting a woman instead of threatening to cause her bodily harm? He watched her lips purse into a thin line. Right, well, politeness was surely lost to him the minute he realized how dangerous the girl truly was.

"When do we wed?" She swallowed slowly, drawing his eyes to the expanse of her beautiful neck. A neck, that although he had just touched it with a dagger, he would much rather kiss than threaten.

"Immediately," Hunter chimed in from behind them. "Sorry. Didn't mean to interrupt this obvious lover's quarrel, but the old captain here said he can marry you straightaway. Isn't that fortunate?"

"So convenient," Isabelle agreed in a monotone.

"Splendid!" Hunter clapped his hands. "Now if you just stand here, Isabelle. Oh, merciful saint of my mother, do you bathe in lavender? Well, it's positively delicious drifting from your skin. I have half a mind to take a small nibble just below your ear there to—"

"Enough." Dominique pushed Hunter away. "Get on with it, captain."

Isabelle narrowed her eyes at Dominique but said nothing.

The captain cleared his throat. "Do you take this woman—"

"I do." Dominique interrupted.

"Um, yes, well." The captain turned to Isabelle. "And do you take this man—"

"Beast. Do I take this *beast*, and yes I do. Unfortunately." She continued to glare.

An exhale of relief from both Dominique and Hunter followed as the captain finished the small ceremony and announced that they could kiss.

Throat suddenly dry, Dominique wasn't sure if he should kiss her or merely give her a pat on the head and apologize for being the condescending monster that he was.

Instead, he decided on kissing her hand. As he lifted it to his lips he suddenly felt quite wicked, and although he wouldn't truly harm a hair on her head, he felt the need to give her another reason to fear men like him.

Closing his eyes, his warm lips met her cold hand and he bit, just slightly, then suckled, and nipped until, with a gasp, she pulled it away.

"Well done!" Hunter slapped him on the back. "Champagne for everyone!"

CHAPTER FIVE

I find that I cannot entertain a woman without feeling the betrayal of their entire race. It is for that reason alone that I have chosen to keep my heart protected. My mistress will always be music, my love will always be for myself, and my heart will never be in jeopardy again.
~The Diary of Dominique Maksylov

ISABELLE WAITED IN THE captain's quarters. After the ceremony, she was escorted to the room and told in no uncertain terms that it would be shared with Dominique, considering it was their wedding night.

Lovely. A nightmare to accompany everything else that had gone horribly wrong. She wasn't necessarily afraid he would force himself on his own wife.

No, despite all of his beastly habits, he didn't seem the sort to harm a woman, regardless of what he had just threatened to do to her. Fear pooled in her belly for an entirely different reason.

Isabelle was afraid he would be kind.

And a kind man would be so much harder to hate. A

passionate lover would surely break her heart, and if she wanted to escape the beast without heartache, he must continue to be horrible to her.

His kiss spoke of passion.

His touch ignited fervor within her.

And his smile was wickedly delicious.

Those weapons were much scarier to behold than his silver tongue.

The door slammed. Dominique stormed into the room like a raging lunatic. Nostrils flaring and hands gripped into tight fists, he didn't even acknowledge her. Instead, he poured himself some brandy and threw back the contents before turning his blue eyes onto her.

So, he was to play the beast tonight, was he?

Isabelle had lived her entire life with her mother, a woman who, in her mind, would scare even Dominique out of his dark humor. She could handle him being threatening.

As long as his warm hands didn't touch her.

And his lips didn't caress hers.

"Well." He poured another glass, sipping it slower than the first. "Let's get on with it."

Isabelle felt herself pale. Get on with what? Did he want some sort of performance? "I'm no courtesan, as you so blatantly stated earlier this day. I find myself confused. What are we to get on with, my lord?" she asked, buying herself more time, for the look in his eyes, a look of pure hate, seemed to billow from him in waves.

Perhaps she should throw up her countenance again to gain some sympathy. Then again, sympathy was more dangerous than hate.

"Take off your clothes. It is, after all, what women do, is it not?"

Isabelle rolled her eyes; he truly was dramatic with his moods. "I only undress when it is time for a bath, husband. I know no other type of undressing unless it's to ready for bed."

"Which is exactly what you are doing now, my love. I need you to ready for bed." He loomed over her, gloves still on his hands.

"After you," she challenged with a tilt of her head. "After all, it is my understanding that a husband and wife are to share the marriage bed."

"Indeed." He growled, making quick, awkward movements with his gloved hands as he tried to take off his fitted jacket.

The task would truly be impossible without someone to help him; anyone could see that it was tailored specifically for his large muscular form.

With a sigh, and the last bit of patience Isabelle possessed, she slowly walked toward the man and touched his shoulders, just slightly.

His muscles tensed, but he indeed froze in place as her other hand trembled and moved across his shoulder to help him remove his jacket.

She must be losing her mind, for what woman would willingly help a man disrobe when the result would be her on the receiving end of his savagery? Yet, she moved to help him and noticed that the minute her hands touched his body, Dominique calmed.

So, the beast it seemed had a weakness for touch, which she found quite odd. Once the jacket was removed, her hands lingered, their warmth pressed against the giant expanse of his muscled back. One could see the dark skin underneath and again it reminded her of his heritage. What, she wondered, would this beast of a man look like if he was to take care of his appearance? If he shaved his beastly overgrowth and cut his hair?

Devastation, it was the obvious choice, for his form, everything about him was perfect. Perhaps his one boon to women everywhere was that he kept his perfection hidden beneath a scowl and a devilish amount of hair.

"We shall begin," he said stepping away from her touch, his body giving an involuntary shake as he did so.

Isabelle lifted her eyebrow. What the devil did he want to commence? Truly, she was ignorant and had no idea what mood Dominique was in other than he was surprisingly sure on his feet after drinking the brandy.

A small gasp escaped her lips as he removed his crisp, white shirt. Turning quickly so she wouldn't see him in a state of undress, she shook her head and closed her eyes, but the visions of his hard-planed stomach and tanned skin were burned into her memory.

Suddenly, she felt heat behind her, and then Dominique's gloved hands were on her shoulders, slowly pulling down her traveling dress with the ease and knowledge of a man who had stripped many a woman in his lifetime.

Although his touch sent chills, it was distant and cold, merely because he kept his gloves on. But the heat from his chest began to spread across her back, and then his breath was hot on her face as his tongue reached out and trailed a design on her neck.

Hot desire pulsed through her in the most wanton of places. His grip tightened on her shoulders and then she heard a rip of fabric. Was he ripping her dress from her body? So he truly meant to rape her?

His touch sent a nervous tremble through her body—she refused to believe it was fear of any kind. A sick feeling swirled in her stomach as she felt those same gloved hands move to her corset strings and begin tugging away; almost desperately he pulled until she thought she would topple forward, and then his arm was bracing her, pulling her body against hard masculine flesh. As the corset was finally loosened, his hands, with agonizing slowness, moved it and the dress down to the floor. Warm lips and that silver tongue of his licked and bit trails down her body through her chemise, until the clothing was a heap at her feet. Isabelle stepped out of the dress and corset and immediately covered her body with her hands. She didn't need to look down to know that her chemise was nearly transparent.

Every girl dreamt of a moment when her husband-to-be gazed upon her, gave her the pretty words she craved to hear, and walked down the aisle with such fervor as to claim his prize. With each strip of clothing removed, her vulnerability increased and the dream became harder to believe in.

But nothing was so horrible as when, Dominique her husband, her protector, and soon to be lover, sneered at her near nakedness. "As I said before, a cold English fish. At least you have curves. I'll give you that much. Now hop into bed before I change my mind about taking the only valuable thing you possess, your virginity."

The tears that Isabelle had been holding in burst. Unable to even see which direction the bed was in, she stood and cried like a small child. Bitter tears choked her throat threatening to close it.

And then Dominique was there, cradling her in his arms. "Shh," he said softly in her hair. "Believe me, it is better this way." He tucked her into the bed and wiped a tear from her face and scowled. "I do not take kindly to tears."

"Well, I don't take kindly to being insulted and forced into marriage, then threatened to be killed!" Isabelle jerked her head away from his touch.

"Regardless of your feelings, Isabelle, I mean to protect you from evil men like the man who sold you to me, to keep you from the darkness, so you may possibly mature into a young woman without vanity and selfishness. And my protection must be firm with you, for I must protect you from the biggest threat at present."

"And what threat would that be?" Isabelle sniffled.

"Myself." Dominique gave her a sad smile and moved to the hammock on the other side of the room.

Confused and hurt, all Isabelle could do was watch.

He was going to Hell.

At least he would be in good company. Hunter's many sins weren't doing well to earn him a spot in Heaven.

Dominique wanted to break something. He was no better than the man Isabelle left, but he couldn't find the balance between keeping her fearful and leery of him, and wanting to protect her from everything.

The truth of it was she reminded him of when he was a small boy. When he wrote music about princes slaying dragons. His mother told him stories at night about such things; she said that since he was a prince, he would one day need to find a princess and rescue her.

Apparently he had found his princess.

Unfortunately, he treated her as a nuisance.

It wasn't just his mistrust of women. No, it was the absolute loss of control he felt in her presence. What had he been thinking? To bite her? And lick her milky skin? His thoughts had been initially to shock her into submission so she wouldn't cry. Instead, he had gotten entirely carried away, almost following through with his urge to bed her.

But as his hands moved down her supple body, his eyes caught a glimpse of his gloves and he remembered. Everything.

The blood, the scars, the pain, and the betrayal. But most of all he remembered the monster he was, and realized that he would rather hurt her beyond saving and have her hate him than have her pity, for if she pitied him, his heart just might break, and he hadn't the strength to put it back together again.

For how could a Beauty such as she ever hope to love or care for a Beast?

CHAPTER SIX

The melody haunts even my dreams, it seems every time I write it down I never allow myself to play it. I merely throw it in the fire and pray that God sent my father into the very fire he dipped my hands in. For I would give my soul, my gift of music, I would give my life, just for a chance to go back…

~The Diary of Dominique Maksylov

THE FOLLOWING MORNING DID not start off as Dominique hoped it would. For one thing, the sheet on the bed had fallen completely off, leaving Isabelle draped across the mattress looking like a goddess emerged from the sea. Temptation to take his wife, because after all, she was his, was so strong that he poured himself another brandy and then another.

Hunter chose that unfortunate time to barge into the room. His golden eyes fixated on the goddess in question before turning an amused expression to Dominique. Laughter soon followed when he approached the woman and watched as she dozed, looking completely untouched. Dominique scowled as Hunter motioned to the drink in his hand.

He had half a mind to throw it at his hateful friend. Hunter shook his head in merriment and made a motion for Dominique to follow him out to the deck.

The salty air rejuvenated him, but only slightly. "What is it?"

"Snappy this morning, eh?" Hunter elbowed him. "Your tone speaks not of a man who was satisfied throughout the evening. A little cold was she? Perhaps I should warm her up first? You don't mind, right? After all, you mean to push her away until she hates you as much as you hate yourself."

Dominique cursed. "You go too far! Don't for one minute think that because we are friends that I wouldn't shoot you for touching her."

Hunter eyed him patronizingly. "Come, Dominique, we both know you excel in fencing, not shooting. Besides, I was merely jesting, at least about the warming part. I stand by everything else."

Dominique glared and chose to ignore his friend's ramblings. "We should make haste. The ship will be docking soon, and we have a long journey ahead of us through the woods."

"And through the trees to Dominique's house we go!" Hunter added with his singsong voice. Oh, what Dominique wouldn't give to punch his happy friend in the face.

With a growl, he turned on his heel and marched back into the captain's quarters. "Get up!"

Isabelle's eyes fluttered open, a look of confusion passing over her features.

"I said get up!" Dominique yelled. "Make haste, we arrive within the hour and still have a grueling journey ahead of us."

Isabelle nodded solemnly and pulled the sheet tighter around her body.

Must she be such a prude? After all, hadn't his hands spent the better part of the night running up and down her curves? Thirsty for her touch, hungry for her lips, he pulled his gaze away. Such torture to constantly want something he could not have. His hands clenched at his sides. "I'll await you on deck. It matters not if your hair is arranged, nor if your dress is beautiful. Wear something comfortable and be quick about it."

With that he slammed the door behind him, waiting a good five minutes before he was able to speak to anyone without wanting to bark or rip their heads off. Just being in the same room with his wife was becoming difficult. The sooner they got to his castle, the better, for at least in the castle he could lock her off in her own wing while he spent the remainder of his days writing music and ignoring the hammering of his heart and pounding of blood whenever the woman was in his presence.

Isabelle kept her eyes focused on the door that Dominique had just escaped through. What the devil was wrong with him? His eyes held anger, pain, but most surprising was guilt.

Perhaps he was having second thoughts about treating her like a common prostitute. Though, to be fair he didn't take advantage of his owning of her the night previous, though she hated herself for wanting him to.

Slowly, she moved out of bed and dressed for the day. Whatever horrors this morn held for her, it could not be worse than what she had already experienced at the man's hands.

The sun shone brightly, reflecting off the dark blue ocean. Isabelle inhaled the salty scent of the water. The ship moaned and creaked as it moved toward the docks ahead. Men scurried about trying to ready the ship for arrival. Dominique was nowhere to be seen. Isabelle fought the edge of disappointment creeping around her heart. Why did she care where her husband was? He had made it perfectly clear that they were to have the type of marriage that the *ton* boasted of. An arrangement where he offered his protection and nothing else save a roof over her head, a cold bed, and no love.

She shivered, remembering the way his wicked hands smoothly caressed her body. If only he would have taken off his gloves; then again it seemed even his gloves, his clothes, his hair, everything he wore was as a shield. A cage surrounded his heart and his black soul. And she wondered if he had ever let anyone in.

"Shall we stop at Madame Buchens' house?" a hoarse male voice asked. Isabelle walked around the corner of the ship and hid behind some boxes. Dominique stood with a few men, a rare smile plastered across his face.

She had to fight to keep from gasping in outrage. Visit a house of ill repute? "We will not have time," Dominique answered. "Though it is a pity, wouldn't you agree, lads?"

They chuckled in unison. An elderly sailor spoke up. "The pity is that you won't allow us to visit the Madame without you, sire. Would be kind of ya to let us have our pick of the best whores rather than take them all fer yerself!"

The sailor smiled, revealing missing teeth, and nudged his friend next to him. "After all, a night with the great prince is a prize indeed. Last time, my girl wouldn't stop talkin' about him and the way he brings pleasure to a woman."

Dominique rolled his eyes and looked away as the rest of the sailors chuckled amongst themselves. "Fine then, you gents may stay an extra night before bringing in the cargo, but only one night."

"And will ya be joining us, sire?" the same sailor asked.

"I have a wife now." Dominique answered, though he seemed to be irritated with having to say it. "Though I'm loath to admit it." He chuckled and threw a pouch of money to the men. "Enjoy yourselves, since you know that I cannot."

Blind rage poured through Isabelle. She had thought him sensitive last night, not wanting to take the one thing she had. Instead it was as if he never wanted her in the first place. Could she truly not bring him pleasure? Because of her innocence and looks? He hadn't said as much, but she figured he found her quite unappealing to leave her alone the night previous. Well, she wasn't one to allow everyone to suffer, and if this would put him in a more amiable mood, why not? Perhaps she could use this weakness of his as a way to coerce him into letting her return to her family, or better yet, annul the marriage!

With a huff, she walked out of hiding and into the group of men. Dominique's features hardened, the sailors around her hushed. "Why husband, if you have such a relentless appetite, why not stay with the men? After all, it seems the whores wait for your arrival with bated breath, we wouldn't want any of them dying of asphyxiation."

Dominique's cold eyes pierced through her. "Excuse us, lads, my wife is in need of being taught a lesson about spying."

The sailors averted their gazes and scattered about as Dominique took purposeful steps toward Isabelle. Frightened, she stepped back only to come into contact with a flat, hard surface against her backside. Stuck, she looked down instead of into the rage-filled eyes of the beast.

"Look at me," he ordered.

Slowly, Isabelle raised her eyes level with his.

"You will never disrespect me in front of the men again. If you do, it won't be whores they'll be spending their evenings entertaining, do I make myself clear?"

Was he suggesting he would give them use of her? Outraged, she pushed at his chest. "No, you do not make yourself clear! How could you even suggest such a thing? You would throw your virgin wife into the clutches of your crew? Without a second thought? Does my presence repulse you that much, my lord?"

A smile cracked at the corners of Dominique's mouth, and his blue eyes looked almost cheerful. "Repulse me?" His hand reached around her neck, drawing her face closer to his. "Hmm, if this is repulsion, I find myself in agreement with your statement." His lips descended, raining feather-light kisses along her brow before pushing her against the wall behind her. "What's mine is mine, beauty. Although your assumptions amuse me, I feel the need to correct you." His teeth nipped her ear as he whispered, "I meant they would be spending their nights entertaining us with dinner and music, not with my beautiful wife. After all, I have quite a talented group of men aboard this ship. I understand you wouldn't be aware of such things, considering you are so talented at jumping to the wrong conclusions."

Unable to speak, she nodded as his hot breath tickled the inside of her ear and his teeth nibbled again. "Now, would you please, yes I said please—and you don't have to go stiff as a board underneath my touch when I show manners—return to Miss Ward and notify her of our arrival."

Isabelle nodded her head.

Dominique released her and stepped away. Thinking she was free to go, she made haste in removing herself from his presence, but his hand leapt out and caught her wrist, pulling her back firmly against her chest.

"I do not share," he barked, then aggressively turned her to face him and took possession of her mouth. His tongue bewitched hers as he drew her mouth open. He grasped her hands within his, pulling her arms around his neck. She fought against his grip and tried to pull away. But he caught her lip between his teeth. The sharp pain made her gasp and then his tongue grazed her tortured lips, plunging her into oblivion. His mouth covered hers and made her so weak, she had no choice but to hang on to him. Her hands gripped his hair. He moaned into her mouth, his tongue arching against hers with such fervor, such passion, that she could do nothing more but grasp at his jacket for balance. As abruptly as the kiss started, he ended it and pushed her away, nearly sending her tumbling.

"Be gone," he said softly and turned to walk in the other direction.

Horrible liar that he was, Dominique had been grasping at any sort of excuse he could find for his wretched behavior. Truthfully, he had said those words about throwing his wife into the clutches of the sailors without thinking. Apparently another side effect of being with the chit. He was starting to care about hurting her feelings. It was becoming more difficult to be cross when all he wanted to do was ravish her where she stood.

Confusion blurred his thoughts. The trip to the first coaching inn was going by faster than he expected. It was, however, helpful that Isabelle had been asleep most the journey so he was able to try to gather his thoughts as well as resolve not to touch her once they were again alone.

Hunter found the entire situation most amusing. Unfortunately, he had chosen to ride in the carriage rather than use one of the horses, saying that his back had a dreadful ache that riding in the carriage would surely fix.

But what he meant was, his back ached and the only remedy was sitting next to Isabelle and irritating the devil out of Dominique each time he leaned in and closed his eyes, breathing in her scent, like the true wolf he was.

"If you value that nose of yours, cease from sniffing my

wife." Dominique groaned and looked around the carriage for something to hit. Something that wouldn't give his friend a bloody nose or a bruised eye.

Hunter just chuckled and crossed his arms. "I'm here to help you, friend, not steal your lady, though the idea of it seems rather exciting. In her current state, it would be too easy and you know how much I enjoy the chase."

Yes, Dominique knew his friend's secret past. It seemed the very goodness that made Hunter a loyal spy still wasn't enough to blot out the darkness that often made itself known within the man. As a friend he was irreplaceable, as a spy he was the best London had to offer, but as a foe, he would be deadly.

"Control your urges, Hunter."

"Fine." He sighed heavily. "I still don't know what else you expect me to do."

"Help." Dominique looked out the window at the passing trees. "Support. The usual. I need to know her character. I need to see that she is safe, well, healthy. But I refuse to be the one who looks after her. I cannot allow myself to grow—"

"Close," Hunter finished knowingly.

Dominique shifted. It was becoming increasingly difficult to see to the woman without crossing his own emotional boundaries, never mind the physical ones. He couldn't see straight when his physical needs were present along with Isabelle. But Hunter, he trusted. His friend would be sure that Isabelle was well-received within the staff, was happy, could find enough to occupy her time, and in the end that she would feel grateful for her position as a Russian princess and English countess.

So lost in thought was Dominique that when the carriage pulled to a stop, he jumped. Isabelle's eyes slowly opened. "Get up." He tried not to issue orders this time, softening his voice as he commanded.

Dominique groaned when they entered the inn. Apparently someone had notified, not only the patrons, but the innkeeper himself. For the minute Dominique's boot touched the threshold of the place, a cheer erupted from everyone's lips.

"Here, here! To the Royal Prince, may God preserve him!" the innkeeper shouted.

"Here, here!" The audience joined in lifting their ale to the ceiling. Dominique was always uncomfortable with praise but even more so with Isabelle on his arm. Her shocked expression also didn't help.

"Close your mouth, beauty." He chuckled.

Her eyes widened even more when the crowds parted for them as they went to the innkeeper to obtain rooms.

"Your Highness." The innkeeper bowed low to the floor. "In honor of your return, we have set out a wonderful dinner in your room. Is this lovely lady to be staying with you tonight?"

Dominique fought back a smile. No doubt she thought he the type of man to throw her to the wolves, proclaiming she was nothing more than a cheap courtesan. "This, my dear fellow, would be Lady Harris, the new countess and, as you all see, the new Princess of Maksylov."

"Princess!" The innkeeper's face turned red with excitement. "Another toast!"

Hunter came up behind them and lifted his ale in the air. "Yes! A toast, to the most lovely princess I have ever laid eyes on. May your smile enchant, your heart captivate, and your lips proclaim the goodness that is our dear prince. And if for some reason he should meet his death, may I be the one to warm your bed during the cold nights!"

Cheers erupted. Dominique's hand clenched her shoulder as he sent a seething glare to Hunter, who was already off dancing with a tavern wench.

CHAPTER SEVEN

It is worse at night. I cannot help it. The melody haunts my dreams until I awake in a pool of my own sweat. So I hardly sleep, instead I play the music until it finally quits, until I have peace. It is harder when I am away from my piano, for it seems every time I close my eyes, the demons of my past threaten to kill me. One day, I fear they will succeed.

~The Diary of Dominique Maksylov

ISABELLE AWOKE TO DOMINIQUE tossing and turning. His thrashing in the bed could have woken the dead, and she was already having a difficult time sleeping knowing that his hard muscled body lay only a few inches away from hers. Dare she wake him?

She hadn't even known he was in the same bed with her until his thrashing woke her. The minute he had escorted her into the room they would be sharing for the evening, he had grumbled orders about her getting her rest and slammed the door behind him, making it the second night in a row that he refused to touch her.

Lonely, Isabelle had swallowed down her tears and readied herself for bed, with the help of Miss Ward, who tried to keep Isabelle's spirits up by chattering about Dominique's grand castle. If anything, it made Isabelle feel worse to know Miss Ward felt sorry for her.

Dominique groaned and then his lips moved, he moaned again and then shuddered, the blankets fell from his chest and she gasped. His golden body was evident even in the night. With a tentative hand she caressed the muscles of his lean form. It seemed to relax him, for the moaning stopped. Only, something more dangerous occurred—Dominique pushed closer to her. His body moving slowly toward hers.

Abruptly, she stopped caressing him, and the moaning began again, this time so painful, so full of sadness that she brought both hands to his back and continued to rub. Within minutes he stopped again, rolled over and pulled her into his arms breathing heavily into her hair. His touch would have been intimate, had his gloves been removed before bed. But when she asked if he was going to remove them, he sneered and looked like he wanted to roar or at least strike something.

So she quickly pretended to fall asleep all the while wondering why he would need to protect his hands. Being eccentric, it made sense that he would choose to protect something so precious; after all, his hands were his life. Then again, what could be so horrible at night-time to cause harm to the very instruments that brought life to music?

A low moan escaped his throat as his grip tightened around her body, and then because she didn't know what else to do. She began to caress not just his back, but his arms, his face, every piece of warm, golden skin that was exposed.

Just as she was about to fall asleep again, as her hands were beginning to fatigue, she heard him mumble in her hair, "Thank you."

The next few nights followed suit. They would eat and go

to bed, and eventually she would awaken to his nightmares, only to lull him back to sleep with her touch. And every night just as she was about to close her eyes, she would hear him mumble, "Thank you".

She never asked him about it in the morning. It didn't seem necessary. Besides, her own sleep was affected enough that she began sleeping during the day and staying awake during the night to make sure she could chase his demons away.

Not that he had done anything to deserve it, for he was still just as monstrous during the days as he had been since she'd met him, but he had said "thank you" and for some reason, those words on his lips were enough to forgive a multitude of sins.

On the final day of travel, Isabelle was awakened by a loud screeching. It sounded of a gate that had not seen the benefits of oil.

Stretching, she looked out the window and gasped.

"Welcome, Princess Isabelle, to Castle of Ogan."

It was a fairy tale, every bit as dark and dangerous—as well as insanely beautiful—as a gothic horror story. The iron gate squeaked as it was forced open, the carriage came to a stop and Isabelle jumped out, craning her neck to see the giant fortress in front of her.

Hundreds of rooms must occupy this space! It had a moat! And boasted of a maze of gardens before one even entered the door! Magic, she felt magic everywhere she glanced. She didn't even notice she was smiling until Dominique scowled in her direction.

"Pay him no mind," Hunter said next to her as Dominique made great haste entering his home. "It is one of his many summer homes. He rarely goes back to his country, rather he favors rusticating, or as I like to put it, molding away here in Belgium."

"It is beautiful," Isabelle whispered in awe.

"Might I make a suggestion, my lady?" Hunter hooked his arm around her shoulders and led her into the grand entrance. "Perhaps you should keep your admiration to yourself; my friend despises this house. But as you can see, it is closest to your home. I believe he wants you to feel comfortable."

A laugh escaped Isabelle's lips. "Comfortable? That is his desire? Have you met the man? If anything he has been going out of his way to make me uncomfortable."

"Give him time, Princess," Hunter mumbled.

CHAPTER EIGHT

What do you suppose a broken man looks like? Is he wealthy but poor of spirit? Does he plunge himself into debauchery trying to make himself whole again? Is he the fellow that laughs in the face of danger and challenges Hades at every turn? He is all of the above, but most of all, he is me. His reflection is the one I see in the mirror, and his eyes are hollow, for the love that once lived behind them was stolen, the day my father took his last breath.

~The Diary of Dominique Maksylov

DOMINIQUE SHUDDERED AS HE imagined blood-curdling screams echoing off the walls as if his mother's spirit was still in between Heaven and Hell. He began to sweat as his boots clicked against the hard marble floors. He knew where this path would lead. It would be the same destination his tiny feet had taken him some fifteen years ago.

His trembling hands reached out to touch the smooth wood of the door before pushing it open. Dust-filled air greeted him. His instructions had been clear. No servant was to enter the practice room, lest they wish to find employment elsewhere. And by no means were they to even contemplate cleaning up the mess.

His heels clicked across broken glass. Cold air swept over him and he shook with the memory laid out at his feet. A mother's betrayal, a father's jealousy, and finally a little boy's confusion.

Blood still stained the floor where the bodies had lain, and the fireplace still held burnt pieces of music. The same music he swore he would never play again. And the piano. Dominique swallowed as he neared the piano, its keys dusty from sitting in such a frozen state.

His white glove caressed the keys, coming back with dust and debris. He imagined that his tears still stained the keys, never had he cried as much as he did that night.

With a heavy sigh he took one last look about the room. The air was thick with memories of early death and sorrow. Perhaps it was a mistake returning to this home. But it seemed if he was to keep Isabelle for himself, as a monster would keep his princess in a tower, then he should at least have her close enough to her home that she could easily visit her family.

After all, Belgium wasn't as far away from London as some imagined. Though the political unrest in Brussels was something to be leery of, they were far enough away in the woods to be safe. And the stories surrounding his haunted castle did wonders for the travelers and French soldiers occupying the area.

As he closed his eyes to shut out the view of the room, his mind conjured up a perfect image of his father. Of his sad smile the night Dominique's mother died, and of his horror stricken face the night his life was stolen from him; in the same room where he took a life, his was forfeited. Was he truly a beast? Just like his father? To save a girl only to condemn her with a life shackled to him? Her alternative would have been far worse, though he wasn't sure why he believed so. Perhaps it was instinctual, but she wasn't safe in London. At least here, she was safe.

Even though, with her presence, his own safety had been called into question. With one final glance about the room, he made his exit, shutting the doors quietly behind him.

Tonight, at dinner, he would notify her of his expectations during their marriage. Intimacy being at the top of the list, and running the household at the bottom. Isabelle must understand that he would claim his husbandly rights, horrid as she may believe them to be.

Above all she needed to understand that he would protect her at all costs; he would gladly die for her, give her everything a person could want. Everything but the thing he had lost long ago. His heart.

"Dominique?" Hunter's voice echoed in the grand hallway just as the door to the practice room shut. "Your pretty little wife needs to be shown to her rooms."

Dominique grunted and followed his voice to the entryway. "The butler will see to her comfort—"

"Alas, I felt that you, being the master of the house, should give her a grand tour, after all, the butler has suffered a serious injury to his…" Hunter looked at Brinks and made a choking sound. "Foot, his foot is ailing him." He nodded his head to Brinks who must have remembered he was supposed to have some sort of injury and began hobbling on one foot. The theatre was not in his future, although it was comical to watch the normally stoic and oddly tall man hop around with such a lack of grace.

"And what about Miss Ward?" Dominique turned to glare at his friend.

"Lost." Hunter shrugged.

"Lost?" Dominique crossed his arms and examined Hunter. Though he was a fantastic spy and even better master of deception, it seemed he was out of sorts when his actors forgot their lines.

Hunter nodded gravely and lifted hands as if to say, *whatever is a fellow supposed to do*?

"And the footman, I imagine something dreadful happened to him as well?" Dominique inquired, searching for any of the staff, though he knew it was in vain. The castle had been without a full staff for a great while. It would be up to Isabelle to hire whom she saw fit. Until then, they would have to make due.

"I regret to inform you, highness—" Brinks put both feet firmly to the floor, then remembered his ailment and began limping with the wrong foot, "That the footmen are busy helping the stable hands with the horses. We are, after all, without much help."

Dominique let out a hearty sigh. "Indeed. Well, where is the girl?"

"Your wife," Hunter began, putting unnecessary emphasis on the word *wife,* "is at this moment getting the sordid tale of the origin of the castle."

Letting out a curse, Dominique hurried in the general direction of his retired butler whom he hadn't the heart to let go when the man grew too old to run the household. Instead he stayed in his employ and often told those who were brave enough to visit, the different stories the walls of the castle held. There was only one place he could be, in the kitchens. For he was convinced that nobody should ever be without a warm meal and drink. If Dominique had any luck at all, he would be able to steal away his wife before she became completely foxed.

Cuppins Port was also a strong believer in spiking one's tea, something Dominique was convinced Isabelle had never been privy to until this disastrous day.

His quick footsteps took him to the kitchen. Laughter soon echoed off the walls.

"And then, the young master ran through the house with nothing but the skin God gave him, he was such a wild boy that one." Cuppins laughed. "How's your tea, my lady?"

Within fifteen minutes of their arrival, the elderly man had not only regaled Isabelle with embarrassing stories, but attempted to get her foxed. If Cuppins were thirty years younger, Dominique would have his head. But as it was, he didn't have the heart to throttle an eighty-year-old man.

Just as he was ready to step into the kitchen, his eyes beheld something he had never seen before in his existence. Rather than be scared off, put off, upset, or even disgusted that the retired butler would take a well-bred lady into the kitchens and attempt to pour ungodly amounts of brandy in her tea, Isabelle reached out her hand and laid it across the knotty one of Cuppins.

The old man's grin was enough to send dangerous constrictions to Dominique's heart; he watched, unable to look away as Isabelle squeezed the man's hand and said, "Tell me more."

She was mad! But she was also the most compassionate woman to say such a thing, for Cuppins lived for his stories; they were all he had after his strength was taken from him.

So, Dominique, in a moment of sheer insanity, leaned against the wall and listened for the next few minutes as Cuppins told another story. When Dominique thought it was acceptable to interrupt, he walked into the dimly lit kitchen.

The bright smile that occupied his young wife's face darkened. Suddenly aware that it was his old, retired butler who had brought such joy to her face, and not himself, Dominique wanted to curse.

"Pardon us, Cuppins, but I thought the lady might wish to see the rest of the castle, now that you've scared her out of her wits, I'm sure, with your stories."

Cuppins let out a hearty laugh. "Oh, we were just having

ourselves a bit of fun, weren't we, milady?"

Isabelle giggled and kissed the man on his cheek. She kissed him! Dominique's jaw dropped. Why was it that he had to steal kisses and she freely gave them to a man more than twice his age! And a servant no less! It just proved the point that women were fickle in their feelings, something he needed to be reminded of after spending a lust-filled ride in the carriage with her.

"Until tomorrow, Cuppins," she whispered and then turned her beautiful eyes on Dominique. With a nervous throat clearing, Dominique wasn't sure if he should grasp her hand, offer his arm, or merely snap orders.

Unfortunately he chose the latter. "Hurry along, Isabelle. This way."

CHAPTER NINE

At times I wish I had no memory, for then I wouldn't have nightmares. I would have peace. But my wish is a double-edged sword, for if I had no memory, how could I remember the notes? The Music? And in the end if I did not remember my scars, the very ones that rip away at my soul—then I would have no excuse to be what I am—The Beast.

~The Diary of Dominique Maksylov

ISABELLE COULD NOT HELP that her nostrils flared in annoyance. Nor could she help the irritated flip flop of her stomach when Dominique had first entered the room. To think that the man she wanted to stab with a knife was the same one who evoked such desire in her belly was appalling.

Surely she was mad, for he was nothing more than a animal set to imprison her in the cold, dead walls of the rocks around her. It would be so much easier if it were ugly instead of beautiful. Or if the servants were mere shades of Dominique's personality. Instead, they were lively, happy even. A trait it seemed Dominique hadn't acquired in all his years.

"And here we are," Dominique said, his voice a deep echo in the great hallway.

"And here is?" Isabelle asked.

"The wall of the strange and even stranger."

"Pardon?"

"Strange, this wall. It's ugly and haunting, and well, to be honest, I despise it, but I've been given the task of revealing all my family secrets to you. And reveal I will."

His personality had changed again. Dominique looked irritated, nervous and uncomfortable as if the very pictures he looked upon would suddenly spring to life.

"Your ancestors, then?" Isabelle prodded.

"All of them, even Alexander the first."

More evidence that he truly was a prince, the remainder made her all the more uncomfortable. "I imagine your family is proud of your musical accomplishments."

"My family ceased being proud of me a great while ago, wife."

What an odd statement to make.

Dominique pulled her hand as he led her hurriedly to the end of the hall. Just as she was about to round the corner, her eyes caught a glimpse of the most beautiful woman she had ever seen. With ebony hair and crystal blue eyes it was undeniable that it was Dominique's mother. Next to her picture was a man, his large aristocratic nose framed by a harsh face. He looked every bit the type of diplomat that people would follow. A man who could lead.

"Who are they?" She pulled Dominique's hand, hoping he would stop.

He looked at the pictures, his face a mixture of hurt and anger. "They are dead, and that is all you need to know."

"But..."

"Enough!" His voice snapped and his icy blue eyes

burned holes through her. "I will show you to our room, but there are a few things you must first know about the castle."

"Other than it's haunted, you mean?" Isabelle whispered.

"Cuppins likes to talk, do not take his words for truth."

"So you didn't run around naked during a royal dinner?" Isabelle wasn't sure what made her feel the need to tease the man who merely seconds ago had scolded her so harshly. Perhaps she was going mad.

Dominique actually smiled, though she could tell he took great pains to hide it, which proved a simple task considering all the scruff on his face. "Yes well, when I was a boy I had a great need for affection. I thought nobody would ignore my presence if I were, uh, naked."

"And did they?"

"Did they what?"

"Ignore you?"

Dominique swallowed and looked down. "Always."

Isabelle reached a comforting hand to Dominique's face. His eyes closed as her skin made contact with his.

"Please, don't," he whispered.

"Don't what?"

"Pity me. I would rather you hate me, rather you dream about my death, than extend the same pity and compassion to me that you do Cuppins."

It made no sense that the man wouldn't want comfort, after all, hadn't he just finished explaining the lack of attention he received as a boy?

"Why?" Her other hand went up to touch the other side of his face, bringing it dangerously close to hers.

"Because, I am undeserving. Of your loyalty, your goodness, your compassion. Everything. I would rather die than receive it."

"Do any of us truly deserve loyalty? Love? Forgiveness? How can you earn such things in the first place, Dominique?"

Her heart leapt as she said his name. She pulled back as if burned, noting the fierceness in his gaze as he looked at her lips then back at her eyes.

"What I have done has earned me a spot in the inner most circle of Hell." His hand caressed her neck up and down, until she leaned in wantonly, needing more of his touch.

"The rules." He cleared his throat and stepped back. "As I stated before, are simple. Dinner is always at eight, you are to dine with me every evening." She opened her mouth to speak but he shook his head and continued talking. "You have free reign of the castle, but you may not under any circumstances enter the second practice room located near the stairs. It is locked, so it shouldn't pose a problem to your morbid curiosity."

Isabelle watched as he bit his lip in obvious frustration. "What's in the room that you've forbidden me to enter? Corpses?" Her sarcastic remark was met with so much rage in his face that she took a step back. Truly, she had meant to lighten the mood with humor. Was it truly littered with such as she said?

"It is none of your concern! Do I make myself clear?" he roared.

"Y-yes," she stammered.

He cursed and turned on his heel, pausing after only a few steps. "And Isabelle?"

She lifted her head just in time to see a devilish smile dance across his face, bringing wicked intent into his eyes. "You will share my bed. Every night."

"But—"

He marched back in her direction and grabbed her arm, pulling her against him. "You are my wife, and you will act as such. In *every* way." His eyes dipped to her bodice and then back to her lips. "If you find the idea so repulsive, then close your eyes. Hum a song, think on happier things. Blast it all, you can even pretend it's Hunter rather than myself, but you will be mine."

Cursing, he left her in the dark hall, his boots stomping all the way down the stairs.

Isabelle sat in silence, and watched as Dominique's form disappeared. She still had no idea where her rooms were, nor in which direction to go. Within minutes, Miss Ward came up the stairs that Dominique had just exited and led her to a bedroom on the second floor of the castle.

By the time Miss Ward had helped her dress for bed, she was a bottle of nerves. The house did not boast of any lady's maids, something she was told to take care of whenever she was ready, so Miss Ward took it upon herself to regale her with stories of the enchanted castle, all the while Isabelle had to fight to keep her teeth from chattering.

He would stay with her tonight.

He would be in her bed. Yes, he'd stayed with her before, but there had been something in his tone earlier that lead her to believe that things would change…and soon.

When Miss Ward left, Isabelle's shaky legs took her to her side of the bed. She extinguished the candle and dove under the covers. The minutes went by with agonizing slowness, until finally she heard the unmistakable click of boots against the marble floors.

The bedroom doors opened in a rush.

Dominique stepped inside, though she could only see his shadow, nothing more. With jerky movements he pulled off his clothes, making Isabelle's face heat even though she couldn't see his form. She could imagine it, and an involuntary shiver ran down her spine. Soon, his weight forced the bed to dip almost causing her to topple towards him. And then, he exhaled and was still.

How in the world could he be still? How was it possible that the man wasn't the least bit affected sleeping in the same bed as her?

At the Inn, they had both been exhausted, but now, here, in their bedroom, in the castle they would share…

He was sleeping.

And her body was refusing to relax.

Every muscle was clenched tight. She tried to breathe evenly but her breaths came out in short gasps, and then something touched her.

His leg moved next to hers, body heat radiating from his person. Her stomach tumbled and tightened. The feeling was foreign as if she was almost weak or exhilarated from his touch.

As she scooted to the farthest edge of the bed, a thought occurred. How was she to survive sleeping in this bed every night for the rest of her life?

CHAPTER TEN

Those who cannot carry a tune should not attain to try, for they try in vain and my ears can only take so much torment before I contemplate removing them with a blunt object to rid them of the ringing horrid music brings. If society stopped teaching young girls to sing and play piano when they showed no true talent, I would be much obliged. Yet, every year it seems a new debutante finds a way to torture me with a note not yet found on the scale.

~The Diary of Dominique Maksylov

DOMINIQUE WINCED. "WHAT THE devil?"

"Ah, so you hear it too then. I was wondering how long it would take for you to catch on to the little lady bird." Hunter smiled and folded his broad arms behind his head as if readying himself for sleep.

How was the man even closing his eyes at such a time?

"Hunter? What the blazes is that noise?"

"Your lady bird."

Dominique paced in front of him. "Do you truly think that pet name fits at this point in time?"

On cue another ear splitting noise broke into the room. Apparently the lady bird had discovered a new note that hadn't yet been sung. Brave of her.

"I believe," Hunter kept his eyes closed, "That she was trying to reach for a high C?"

"I believe," Dominique mocked with a curse, "that she was trying to kill us off. That blasted noise has been waking me from sleep every single night this week! I thought it was—"

Hunter opened one eye. "A badger in heat?"

Dominique forced himself not to smile. "Yes, well, apparently I was wrong."

The shrill voice continued to try at higher notes until Dominique was sure he was going to have an apoplexy.

And then an expensive vase, one purchased by his mother in France, chose the opportune time to shake and fall to the floor.

"Did you know?" Hunter slapped his knee and laughed. "I thought that only happened in books and plays! But her voice truly just made a vase commit suicide. Pity. It was such a beautiful vase."

"Family heirloom." Dominique grumbled, looking at the glass shards on the marble floor. "At any rate, we simply cannot have her continue to sing like this. My entire staff will quit!"

"Oh they'd never do that." Hunter sobered. "They're in love, every last one of them. Lucky sods, just yesterday I saw the groom nearly fall prostrate in front of the woman."

"What the devil did she do? Offer him his weight in gold?" Dominique cursed and took a seat next to his nosy friend.

Hunter grinned wolfishly. "No, dear friend, she smiled, and I believe she said 'thank you'. Though I couldn't be sure, you asked me to spy and make sure she was comfortable and adjusting to castle life, not make myself known as to her exact wording in every conversation. Say, would you prefer I take notes? I imagine it would be in my best interest to follow her around and write down every beautiful word flowing from her mouth."

The voice heightened.

"Care to retract that last statement, friend?" Dominique smiled this time and then covered his face with his hands. He hadn't slept in days. Make that weeks! The woman was impossible!

"She likes music," Hunter pointed out.

"Yes, well, music doesn't like her," Dominique retorted.

"Teach her."

Dominique froze, hands still covering his face. "You cannot be serious? Please tell me this is just another one of your jokes you say to amuse yourself at everyone else's expense. She is unteachable!"

"You don't know that," Hunter argued.

"Yes, yes I do!" Dominique shot out of his chair. "She refuses to dine with me, she scowls at me at every turn, and her voice makes me want to cut off my own ears!"

"Only her singing voice. Her conversational voice is quite pretty." Hunter let out a besotted sigh.

"The devil you say!" Dominique kicked a chair. "She converses with the great Wolf of Haverstone and refuses to even greet me in the morning!"

Hunter laughed and shook his head. "It does help to be polite. You do know what being polite is, correct? Perhaps it would help you to teach her. Mayhap it will help both of you to build some semblance of a relationship since you're stuck together in holy matrimony."

It was aggravating to say the least, that his friend had conjured words from the very woman that Dominique shared a bed with every night. She refused to acknowledge him in the morning, and often took her dinner in her room claiming she was sick.

Admitting defeat, Dominique took another seat and cursed. "I have no idea where to start."

"Hello."

"Pardon?"

"Start with *hello*, or perhaps *sorry*. You do offend her with every other word pouring forth from your mouth." And with that Hunter stood and began walking toward the door. "Oh, and Dominique?"

His head jerked up.

"Do try to write a song worthy of the woman you're teaching it to. It wouldn't be right to have her throw herself from the highest balcony because your music depresses her very soul."

"They couldn't prove that!" Dominique argued.

With a laugh, Hunter waved him off and exited.

The cur! It had been years since anyone had brought that up! And it wasn't his fault that someone found his music so moving that they wanted to promptly float into the afterlife! Or in the gentleman's case, plummet into the eternal.

Though that cursed note he left gave Dominique pause. Perhaps Hunter was right. Not that he would ever say anything of the sort aloud, and to Hunter nonetheless, but the girl did like music, even if *it* despised her.

Perhaps it would be the only thing that would put them on common ground. With a sigh, a few curses and ten minutes of senseless pacing, Dominique had made up his mind. He would go to her, he would ask politely, and he would face rejection—again.

"My lady?" Miss Ward knocked on the door. "The master wishes an audience."

"Perhaps he can pay some servants to listen to him roar and bellow orders. I'm busy." Isabelle shifted the book between her tired hands and sighed. She wasn't sure how much longer she could sit and read. Not that she hated reading, but only three books were in her room and though Miss Ward had hinted that Dominique had an expansive library, the last thing she wanted to do was ask him if she could see it.

He'd probably demand she see it at a certain hour and then blame her if for some reason all the books weren't returned promptly the next day. Blast, he'd probably charge her too.

The man was a conundrum. Nothing and everything seemed to faze him. Yet, a shiver ran down her spine. When he smiled, which had only been twice since she'd met him, the world seemed to fade away.

If only he would shave that blasted beard! And at least try to pull his hair back! He looked like a beast! A Russian ruffian!

"My lady?" Miss Ward's voice was now more urgent. "He says it's of the most importance. It is in regards to your instruction on how to be a proper wife."

Furious, Isabelle tossed the book aside, leapt from her chair ran for the door and threw it open. Miss Ward was waiting on the other side, wringing her hands within her apron. "Just this way, my lady."

Miss Ward was silent, which truly was a first, as she led Isabelle down the long hallway into the East Wing of the large castle.

She was ushered into the spacious room and waited for her husband to make his appearance. Isabelle tried her best to appear bored, but it was impossible. The room was built for movement. A large piano lay in the corner and giant windows lined the far wall. And everywhere she looked were places to sit and enjoy music, including an elaborate fireplace that seemed to take up an entire side of the room.

The room itself seemed to sing, giving her the all too familiar urge to belt her favorite songs from her lungs. It didn't matter that she couldn't sing, or even whistle for that matter. Passion ignited within her every time she was moved in such a way and the only way to express such passion was to make a joyful noise.

With a giggle she opened her mouth.

"If you value your life, you will refrain from making any sort of noise from those delectable lips of yours," Dominique said from behind her. How had he snuck up on her? His breath was hot on her neck. Trembling, she clenched her jaw.

Dominique seemed to relax behind her. "God be praised, at least you listen to reason."

Isabelle took a deep breath.

His large hand covered her lips with such haste her mouth was still wide open when he clamped it shut.

"Shh..." Dominique mumbled in her ear. "One cannot appreciate music if one is constantly blocking it out with a voice."

Enraged, she fought to kick him, but he embraced her even harder.

"Listen, love."

Listen? Love? Was the man insane! He made demands of her day and night, didn't as much as ask how she was doing, and he was calling her *love*? And ordering her to listen? Her, of all people? The man couldn't listen if he was ordered by royal decree.

And then Dominique began to sway behind her. "Shh, just listen."

Defeated, Isabelle stopped struggling and did as he said. Only there was nothing to listen to, save her own treacherous heart as it slammed against her chest.

Insane, yes he was insane, but she continued to listen, and again all she could hear was her own heart. It sped up, slowed, and then sped up again like she was taking flight in the air with the birds.

"One, two, three—" he breathed in her ear and moved his hand down her throat to her chest. "One, two, three." He repeated this time, lightly patting her chest with his hand in perfect cadence with her heart. "Feel it, Belle, feel the music."

Her eyes closed of their own accord and she began to concentrate on her breathing as Dominique's hand grew warm on her chest.

"One, two, three." His other arm encircled her waist, leading her toward the far end of the room where the piano stood.

"Listen to the rise and fall of your own breath, the rise and fall of the music of your heart. Do you hear it?"

"Y-yes." Isabelle stumbled on the word all too aware of the warmth his body gave her. Of the way his touch burned her skin. Though he still wore his gloves, his fingers blazed a fiery trail of need into her flesh.

"Now, keep your eyes closed," he whispered, leaving her body aching, wanting, and alone.

A single note was played, followed by another, as her heart kept perfect rhythm with the music, perfect timing. And then more notes flowed forth.

A deep male voice penetrated the music, so beautiful, so achingly beautiful. She opened her eyes to see Dominique hovered over the piano, singing. The song was unlike anything she had ever heard.

Or Dominique had ever composed.

It was heart-breaking and beautiful at the same time.

"Merciful Heavens!" A female voice burst into the room. "I thought—"

Miss Ward promptly dropped her tray onto the floor and

began hopping on one foot. "Oh dear me, I've ruined everything. My apologies, master, I thought you were—"

"Killing her?" he offered with an amused smile.

"Well." Miss Ward crossed her arms and turned slightly pink. "You have to know we haven't heard such glorious music in an age! What else was I supposed to think?"

Isabelle gasped. Dominique's once cheerful face turned hard as granite. "Yes, well, I won't make the same mistake again. Apologies." He turned to Isabelle. "I will expect you tomorrow at the same time for lessons."

"Lessons?" Isabelle squeaked.

"Yes. Lessons," Dominique ground out. "So vases cease from breaking and stray animals stop arriving at my front door in hopes of mating with one another."

"Dominique!" Miss Ward stomped her foot. "Of all the asinine things to say!"

Isabelle felt hot tears at the back of her eyes, forcing themselves forward and down her cheeks. The knot in her throat increased until, with a cry, she quit the room and ran up the stairs, away from the insufferable man. It wasn't until she slammed the door that she remembered the reason for going down to the practice room in the first place.

Were lessons his twisted idea of wifely duties? And why did it leave her feeling even emptier than before?

CHAPTER ELEVEN

Where words fail me, music never does, for its very essence explains what I cannot, yet not everyone understands the language of a song, so I am brought back to words. And I am loath to admit, I do not understand how to use them.

~The Diary of Dominique Maksylov

"BRAVO!" HUNTER CLAPPED. "MAGNIFICENT performance, wouldn't be surprised if the girl was at this moment trying to scale the wall in hopes to escape you."

"Glad I amuse you..." Dominique had been sitting in the practice room for two hours since Isabelle's hasty departure.

"She's not coming back down here," Hunter observed. "Perhaps you should seek her out?"

"Seek her out?" Dominique repeated. "I'd rather stay in here without food or drink."

"No you wouldn't." Hunter scowled. "Admit it, you like her, even if her voice reminds everyone why women would be best to be seen and not heard."

Dominique couldn't help but laugh.

"Go after her. Rumor amongst the servants is she likes books."

Dominique's head snapped up. "Truly?"

"No, I'm lying in order to see you more depressed, if that were possible. Yes." Hunter shook his head. "Now go after her. You do realize I'm only giving you a few more weeks before I seduce her and steal her away from you, right?"

"Remind me why we're friends again?" Dominique cursed and rose to his full height. "What do I say?"

Hunter tilted his head. "Good to know you've forgotten my instruction after being in her presence only an hour. I believe my earlier suggestion was *hello* and *sorry*. You would do well to remember both of those words considering they will be put to good use with the girl."

Dominique wanted to tell his friend several things; sorry was not one of them, but he listened to his advice and found himself standing outside Isabelle's door without a clue as to how to proceed.

He thought of bringing flowers but as it so happened, it was winter, and everything was dead, just like his heart. He hadn't even kept the orangery up to standard, meaning all he was left with was himself.

He was nothing, no gift suitable for an apology.

Harsh words habitually flew out of his mouth before he was able to stop them, and spending time with Isabelle made it worse than usual. Her happy demeanor, beautiful body and captivating smile threatened his very existence.

The Royal breeding of his ancestors ran thick within him, even though he despised himself for it. His training shaped his actions even when he didn't want it to: he'd been taught to treat women with courtesy even though he knew from experience they rarely deserved it.

Cursing under his breath, he knocked on the door.

"Who is it?" the sweet voice asked.

"Dominique," he snapped and then winced at the gruff sound of his own voice.

"Go away!" Her shout was followed by something breaking against the door. Great, not only her voice was causing things to shatter, the girl herself was now destroying his property.

"See here—"

"Ouch!" Isabelle screamed.

He couldn't breathe, couldn't think. Using all his strength he slammed his body against the door. His shoulder throbbed with the impact. The door remained unmoved. He backed away and hit it again, this time bellowing profanity. Finally, it opened.

Isabelle sat in a heap on the floor, holding her hand out in front of her as blood began trickling down her arm onto her dress. Face pale, she looked fit to swoon. Luckily she was already sitting.

Dominique's heart lurched at the sight. Blood reminded him of his mother, of her death, it was as if the red substance could conjure up memories he'd rather keep trapped in the darkness inside. His mouth went dry as he fought with his conscience; he wanted nothing more than to pull away, to fight the dread that wrapped around his heart, the smell of death as it permeated his nostrils.

But, Isabelle whimpered and he knew he needed to help despite his horrifying reaction.

"Let me see." He reached out and grabbed her hand within his glove. "Hold still."

Isabelle swayed toward him. He picked her up off the floor and laid her across the bed. Blood trickled down her finger.

"I-I threw something," Isabelle mumbled.

"Yes, but that something seems to have bitten you, hmm?" Dominique smiled. "Choose carefully when destroying my property. Might I suggest throwing a chair next time? No shards of glass on the floor. On that note, if Hunter is near you next time you feel the need to take out your anger, please feel free to throw him out the window. It would save me from having to do so, you understand."

Isabelle giggled through her tears.

Relieved, he felt the weight on his chest lighten, just a little, even though her tears shone brightly.

"Ah, there it is," Dominique examined her finger. A bit of glass poked out from the top. Carefully, he tried to pull the infuriating piece out, but the blood began to trickle, making his gloves slippery against the piece. Isabelle moaned.

His stomach lurched. How he hated to see her bleeding and all because he couldn't find the words to be polite. It was his fault, just as everything was always his fault. Would he never learn?

"You must take off your gloves so you can grasp it," Isabelle urged.

Dominique swore, dropping her bleeding hand. Shaking, he walked a few paces away from her and returned. "I cannot do that."

"They're just gloves!" she wailed. "Surely you have more to replace them?"

"It isn't the gloves. I dare say what's beneath the gloves would cause you to swoon in earnest. Now, hold still." He grabbed her hand again and lifted her finger to his lips and into the warm encasing of his mouth. Gently, his teeth nipped the piece of glass out of the wound, spit it in his gloved palm and placed it in his pocket. He continued to suckle, cleaning the wound so he could wrap it in fabric and have Miss Ward take care of it.

At Isabelle's sharp intake of breath, he stole a glance at her eyes. Wide, innocent blue eyes peered back at him through dark, sooty lashes. His heart began hammering inside his chest as the music surrounding her aura picked up.

A single tear ran down her cheek. Reaching out, he caught it with his fingers. Slowly, he finished suckling the wound. Without thinking, he pulled his shirt loose and ripped off a generous piece of fabric, carefully wrapping it around her finger.

"T-thank you." She looked down. Her face flamed red.

Not wanting to embarrass her further or impose on her any more than he already had, he nodded. Making a move to leave, he stopped when her hand reached out and caught his arm.

"I'm sorry I broke another vase," she whispered.

"I'm sorry I yelled."

Isabelle's eyes snapped up to his.

All calming thoughts flew out of his mind when her tongue peeked out to wet her lips as her breathing continued to hasten.

He reached out to cup her chin, and with a smile he leaned down and kissed her across the lips. Quickly, he ended the kiss but was surprised when the girl who had every reason in the world to hate him pulled him flush against her body and opened her mouth to him.

Unable to quench the burning fire of temptation her lush lips and beautiful form presented, he could do nothing as his hands reached from her chin to her hair, diving into the luxurious golden brown tresses.

Dominique cursed his beard. For he couldn't kiss her as he wanted to; it would rub her perfect skin and he had no desire to scar her beautiful face with his roughness. He decided right then and there to do something about his appearance, for no other reason than he wanted to be able to feel her soft skin across his face.

"Will you—" He cleared his throat as he pulled away from her, struggling for the correct words "—do me the honor of joining me for dinner?" Fighting for a breath and swallowing the curse words that threatened he added, "Please."

One would have thought he had just promised her a unicorn or perhaps a castle of her own. She threw her arms around him and pulled him into a tight embrace. "You said 'please'!"

Dominique bit back a retort. "Yes well, it was difficult for me and now I find I'm completely exhausted, so don't expect any fancy words at dinner tonight." Trembling, he walked away from the bed, away from the girl that threatened to destroy every wall he had fought to erect around his heart, and muttered, "Dinner will be served at eight as usual." He paused at the door remembering Hunter's words. Awkwardly he turned on his heel and gave a curt bow before quitting the room, all the while thinking of ways he could strangle his friend without anyone being the wiser.

CHAPTER TWELVE

Manners? They escape my notice, for what good are manners when one lives in solitude? Now, rules, I understand. I exist on the bread of notes and the water of my piano; to practice manners for the very society that failed me seems fruitless. After all, when would I need them?

~The Diary of Dominique Maksylov

DOMINIQUE PACED IN FRONT of the fireplace, no doubt ruining the rug he had placed there for Isabelle's enjoyment. "She's late," he roared when Miss Ward presented herself to him.

"She is getting dressed, my lord, try to have some patience."

He lifted an eyebrow. So now his staff was arguing with him. He opened his mouth to speak just as someone cleared their throat. He turned to see Isabelle entering. A gold dress draped off her shoulders, his mother's diamond necklace plunging between the curves of her breasts.

Mouth completely dry, he struggled for any sort of reaction but all he could muster was an awkward hand gesture for her to take a seat. Blushing, she curtsied and went to the far side of the table.

"My, my, what have we here? Hmm?" Hunter floated into the room, took one look at Isabelle and fell to his knees in front of her. "Oh, thy beauty is so great, it pains my eyes to look upon—"

"Hunter, if you value your life, you will refrain from finishing that sentiment." Dominique glared.

Isabelle tilted her head, her eyes twinkling with amusement. "Does that mean you will compliment me, since you've taken away Hunter's privilege to do so?"

Hunter grinned cheerfully.

Miss Ward crossed her arms.

Isabelle leaned forward in expectation.

"You, um." Curse Hunter for setting him up! "You look…agreeable."

Miss Ward rolled her eyes and left the room. Hunter shook his head. "Perhaps while this young bird practices singing, I'll give you a lesson in the art of seduction. Or perhaps compliments. Women do so love them. Shall I show you how it is done?"

Hunter opened his mouth. In a fit of rage, Dominique charged him but was stopped suddenly when Isabelle stood in front of him with an icy glare. "You may fight like a beast after I've had my dinner. Now, mind your manners, take a seat, and we are going to have a nice meal." She turned on Hunter. "And you! Stop provoking him! It's like living with children!"

Hunter hung his head and walked to his seat, playfully defeated.

Honestly! Never had she been in the presence of such immature gentleman. They actually enjoyed provoking one another. And it was driving her to Bedlam! This was the first meal she had agreed to. Looking across the table, she couldn't quite figure out why she had been so against it in the first place.

Dominique was still cross and more often in a bad mood than a good one, but tonight he seemed different, changed in a way. And that's when it dawned on her.

"You shaved!"

Dominique dropped his spoon; it splashed soup onto his neatly tied cravat. Hunter's laughter echoed through the room.

"And your, that is, your hair, it's, it's..."

"Quite glossy, don't you think?" Hunter interjected. "Apparently all of the Russian princes can boast of such a thick mane. I used to be envious, that is until I discovered I had the larger—"

"Fortune!" Dominique yelled as he turned bright red. "And that has yet to be proven, friend."

Something in their tone told Isabelle it was not fortune they spoke of, but she was too focused on her husband's beautiful face to form a question. Perfectly sculpted lips so full they looked painted. His hair, now with tighter curls, hung loosely around his eyes, dark shadows of his cheekbones poked out, drawing a perfectly symmetrical line. If she were an artist and in need of the perfect male specimen, she would have chosen Dominique, for he didn't seem real. Her eyes must have betrayed her interest, for it wasn't until Hunter cleared his throat the third time that she managed to look away, a burning blush heating her cheeks.

"It is agreeable," she mumbled, dipping her spoon into the soup.

Silence met her declaration. She looked up to see Dominique's hungry gaze. Warmth spread throughout her body, tingling her until she thought she would go mad.

"Perfect, now I'm surrounded by people who know

nothing of how to give a compliment," Hunter interrupted, looking between the two of them. The air was thick with tension. Hunter cleared his throat once more. "Great soup. I always say soup is the best course to start with, it warms the soul when the bed is empty."

"Your bed better stay empty while you're in residence, Wolf." Dominique turned his eyes toward his friend and glowered.

Hunter didn't seem the least bit bothered. "Excuse his hidden meaning, Isabelle. He's merely trying to warn me to stay away from you, lest I find my head removed from my body in a most painful manner."

"Couldn't have said it better myself." Dominique smiled.

Isabelle gasped.

Both men turned to look at her, humor dancing behind their eyes. "Something amiss, my lady?" Dominique asked, the candlelight beaming off of his erotic mouth.

"I, was just, um... Frightened!"

"Of?" he prodded.

"The…" Isabelle looked around for anything to excuse her behavior. But saints alive, without the wild hair covering his face, he looked like a fallen angel. "The dark." She winced. "I thought I saw a shadow…"

Isabelle inwardly rolled her eyes.

Dominique narrowed his gaze, making her shift uncomfortably. And it was that same gaze that held her attention throughout the entire meal. Finally, he relented, but only when Hunter retired for the night.

"Would you like to share a glass of sherry?" Dominique's deep voice interrupted her thoughts.

"Yes, that would be lovely."

They adjourned to one of the practice rooms; the same one Dominique had assaulted her in, earlier that day.

The lit candles cast a haunting glow upon the piano. She

wondered silently what secrets the piano held, for it seemed every time she tried to figure him out, she ended up more confused than when she started.

"Tell me, Isabelle…" Dominique came up behind her his breath a soft whisper across her ear, "Why is it that you love music so much?"

What she wouldn't have given to have been blessed with musical talent. "I love something that does not love me back, it seems." Her intake of breath made her nearly fall backward into his chest. He wouldn't think it a double meaning, would he?

"And you love music?"

"Desperately."

"Do you feel music? Did you feel it this afternoon when I was teaching you?"

"I tried." Her shoulders slumped. "I admit to being distracted."

"By?"

"My own thoughts, your nearness, the room and dazzling view out the windows. It is so hard to concentrate when life goes on around you." Never had she realized how much she was driven to distraction until she said the words aloud.

"Don't move," he breathed.

Terrified, she stayed immobile. Dominique withdrew a black piece of fabric and grinned. "Now, close your eyes."

Not quite sure why she trusted the man, she closed her eyes as he wrapped the blindfold around her eyes. "Now… I begin your second lesson of the day."

She nodded. His presence left, and she was immediately cold. Where did he go? She wrung her hands and finally clasped them behind her back as her ears listened for any sort of movement.

"Feel." It was one word, one single word from Dominique's lips. She couldn't see his lips but knew the way the word would look as he formed it. No doubt they pressed together just slightly before he exhaled. Her breathing became ragged.

He pulled her body firmly against him, he held her from behind, his strong arms wrapped around her.

"Feel," he said again, this time lifting her hand to his lips. Swaying, she managed to stay standing, but it was not without effort.

His skin was warm beneath her touch, his lips slightly wet as if his tongue had just licked the bottom half of their plumpness. Slowly, he grasped her hand and drew it down his neck until it stopped at his pulse. A healthy rhythm pulsed beneath her fingers, and again he moved her hand lower repeating the same word as her hand went to his hard lined stomach. "Feel." His voice came out hoarsely as she felt his inhale and exhale of breath.

"Your body—" He wrapped his hands around her waist bringing her closer, "is the instrument, much like the piano is mine. You desperately want to sing, but have no idea how to control the one tool you have to your advantage. Much like a child who wants to play the piano but hasn't a clue what the notes sound like, that is how you sing. Now, I want you to feel."

"I did, I just felt…"

"Not me, I was merely demonstrating what you were to do to yourself. I want you to understand your body, understand your femininity so you may finally take ownership of what God has given you." He grasped her hands within his own and laid them across her own lips. "Now, feel."

Breathing heavily, she listened, the silent torture nearly killing her as his hands helped move hers over her own body.

Never had she felt so alive or so in desperate want of the man holding her so close to his warmth. "Touch, just here." He cupped her hand and pressed it against her neck. "Listen to your pulse, listen to the rhythm." Sliding her hand downward, he pressed it against her heart. "Your breath, it is shallow, is it not?"

She could only nod as he slid her hand further down to her abdomen. "Breathe from here, not here." His hand left hers as he pressed it against her ribs. It was enormous and warm almost taking up the expanse of her chest as he pushed against it with each breath.

Now, his hands skimmed the tips of her breasts as he met hers across her stomach. "When you sing, I want you to remember to feel, to have confidence in that feeling you have. Do not make noise for the sake of making noise, make noise for the sake of making music."

With little effort, he lifted her into his arms and set her across a bench. He began to play a soft, haunting melody. The blindfold was still on, but it seemed with her eyes blackened she could finally hear the music the way it was supposed to be heard. Dominique's gift was evident as he continued playing, almost as if he was telling her a story with his hands. Something he dare not communicate with his words.

"Don't stop," she pleaded when the music ended.

"I wouldn't dream of it." He played a new song, one that brought pain into her lungs. Tears formed in her eyes, without thought she reached out to touch his hands as they played, the minute she came into contact with them she knew something was horribly wrong.

He jerked away; the music came to a crushing stop. His hands were without gloves. Not knowing what else to do, she waited. Finally, after a few minutes he removed her blindfold. A sad smile played at the corners of his mouth. "I believe this is where I bid you good night." He lifted her hand into his gloves and bestowed a gentle kiss on the tip of each finger.

"Goodnight." She gulped and wandered out of the room

all the while keeping her eyes trained on his form as he too exited without another word. So close, she was so close to knowing him she could feel it, even see it at times in the way he looked at her, the way he touched her. The problem, it seemed, was he didn't trust anyone, not even himself.

CHAPTER THIRTEEN

I can no longer write music. For every time my hand stretches across the parchment to give life to the note, my mind thinks of her, and when my mind replays her image, all I see is blood. My compositions are my blood oath, to avenge her one way or another. To push forward when all I want to do is relinquish music's hold upon me.

~The Diary of Dominique Maksylov

ISABELLE AWOKE EXHAUSTED THE morning after her first music lessons. The feel of Dominique's hands across her stomach, and her neck, made her body tingle with awareness. His touch did things to her, funny things, that she never knew possible. For how was a woman to feel this, this feeling when the man touching her was so harsh?

Perhaps she would never figure out her own fickle emotions. She hastened through her morning toilette and went down to the dining room to break her fast.

Hurrying down the marble staircase, she didn't notice that the room, usually empty when she ate in the morning, held not just Dominique but Hunter as well.

"So the princess is awake?" Hunter looked up from his plate. "We were beginning to worry about you."

Isabelle lifted an eyebrow. "We?"

"Yes." Hunter wiped his mouth with a napkin. "Well, to be quite honest, I knew you were just fine, most likely exhausted from beating off the swine and his snoring through the night. But, I am glad you are here." He chuckled when Dominique rolled his eyes. "It seems Dominique has discovered close to twenty ways you could have injured yourself this morning, all of them most likely a figment of his own imaginings. But alas, I see you are in one piece."

Isabelle snapped her attention to Dominique. With his face clean-shaven it was apparent that he was fighting not to blush, as his neck turned a light pink color.

"See, old friend? I told you it was impossible for someone to fall from her bed and break her neck, or take a tumble down the stairs, or for a bird to jump through the window and peck her to death. Truly, does your own imagination never frighten you?"

Still, Dominique said nothing. Peculiar. It wasn't often that he didn't yell back at his friend when provoked, or at least growl.

Isabelle walked closer to where he sat and leaned in toward his face. Perhaps he was foxed? At her inspection Dominique leaned back, which of course just made her lean forward even more until she was only a few inches away from his face, her eyes squinted.

"Saints alive, I think she's inspecting me," Dominique said cheekily.

Hunter's laughter brought Isabelle back to the present. Embarrassed, she jerked back and went to the sideboard to obtain some toast.

"Are you ill, my lord?" she asked, her back turned to both of the men.

"Ill?" Dominique repeated. "No, I believe I'm quite healthy."

"Foxed," she guessed.

"I do not drink in the mornings."

"Perhaps you are in good humor because Miss Ward snuck some herbs into your morning coffee?"

Suddenly Dominique's hands were on her shoulders, and she nearly dropped her plate. She stood, rigid, as he whispered in her ear, his voice sounding like music. "Or, perhaps I'm overjoyed at seeing you first thing this morning."

"Impossible," she breathed. Never had he taken his breakfast with her. His only demand had been dinner. If anything, he had been avoiding her for the past week. But everything changed last night. She felt it, felt the way his touch sent a shiver down her spine. It seemed he was actually trying to be agreeable.

"I have a surprise for you." She felt him step away. His abrupt subject change was welcome. Grabbing an extra piece of toast, she reached for the jam and went to join the men at the table.

"You're leaving?" She added some jam to her toast and waited for him to bark at her for saying such a hurtful thing.

"If I left, you would be coming with me," he answered, his words short as if he was trying to keep himself from yelling.

With a sigh, she looked up and into his blue eyes, eyes that were a whirl of so many emotions. Perhaps he was trying to be a good husband. Maybe, he wanted things to be different between them. Music, it seemed had united them in some odd way, though she couldn't imagine how, considering he was so agitated with her lack of talent.

"What is it?" Taking a bite of her toast, she waited.

Hunter folded his hands and leaned in toward Isabelle. "You mean the actual surprise, not the fact that Dominique is doing such a wonderful job of keeping his temper in check? I take full credit by the way. You may thank me how you see fit." He winked and stared blatantly at her lips.

The air in the room stilled. Isabelle stole a glance at Dominique, who against all odds still appeared to be calm. Suspicious, Isabelle promised herself that she would sniff his tea to see if there *was* any sort of calming herb mixed in.

"Finish your breakfast. Take your time." Dominique rose from his seat. "I will await you in the stables."

Isabelle nodded at his retreating form then glanced back at Hunter, who merely shrugged and winked at Miss Ward who had just entered the room.

Dominique paced back in forth in the stables, watching for a glimpse of Isabelle's honeyed-brown hair glinting in the sunlight, waiting for her luscious voice to break the silence, or at least keep him from going mad.

"This better work," he mumbled to himself.

Last night after watching her sleep, which he later admitted was a grave mistake for she slept so beautifully it made his chest hurt, he had decided he would try. The nights had been torturous, but nothing compared to the absolute pain he felt every day that went by that he was stripped of the chance to touch her with his bare hands.

The idea that he could be anything other than what he was hadn't at any point crossed his mind, that is, until Isabelle entered into his life. And oddly enough, after spending time in her company, he found he quite enjoyed himself, at least enough to want to see her smile, to hear her quick intake of breath when he was close, to smell the scent of lavender floating off her skin.

After all, he had self-control. He had been in control of

his baser instincts these last few years. He'd had to be. And now, well, he imagined he would try to keep the walls around his heart firm, for they had to be impenetrable. But, he justified his actions with his wife. After all, she was lonely, and he would be just as bad as his father before him if he left her to her own devices.

Hunter suggested he ravish her, but that would prove difficult, for he could not imagine separating his soul from bonding with hers if he joined her physically. And Hunter always had allowed his body to make choices before his mind when it came to women.

Miss Ward had suggested he dine with her in the mornings in order to familiarize himself with her character.

And Brinks was so besotted with the girl that his suggestion had been to let her have free reign throughout the castle as long as she smiled at him the way she did. In fact, just this morning, Brinks had told Dominique how lovely it would be to allow her to pick out a horse.

Fools. All of them.

He hoped he would trust her, eventually. But it would take time.

As all good things did.

"Dominique?" Isabelle called out his name. The sweetness of her voice gave him pause. Without taking as much as a breath, he peered around the corner and watched, fascinated as she glided along the ground, dancing as she made her way to the stables. Her long, graceful arms tickled the sides of her dress. If he closed his eyes he could almost feel the way the fabric would grace his fingers. It had been ages since he had felt any sort of texture against his hands. Would her dress feel silky? And her hair, would it slide through his fingers? He shuddered as he imagined how her soft warm body would penetrate into the depths of his scars.

He shook the treacherous thought from his head.

It was just an afternoon ride.

Nothing more, nothing less.

"Dominique?" she called again, this time closer as her booted foot stepped into the stables, obviously having changed into a riding habit in record time.

Naturally, he didn't want to appear the fool that sat about and gawked at her without her knowledge, so he thought the best course of action would be to ignore her altogether.

His brilliant plan proved not so brilliant when she, in a moment of obvious irritation, kicked a bucket in his direction.

"Dominique? Is there a reason you've been rendered mute?"

He turned on his heel, prepared to give her a tongue lashing for mocking him, or at least a haughty look.

What he had in mind to do, and what actually happened were two different things.

But what could she expect? When she stood, hands on hips, lip jutting out, and pieces of hair tumbling out of her coiffure.

"Uh…" He prayed for a complete sentence, or words.

Again nothing.

"Well?" she prompted, this time taking a step closer. The smell of lavender practically danced in the air, bombarding his senses, weakening his knees.

He shook his head, breaking her penetrating gaze. "Pick one."

Unfortunately, he hadn't noticed that he was in fact in front of an empty stable, not anywhere near the other side of the stables where several horses stood eating hay.

"You have a mind to put me in the stables now? Am I to pick my room? Is that why you've dragged me out here in the blistering winter? So we aren't to go riding?"

So many questions and assumptions in that beautiful head of hers. "No, Isabelle, it seems I'm out of sorts today. I meant for you to pick a horse, but if you'd rather a night tossing in the hay with yours truly, by all means, don't let me stop you."

Her eyes narrowed. "Fine. I want that one." She nodded in his direction, to the horse directly to her left. His horse.

"Any horse but that horse."

"But I thought you said I should just pick one?"

Dominique let out an irritated breath. "I meant for you to pick from the available horses, over there." He pointed to the long row of stables that held the rest of the horses.

"Then you should have made that clear before you ran your mouth and got yourself into a pickle. You said to pick a horse, and I fancy the black one."

"You'll get yourself killed." Dominique knew it was a losing battle, trying to fight with her. She was just as stubborn as he, though she tried to shield her streak with a quick smile and easy manner.

Isabelle placed her hands on her hips, jutting out one and leaned provocatively close to him. *Curse her inability to back down*. He could roar, growl, and throw all sorts of tantrums and she'd most likely smile and ask if he were done. And the worst of it was that he would have be to be standing within her vicinity the entire time, nearly dying from having to keep his hands away from her body.

"Fine." He moved out of the way. "But don't say I didn't warn you when Horse throws you."

"Horse?" Isabelle walked toward the animal and laid a hand across the shiny coat. "Is that truly the beast's name?"

"My name or the horse's?" Dominique tilted his head.

"The horse."

"Is named Horse."

"I'm confused." Isabelle furrowed her brows.

"Yes well, it isn't too hard to understand. The horse is named Horse. Lovely name. Descriptive, straight to the point, no confusion as to what the animal actually is…"

Isabelle leaned across Horse. "Yes, it's also boring and ridiculous. Tell me, were you drunk when you named her or merely practicing the art of stupidity?"

"Both." Hunter interrupted. "Though, to be fair, I believe it was my own fault that he was so inebriated. The stupidity, however, is all his own doing."

"Thank you, Hunter." Dominique felt himself manage a small, irritated twitch of his mouth, which could be mistaken as a smile if one looked hard enough. He shook his head. "Are you suddenly under the impression you've been invited?"

Hunter grinned and peered around Dominique to wink at Isabelle. He gave a little wave and returned his attention to his friend. "It seems our dear Isabelle has forgotten her hat. And I thought to myself, what lady, what princess, could possibly go for a morning ride without her hat? Truly, it would be a travesty! An error of gigantic proportions! So I steeled myself against the morning mist and cold temperatures, to save the day."

"How very heroic," Dominique said dryly.

Hunter looked genuinely pleased that Dominique had even acknowledged him. "Thank you, I thought so. Now, here you are Isabelle. Let us attach this magnificent piece of…er, hat. And get you on to your delightful morning."

Something wasn't right. Hunter wasn't truly the idiot he was portraying himself to be. If he was, he would be the worst spy the Crown had to offer.

He walked forward and gave her another wink, just as the groom entered the stables to speak with Dominique.

"He needs a little push is all." Hunter placed the hat on her head, in perfect fashion.

"Pardon?"

Jolly façade gone, Hunter took a step back, and she nearly gasped. She had always thought he was an attractive man, but his silly attitude made him seem so harmless. She realized it was a mask, merely one of the disguises he wore to keep his true self as well as his real intentions hidden. Humor drained from his face as Hunter leaned forward and whispered, "He needs you."

Isabelle swallowed and looked down at her hands. "I'm not sure I'm doing a good job."

Hunter's hand touched her chin, lifting her gaze upwards toward his face. "Then I'll just have to remedy that. Oh, and if you could take the sting out of your slap I would be eternally grateful."

"Whatever do you mea—"

Before she had a chance to finish her sentence, Hunter was upon her. All of him. Raw masculinity poured out of him as his lips forcibly moved across hers. His hands moved to the sides of her face. And in a moment of sheer madness, his tongue plunged into her mouth. Truly, he was insane!

She pushed against him, beat at his chest, and finally when he pulled away, slapped him across the cheek.

"If that was you taking the sting out of your slap, I pity poor Dominique. How many times have you slapped him, anyway?" Hunter rubbed his cheek just before Dominique charged him, knocking them both into the hay.

"What the devil do you think you're doing?" Dominique brought his fist back to lay what would surely be a devastating blow to Hunter's head, when Isabelle let out a scream and fell to the ground.

Dominique lurched to his feet and ran to her side. Hunter, however, lay back in the hay, hands behind his head and a piece of straw in his mouth.

"Are you hurt?" Dominique inquired. It seemed the only

time he was truly gentle with her was when he thought she was injured. Before, it was when the glass had cut her, and there was the situation with him being afraid that Horse would throw her, and now this.

"My, um, my ankle turned, just a little." She managed a small voice and looked shakily in Hunter's direction. He nodded his approval and gave another wink before slinking away.

"I—I think he was merely trying to provoke you," Isabelle stuttered, in hopes that he wouldn't beat Hunter senseless later. Dominique's hands glided smoothly over the ankle she had pointed at. Each trail he made with his gloved fingers caused gooseflesh.

"Hunter is a fool." Dominique helped her to her feet. "But, he's a smart fool, and he's my best friend. If he decided to kiss you, I can only imagine he either wants me to shoot him, is bored of country life, or truly is making good on his promise to steal you away. Regardless, you are mine." The way he said *mine* was so possessive, so typically male, but she wasn't offended. No, rather, she felt light-headed and important.

He led her to Horse and gave strict instructions to the groom to place a sidesaddle on the animal, all the while cursing Isabelle under his breath for taking the one horse he didn't want her touching.

Within minutes they were ready for their morning jaunt, they led the horses out into the open. Isabelle pulled her fur cloak tight over her riding habit. As his hands wrapped around her waist to hoist her up, she whispered. "I am."

"You are? What?"

Isabelle felt heat rising to her cheeks. Looking down at his curious, chiseled face, she almost lost her nerve but remembered Hunter's words. "Yours."

CHAPTER FOURTEEN

Emotions are fickle. Music, however, is always the same. Notes may change, chords may differ, but the sensation of gliding one's hands over the keys never changes. Exhilarating, provoking, sensual—but music can only play part time lover until you crave the real thing. The real emotions, the real feel of a woman's flesh in your hands, the taste of her tongue on your lips. I pity the day I begin to crave such things, for nothing will keep me from experiencing it, and I fear my own emotions will be my downfall.

~The Diary of Dominique Maksylov

SINCE HIS EARS WERE obviously playing tricks on him, Dominique had no reason for his hands to still be placed across Isabelle's luscious waist, or for his body to react so violently, so possessively, to her admission. Merciful heavens, he was actually perspiring over the simple word. *"Yours."*

Clearing his throat, he walked away and mounted the horse he thought Isabelle would choose.

"You're an idiot." Isabelle's voice disturbed his dream-like state.

Dominique turned his horse to face her. "Excuse me?"

"If you truly think I would pick that horse over this one, you're an idiot." She flashed him a brilliant smile and kicked her heels into Horse so hard that Dominique's sides hurt.

"Race you to the forest?"

Dominique swore as she took off, but forced his horse to gallop after her, and then felt foolish for even trying.

The impetuous girl was a sure judge of horseflesh. For he had assumed she would choose the oldest, most docile creature in the stables like the one he currently rode. Instead she chose the most dangerous one of the bunch. It was a good five minutes before he reached her. And the horse's sides were heaving.

"That was not even a race, Isabelle."

Brown hair spilled from her coiffure onto her shoulders, a bright crimson stained her cheeks. "No, it wasn't." Her teeth bit down on her lower lip as her mouth spread into a smile.

Dominique irritated with his own arousal at seeing her bite her lip, dismounted and gruffly pulled her from her horse making sure to tie them to the nearest tree. "Now, for the surprise."

"I thought the horse was the surprise?"

Dominique grasped her hand. "You thought wrong. Now, try to keep up." He pulled her closer into his embrace and led her through the edge of the forest, into the tiny clearing he used to retreat to as a boy.

The only happy memory of playing at all had been when his father demanded he take riding lessons to have an hour of respite from playing the piano. But this particular memory was something he knew would forever be etched in his mind.

His mother had told him that elves lived in the forest and often made ice sculptures during the night, casting magical enchantments around the land. Of course, he was always such a sober little boy, he never believed her. Until one day, when he took his daily ride, the only hour he had to himself; he went into the clearing and discovered two ice sculptures as if they had been erected out of pure magic.

Later he discovered it was the doing of Cuppins Port. Apparently he had felt sorry for Dominique as a young lad not being able to experience adventure of his own, so he had created magic for him. He never told his father, for surely he would get into trouble if he was caught doing something other than training to be the leader his father wanted him to be.

It had been his sanctuary.

Until the night his father followed him and destroyed the magical sculptures. Dominique cried himself to sleep that night. A week later, out of sheer habit, he led his horse into the clearing and noticed a small sculpture, resting beneath a tree. The scene was a boy playing the piano. It was him. And ever since then, every winter, there was a sculpture waiting for him.

Perhaps it was foolish, but if he could share just a tiny bit of himself with Isabelle, this was what he wanted to share. The one happy memory he could think of. The only memory of his childhood that wasn't stained with blood, pride, or betrayal.

"Where are we?" Isabelle asked. Her hand was still firmly clenched within his.

"You'll see." Dominique's breath danced out in front of him, the temperatures were getting colder, and he only hoped Isabelle wouldn't freeze during their little adventure. Of course, he could always pull her closer and share body heat, but that would mean touching her, and touching any more of her body would surely lead to things he had no business doing, considering they were in a snow-covered clearing. Though, it would keep *him* quite warm.

Isabelle gasped, releasing his hand and covering her mouth. He smiled at her response. For it was truly something taken straight from a fairy tale book. Crystalline icicles hung from the branches of the trees, glittering like diamonds, the poetic rhythm of the melting ice dripping into the pristine snow drifts. Everywhere one looked was a reflection of the icy cold of winter, yet strangely warm and intimate. Trees encircled the small area; it appeared untouched by anything. Isabelle's dark hair was a vivid chocolate against the white snow and her eyes sparkling sapphires as she smiled at him with appreciation. "It's so beautiful! It feels like magic!" She ran into the middle of the clearing and twirled around in a circle. Pieces of snow fell from the trees onto her eyelashes as if they too wanted to touch her and add to the enchanting beauty she was.

Transfixed, Dominique watched, a smile spreading across his lips as Isabelle laughed and then stopped twirling. "What is this place?"

Suddenly feeling exposed, Dominique turned away from her burning gaze. "It was my sanctuary when I was a small boy. If you look just there—" he pointed beneath the largest of the trees "—you'll find something I'm sure you've never seen before."

Isabelle laughed and ran to the tree. "What is it? I don't understand."

Dominique was going to kill Cuppins Port, slowly…The sculpture beneath the tree was that of a beautiful young girl who looked exactly like Isabelle. But that wasn't the most mortifying part. No, the worst part was that the girl was in a man's arms. Dominique's arms to be precise, and they were sharing a passionate embrace.

His face heated as he struggled for words. Isabelle bent down and touched the sculpture. "It's beautiful. Is it us?"

"I assure you, Isabelle, my intention was not to—"

She reached out her hand and lightly touched his arm. Rising to her feet, she stepped toward him. Time stood still, as if nothing existed but her eyes, her lips, and the vision of icicles glittering her hair. Frozen in place, he closed his eyes, as her hand traveled slowly up his arm and cupped his face.

Tender, she was tender and achingly slow in her examination of him. She removed her gloves and then her hands caressed his cheeks, skin-on-skin contact that singed him all the way to his frozen toes. Thawing much more than his body, but his mind. His heart. In that moment he believed in magic.

The magic of touch.

His eyes flickered open as he watched her examine him, and then her eyes closed as her cheek pressed against his and then he felt her plump, wet lips touch the side of his mouth. The words, his thoughts, everything was lost and forgotten in the beauty of her warmth.

He kissed her. It was as simple as that. Different than the other times because this particular moment was theirs, and only theirs. With nothing to prove, no pride in the way, and no hurt feelings.

It was them.

Gradually, she parted her lips. But he didn't push the kiss any further than paying special attention to each corner of her mouth, as if a treasure was hidden behind the curves of her lips. Dominique reached out and touched her hair, smoothing it back behind her ear as he laid lazy kisses across her mouth and finally tasted her tongue. Slow, erotic movements made it absolute torture to keep his hands from traveling down the expanse of her body. He brought his hands around her waist and pulled her tighter against him, their breaths mingling in the air in front of them.

Heat spread through his body at their contact. Feminine curves fit perfectly into his arms, and he found himself needing to be closer to her, needing that completion that only comes with intimacy.

Oddly, this innocent kiss had turned into him wanting

sex. Horrified, because it completely shattered this beautiful moment, he abruptly pulled back. Sex had always been identified with using women, never something so intimate as what he was experiencing with Isabelle. It was hard to fuse the two acts together. One was out of necessity and selfishness, whereas this, well it would be out of wanting to give all of himself to the one woman he knew he shouldn't.

Never had his body been so aroused, so completely ready to give of itself, to take and take until nothing was left of the woman peering at him through thick lashes.

"I can't..." Dominique swallowed and took a few deep breaths. Clearly Isabelle didn't understand the seriousness of the situation. Had she any idea how close he was to utterly ravishing her on the purest of snow? He closed his eyes against the ugliness of his thoughts: Isabelle's dark hair spread across the white covered ground, her cherry red lips swollen with kisses and then his blasted hands *sans* gloves caressing her body. Red, ugly scars ruined the picture of perfection, just as he ruined everything he touched.

He winced, and stepped completely back from Isabelle.

She stepped toward him, trapping him between her body and the tree.

"Don't."

"Pardon?" His breath was coming out in short gasps.

"Don't hide anymore." Her voice was soft, angelic, sensual. He blinked several times trying to break the illusion of the compassion in her face.

"I think it's time for a music lesson," she said taking his hand.

The idea of her teaching him anything musical made him laugh aloud. Isabelle gave him a pointed look. "Never fear. I know where my strengths lie. I sometimes wonder, Dominique..."

"What?" His voice was hoarse with arousal. "What do

you wonder?"

She stopped in the middle of the clearing and let go of his hand. "I wonder if all you know is music. I wonder if you understand things only in musical terms, but fail to comprehend emotions. It seems to me that you lack something important."

He shuddered, unable to help it. This was the moment, the time when she would point out every insecurity, every single thing wrong with him. Just as his father had, and his mother and—

"You do not follow your heart." She interrupted his thoughts. "So I'm going to teach *you* how to listen."

Stunned, he merely stood there as Isabelle began to circle him. "Listen, Dominique, listen to the drops of water falling from the trees. Listen to your breathing, just as you showed me with the music. Listen."

Satisfying her, he closed his eyes and did just that. He listened.

And then, sultry feminine hands wrapped around him from behind. The smell of lavender overwhelmed his senses. How the devil was he to listen when all he wanted to do was turn around and lay the woman flat on her back, possessing every inch of her body?

Her voice, so quiet and steady, whispered in his ear, tickling the side of his neck. "One, two, three. One, two, three." She then put her hand on his chest and lightly tapped it in cadence with the same rhythm he previously taught her. Leisurely, she continued her tapping until finally he was facing her.

"You took a girl without knowing anything about her, saving her, at least you claim as much," she whispered. "What does your heart say about that?"

"My heart—"

"And before you answer," she interrupted. "Remember

your head is not your heart. What does your heart say?"

Dominique exhaled. Truly, his head told him he was the worst sort of human being, that taking her defied all logic. Selfishness drove him to do what he did. Yet as he was thinking on it and as she corrected him, it was as if his heart burst forth with the correct answer—the real answer.

"My heart says there was no other way. It says the moment I laid eyes on you, the rhythm of my heart forever changed…and aligned itself with yours."

If his response shocked her, it was impossible to tell, as she continued in the same fashion. "Relax, listen to your breathing, forget your thoughts, listen to the music of the trees. The music I know you hear. It sings to you, pulls you. Dominique, what does your mind say about me?"

"You said to listen to my heart."

"Answer the question."

Dominique sighed and hung his head. Eyes still closed, he answered. "My mind says I don't deserve you. That you'll run away screaming the minute you see me for who I really am. My mind cannot separate my need to have you and my selfishness for doing so."

"And your heart?"

With a shudder Dominique turned to face her. "It sings your name."

CHAPTER FIFTEEN

I fear losing control. I fear the day when I hold nothing back and there is nobody there to catch me when I fall. But most of all, I fear that someone will be there, they will catch me, and in the end will know all of my secrets, all of my lies. In the end I would rather fall, for then I would feel no shame in my lies.

~The Diary of Dominique Maksylov

ISABELLE FELT TEARS WELL in the corners of her eyes. She blinked rapidly, trying to remove the desperate urge she felt to weep for the man in her arms. For the vulnerability he had just shown.

She reached out to grab his hand. He pulled back, but she pursued, finally able to grasp at his gloves. She prayed her eyes said trust me, when she gazed into his. Fear was marked on his every feature, from the grim set of his lips, to the pale color of his face. Gradually his eyes closed. Black lashes against the perfect lines of his cheekbones. He exhaled, Isabelle pulled and then a branch snapped in the distance.

"Get down!" Dominique hissed, pulling her behind one

of the trees between two large bushes.

Two French soldiers meandered into the clearing. They were armed, but discussing a recent fight that had broken out amongst the soldiers, nothing important was said. Isabelle's heart slammed in her chest. Surely they were safe! After all, they were at least a few days' ride from Brussels. And Dominique would never knowingly put them in danger. She glanced at Dominique, he was frozen in place, did he too understand French? He had to, for the minute the Frenchman cursed the English, Dominique's hand tightened on her waist.

Swallowing the dryness in her throat, she glanced at Dominique. He looked ready to attack, ready to kill. His eyes darkened as the men neared the tree where they hid, and then they were gone.

Isabelle began to shake in Dominique's arms. He held her close and kissed her head. "Are you all right?"

"Y-yes. I thought we were safe here! Heavens! What if they would have seen the horses?"

Dominique grimaced. "Yes well, we were fortunate that they didn't notice much of anything, we weren't exactly concealed."

"How did you know there was danger? It could have been an animal, or even Hunter."

Dominique actually blushed and looked away. "We should return."

Isabelle put her hands on her hips. "Not until you tell me. What are you, some kind of spy? Is that how you and Hunter are friends? You both work for the Crown? Is that just another secret you're keeping from me?"

Dominique's face turned murderous. Isabelle backed up, knowing she'd pushed him too far, and so soon after the progress made!

"I am not a spy," he spat. "And if you must know, I am a trifle mad, at least that's what you're going to think."

"I would never."

"Save me your pity. Yes, you will." Dominique mounted his horse, not giving his aid for Isabelle to mount her own. "I heard the music."

"The music?" Isabelle repeated dryly. "I didn't hear anything."

Dominique let out a heavy sigh. "You wouldn't. You don't have my curse. I hear…" He swore and took a deep breath. "The reason I took you when I did was because I heard music. It was the same music that haunted me when tragedy struck my heart as a boy. And when the twig snapped, I heard it again."

"So you…hear…music." Isabelle had to say it aloud to believe it herself.

"Yes, I believe that's been established."

"And it tells you things."

Dominique cursed and stopped his horse. "It doesn't speak to me. Well, I guess in a way it does. Just...never mind."

"When you saw me, when you took me, you said the music changed, were you…" Isabelle swallowed the dryness in her throat. "Were you worried for my welfare? Was I truly in danger?"

Dominique shifted on his saddle and looked away, before digging his heels into the horse's flesh.

"No…Dominique, wait." She pressed her boots into the horse's sides to catch up to his trot. "I'm just trying to understand."

Dominique laughed bitterly. "You will never understand. Nobody will ever understand me. Don't you get it?" He urged the horse faster; she increased the pressure in her heels to keep up. "No matter how many walls you break down, no matter how many lessons you give me. You will never understand my pain, you will never be close enough to understand what haunts me."

"I want to be." Her voice trembled.

"No, no you don't. You want to fix me; you think you can heal what's been broken, what's been so utterly destroyed. But you cannot redeem the damned, Isabelle. No matter how hard you wish it." His words were just above a whisper when he said, "I thank you for trying. And as I have shown you, I will try as well, but please, do not continue to wish for things that will never be. I will never be more than I am right now. You must accept that."

Isabelle nodded as she watched him gallop off. He didn't hear her say *I do,* nor did he see the slippery tears that ran down her cold cheeks. It was more than the physical scars that kept him so tortured, though she hadn't seen any evidence of such in all her days with him. But she decided then and there that she was going to discover what haunted him, even if it killed her.

She watched him jump off of his horse and stomp through the back door. With a sigh, she brought Horse back to the stables and slowly made her way back to the castle. Hunter greeted her, a grim look on his face.

"I take it things did not go well?" Hunter offered his arm. She took it as he led her into one of the salons.

"You could say that."

"Truly, I do not understand why you would have so much difficulty. He's such a shy, gentle fellow."

At that precise moment a loud bellow was heard throughout the house and then a thunderous yell, followed by something shattering.

"I'm sure he's just redecorating. Hates the color purple, often makes him agitated and prickly," Hunter offered.

Isabelle laughed in spite of the somber mood she was in. Perhaps Hunter would tell her what haunted Dominique so.

"Won't you tell me about my husband?" Isabelle gave him her most reassuring smile, the same one she used to give the cook in order to receive the hottest biscuits in the mornings.

Hunter's eyes widened just slightly before he leaned forward and clasped his hands. "You're good, I'll give you that. Put you in a room with a few French soldiers and they'd blurt out every battle plan and strategy that existed, and all for one of your smiles or for a kiss. But I am made of stronger stuff."

"Of course you are," she said, breathlessly.

"As I said not a few seconds ago, I admire your flirtation, and I would normally take you up on such an offer, though we both know you'd rather be shot than lie with a wolf. Not when your heart so irrevocably belongs to him." Hunter sighed and pushed away from his seat, he walked in front of the large window.

Isabelle watched his taut muscles flex and stretch beneath his fitted jacket. Lifting a hand to his head, he rubbed then cursed. "It is not my story to tell, Isabelle." He looked agitated and uncomfortable before taking a seat again. "Sometimes, it is best for the ones who have been wronged to tell how they were wronged. For me to steal that from Dominique would do irreparable harm to your relationship, for how can you be the salve that heals him when he doesn't trust you with his life? I cannot take that from him. I refuse to steal the one thing keeping you apart from one another."

"Isabelle!" Dominique's voice shattered the moment between her and Hunter. Isabelle looked back toward the door. What the devil did he want? It was nearly time for luncheon and…

"Have you forgotten your lesson?" Dominique stood in the doorway, hands behind his back; whatever scowl he must have worn while shouting minutes ago was gone and in place of it, a demure smile that made her slightly uncomfortable. Perhaps he was *drinking and redecorating* as Hunter put it.

"Apologies, I hadn't realized you wished to commence lessons so soon before luncheon."

"You will join me in the music room for luncheon," Dominique said in a clipped voice then glared at Hunter. "Don't you have some place to be?"

Hunter jumped from his seat. "Yes, well, any place where I'm welcome. Perhaps the local tavern has some wenches I can pay to talk to. After all, I'm merely a man starved for conversation. Besides, I've already had my kiss for the day." He winked at Isabelle. Wide-eyed she could only shake her head. The fool truly didn't know when to stop talking.

Dominique rolled his eyes and pushed the door open as Hunter walked briskly out before returning his attention to Isabelle. "You have five minutes to change out of your riding habit and into an afternoon dress. I'll be waiting."

Clenching her fists at her sides, Isabelle wanted nothing more than to yell at him. She knew why he did it. Why he was so hot and cold. He only gave her glimpses of the man he could be. Instead he hid behind all of his anger, his bitterness. It was easier to push others away when one shielded oneself against emotions. And he had spent the better part of his morning bleeding for her. In all honesty, he was most likely spent for the day and exhausted.

Managing a small smile, she curtsied to her husband and walked toward the stairway. If he wanted to be in lessons the rest of the day, she would be in lessons. Anything to discover his secrets to help him heal.

CHAPTER SIXTEEN

I always hated it when my parents would raise their voices. Often times I was told I spoke too softly. But I felt the need to balance out the loudness, to blot out the anger. Yet, I am my father's son, as much as I loath to admit it. For the anger that destroyed him I see in my own reflection. It scares me more than I care to admit, for I hate giving into fear. But I reek of it. The stench of fear is what I bathe in. For every moment of every day I wonder when I will turn out just like him.

~The Diary of Dominique Maksylov

DOMINIQUE WAS ACTUALLY QUITE patient. He just didn't want anyone to know about it. He would be happy, sitting at the piano and drinking tea all day with Isabelle. But he noticed that the minute he began to sit and think was also the precise moment he was tempted to give into every single feeling he had. Silence made him want to speak, and when he was in her presence he wanted to speak of it.

But she would hate him again if she knew.

She would recoil in disgust, not just because of his

physical scars but because of the sins he committed in honor of them. Isabelle wanted to know, she wanted to fix him, she had said as much hadn't she? Music was the common ground. He needed it to be able to think clearly. If the music surrounded their time together then perhaps he wouldn't be tempted to open himself up too much.

"Dominique?" Isabelle's sweet voice called to him. Sometimes he wondered if she understood how completely beautiful and clear she sounded to him. If he was in a crowded street in London and she spoke his name, he would still know it was her. The inflection of her voice sounded like a bell; unclouded, strong, unwavering, and every time she said his name, she lingered at the end as if she didn't want the word to finish pouring forth from her mouth.

Obviously, he was mad to think so, but he imagined she liked the way his name sounded on her lips. Not that he cared, for any time she spoke he wanted to close his eyes and listen. Her singing voice was in desperate need of help, but he was thankful for it. What would he have done had she had a beautiful singing voice? Along with all the rest of her gifts? He shuddered thinking of it.

"Are you well?" Isabelle was leaning over him, her eyes a mask of worry. Blast, it felt good to have someone other than his servants concerned for his well-being.

He cleared his throat. "Fine, just fine. Now, why don't we have a little to eat while we discuss your lesson for the day?"

Nodding, she took a seat across from him. "Shall I pour the tea?"

"Absolutely." He smirked and watched as she began to pour the hot liquid. Such a perfect little English wife. Posture rigid, face emotionless, and body amply hidden by a prudish-looking afternoon dress. One that hid every curve of her body.

Pity.

"Take off your dress." He heard himself speak, a little

shocked that he was being so rakish.

"Pardon?" Isabelle paused mid-pour. "Did you just tell me to take off my dress?"

"So you can breathe better," Dominique half-lied. Naturally it would help her breathing, but part of him, the part that yearned to see the curves of her body, demanded she take off the one piece of fabric that kept his eyes from feasting on her form.

"I can breathe just fine, thank you."

"No, you can't, it is why you have trouble singing, but if you want to continue to sound like a dying dog, by all means keep your dress on—"

"Fine!" Silverware clattered as she dropped the teapot onto the tray and began hurriedly undoing her dress. After several minutes in which he watched her wiggle this way and that, she asked, "Can you help me?"

"I don't know, can I?"

"Will you help me?" She ground out, nostrils flaring.

Would he help her? Any red-blooded male would trip over himself for the chance to touch her. Trying not to look too smug or pleased with himself, he slowly rose from his seat and walked the few short steps to where she sat. Turning her back to him, she waited.

His hands itched inside his gloves, they trembled, they shook, and they wanted to feel the warmth of her skin. But, he kept his gloves on as he nimbly and quickly loosened the dress's hold on her body.

When he was finished, he adjusted his cravat, because it was quite hot in that particular room, and took a seat, as if he hadn't just been aroused beyond his wildest imagination.

"My thanks." Isabelle's face was flushed. "Now, am I to eat in my corset and chemise, or did you have any other excuses for me to strip the rest of my clothes from my body and sing naked?"

Dominique choked on his tea. Clearing his throat he answered, "I imagine you would sing even better naked, love. But I doubt I would be able to give you any sort of lessons of the musical nature. They would be more…carnal, if you understand my meaning. Now why don't you eat some sandwiches while I discuss our next lesson."

Isabelle snatched a sandwich and lifted it to her lips. Why the devil was he watching her so closely? It was as if his body was no longer listening to him. As if she now commanded its allegiance. Her every move, the way her tongue wet her lips, the look of her chest as she took another breath. Perhaps it was a poor choice for her to remove her dress. But he truly *did* have an educational purpose for it. At least that's what he told himself every time he was tempted to reach across the table and pull her into his lap.

After fifteen of the longest minutes of Dominique's life, they were finished eating and he was able to focus on music rather than her breasts, or her arms, or her shapely legs.

"The lesson," he began, as he rose from his seat, "has to do with breathing."

"Gathered that." Isabelle stood and approached the piano. "Now, what will you have me do? Strip naked? Dance around? Scream at the top of my lungs? Tell me, what mortifying thing will prove to you that I am earnest in taking these lessons? Is your aim to teach or merely gawk at me?"

Amused, Dominique chuckled. "I imagine it's a little bit of both. Now, cease talking and close your eyes."

Taking a soothing breath, Isabelle closed her eyes and waited. The only reason she was able to go through with taking off her dress was because she saw the vulnerability on his face when they were in the forest. If he could reveal parts of himself that he'd kept buried all his life, then she could very well take off her dress. If, and only if, it was for academic pursuit. The cold air in the room chilled her.

That is until she felt warm breath on the nape of her neck. "Now, when a woman wears a corset it is often too tight for her to breathe properly. One must breathe here." He moved his hands to her lower stomach near her hips and pressed just slightly. "When you sing, Isabelle. You often sing from here," he touched her throat but left one hand on her stomach. "I'm going to loosen your corset, just slightly, and I want you to take a deep breath, but I want it to come from here." Again he pressed against her stomach. She waited while he tugged at her corset. Satisfied that it was loose enough, he grunted, and returned his attention to her body.

Was it so wrong that she wanted nothing more than to be held up against him? Was it terrible of her to want to lean back into his arms? His body surrounded hers, he reached around her and played a single note from the piano, and then another, until three notes were given in unison. "This is your chord," Dominique whispered in her ear. "Now, I want you to softly hum this chord."

Knowing she had no talent and that it was quite useless, she had already decided that she would do the lessons to bring them closer, but perhaps he knew something she didn't. After all, he was a prodigy. So without complaint, she hummed the three notes softly. They weren't exactly on tune but they didn't sound like a dog dying either.

"Now, follow me." Dominique sang a few lines of a song she'd never heard before. He repeated the same verse over and over again. "Join me," he breathed in her ear. "But join from here." He touched her stomach. "Not here." He caressed her neck. And she sang.

Again, it wasn't beautiful. But it was better, and it felt better, somehow. "I feel like I can breathe. It isn't as much of a strain as it once was."

Dominique chuckled in her ear. "Does this mean you're going to take back all those nasty things you said about me, not five minutes ago?"

"Absolutely not. You're still a cad for asking me to take off my dress. What type of man asks that of his wife?"

"A human one."

"I thought you were a beast."

His chest shook with laughter behind her. Large arms pulled her even tighter against his body. "Well, I wouldn't want to disappoint, or make you a liar." His tongue licked her earlobe and then traced down her neck. Pulse racing, she tried to focus on anything, but the thrill his touch sent to her toes.

Breathing. She could focus on breathing, and counting to ten and, oh heavens, his hands were moving slowly down her arms, causing chills. And then his teeth grazed her shoulder. With a growl, he bit her, then pulled away.

Beast, definitely a beast.

"Now," Dominique said, voice steady, sounding irritatingly nonplussed by the interaction they just shared. "Would you care to—"

Thunder interrupted his words. Glancing at the window his brows furrowed, and then he shook his head. "As I was saying, would you—"

The thunder boomed, shaking the practice room. Dominique cursed and marched over to the windows. Lightning streaked the sky.

He cursed again as the thunder shook the windows and then seemed to retreat behind Isabelle.

"Am I to understand that the beast is afraid of a silly storm?"

His eyes turned murderous. "I'm not afraid."

"So you make a habit of hiding behind women when you want to show acts of extreme bravery? How very brave of you." Isabelle reached out and touched his arm. "We can always continue the lessons elsewhere."

"No." Dominique backed away from the window, nearly tripping over the sofa behind him. "It will be loud everywhere in the house except—"

"Except?" Isabelle prodded, a chill running down her arms. She really did need to put on her dress.

"Never mind." Dominique gave her a tight smile. "Lessons are done for the day, you can read, or sew, or do whatever a woman does to keep her hands from idleness and I'll just run along and..."

"Drink yourself into a stupor?" Isabelle reached for her dress and began the task of dressing herself.

Dominique scowled. "I was going to do nothing of the sort."

"He lies," a voice said from the door. "Apologies, Dominique, when I heard the impending storm I rode as fast as I could to get here. Are you well?"

"Merciful heavens! What is going on?" Isabelle nearly shouted. "Why wouldn't he be well?"

For once, Hunter was silent, which is something she would normally comment on in order to bring out his usual biting sarcasm, but his eyes seemed haunted, fearful almost.

Dominique was visibly shaking.

Fortunately, Isabelle had managed to fasten her dress in time for Hunter to enter the room. Both men were now talking in hushed voices. Hunter had his back to her and Dominique held his head in his hands.

Something was wrong, but the only cause she could find was the storm. Why would a man, so fearsome to behold, a beast, be afraid of a little thunder?

CHAPTER SEVENTEEN

I can still remember the storm as if it was yesterday. It broke a window in the house. Terrified, I ran downstairs to my father. He may have been a monster, but he was still my father. Even after everything he had done to me, I still wanted his approval, needed him to say I was growing into a good man, even though I was only a young lad. Upon entering the room, I noticed another window had been broken. He was standing in the glass, barefoot. I remember because the blood stained the carpet. He stared at the rain pouring down and then lightning flashed. I noticed the pistol in his hand. Would the violence never end? The music started again, and I couldn't bear it. I still can't describe the pain a child feels when he sees his own flesh and blood blatantly reject him. He lifted the gun toward me, pointed it directly at my chest and snarled. Instinctively, I moved away from the gunshot and plowed into him. He lost his balance. In the span of two years, I lost my parents. But not just my parents, my future, the meaning of life, my contentment, my soul. To say I hate thunderstorms would be a gross understatement, for every time one is upon me, I feel possessed with hatred and sorrow. I fear, that one day, I will die the very same way my father did. The thunder, just like the music will come for me, and I'll leave this world as the same sad little boy who entered it.

~The Diary of Dominique Maksylov

DOMINIQUE FELT THE FAMILIAR chill run down his spine. Hunter's words seemed to be pouring from his mouth at a slow pace. The room spun, and his chest clenched with terror. The thunder rolled again, and Dominique tried to swallow, tried to calm himself, but it felt like his throat was closing, that air could not get through from his lungs to his lips. He choked and coughed. Air released, but only a little. His vision blurred as he glanced at Isabelle.

Beautiful Isabelle with her golden-brown hair and bright blue eyes. Innocent of the evil done in this very house. Blast him to Hades for forgetting that minor inconvenience. The world wasn't fair. The last thing he wanted was for her to see him in such a weakened state, or God forbid, for him to harm her as he had harmed his father. Like it or not, his father's blood ran through his veins and as much as she tried to cleanse his body of the hatred at being related to such a terrible man, it seemed to only fan the flame.

"Leave!" Dominique yelled. "Leave me!"

Hunter slapped him on the back. "Right, then, I'll just be on my way."

"Where are you going?" Isabelle chased after him. "You cannot leave him here like this! Do something!"

"What would you have me do?" Hunter gripped her arm tightly. "Erase the past? Hmm? Tell him to forget the horrors of his life? Knock him on the side of the head? Believe me, none of it works."

Isabelle looked back to Dominique, her eyes full of compassion. "What should I do?"

"Love him," Hunter whispered so softly Dominique nearly missed it. "You must love him."

Dominique closed his eyes as the room continued to spin. He needed to gain control of the fear, but it suffocated him, made him want to scale the walls of the room he was sitting in, yet at the same time he couldn't move. He didn't even have a sound enough mind to be embarrassed.

Isabelle walked over to him. Her fingers brushed his forehead, and her smile made him want to weep.

"It is such a fortunate turn of circumstances that you have taught me how to sing." Isabelle began taking off her dress again, which truly should have been enough for him to snap out of his stupor. Instead, he began to sweat. Which was quite uncomfortable considering it was a cold sweat and he was still in his jacket and wearing his gloves.

The dress fell to the floor in a heap.

Dominique swallowed. Odd, but his throat seemed to be releasing the tension it once held.

"I know exactly how to keep you focused. You are a man, after all, no matter how many times you may bite me, Dominique. Now, pay attention."

Isabelle walked over to the piano and played a few notes. "By your silence, I'm guessing you didn't know I could play piano. I'm not completely without my uses. Didn't want to tell the great prodigy that I knew how to play. I imagine it would be like a small child showing a man his muscles. And you would have surely laughed at me."

No. Absolutely not. He would have embraced her, might have kissed her. But he wouldn't have laughed.

As she lightly played the notes, his heart did indeed clench, but not out of fear. Admiration? Lust? Appreciation? Shock? He wasn't entirely sure. For the song she played was one he had written. An older song, one of the happier ones he could remember.

His throat constricted. It was the song he wrote in his mother's memory.

Her voice, the same voice he had hours ago compared to a dying dog, began to hum the tune. His eyes closed and he leaned his head back against the sofa.

The music stopped.

Disappointed, he sighed, ready to open his eyes and yet again face the storm.

But delicate feminine hands interrupted him, cupping the sides of his face and moving carefully over his features down to his shoulders. Isabelle's strong fingers kneaded his muscles. Wafts of lavender danced around her hands. He felt his body relax.

Eyes heavy, he gave into the sleep that beckoned him.

Dominique had been sleeping for close to two hours. She had left him in the room once the thunder had stopped, and then readied herself to talk with Cook about the menu this week. She still had so much to do when it came to running Dominique's giant estate, not to mention hiring more help. It was shocking how few staff he had, but they were all loyal and wonderful in helping her.

"Cuppins?" Isabelle went into the kitchen where she knew the old man would be sitting with his brandy-laced tea. "I know you are living out your best years without working, but would you mind terribly if I had you help me in getting Dominique a present?"

The cook had let it slip that Dominique would be nearing his birthday in a month and Isabelle wanted to do something special. After seeing the fear in his eyes from the thunderstorm, she knew there was more to the story than just his physical scars, though she doubted they were anything but a myth considering she saw no evidence of physical deformities. Something in his past haunted him, and if she could bring even just a tiny amount of joy into his life, she would try.

Cuppins looked into his teacup and sighed. "The master of the house despises gifts of all kind, my lady."

"Yet that does not keep a certain man from trudging through the snow and making ice sculptures, now, does it?"

Cuppins swore. "Who told you that?"

"Never mind who told me. Will you help me?"

"Don't know what I can do." Cuppins took a swig of tea. "You'll have to make it look like an accident."

Was she killing him now? What was he talking about?

"The gift, I mean," Cuppins explained. "He won't accept it if you wrap it up all nice and present it to him. Sneak attack works best."

"We aren't spies, why do we need to sneak?"

Cuppins shifted in his seat. "The master has never received a birthday present before, at least not publicly. His mother bought him his first piano. It was the first and last present he ever received. His father was a cruel man, and thought that gifts would soften the young lad." Cuppins shook his head. "What are you aiming to do for him? The man's richer than Croesus. Don't know what you could possibly give him that he doesn't already have."

Isabelle searched her thoughts. There had to be something! They were husband and wife! It was necessary that she give him something. Immediately she thought of a child. Wanting to laugh aloud, she merely smiled and told herself to push that notion away. They hadn't even consummated their marriage yet. And she often wondered if it would ever happen. Each night, when they went to bed, always in the same bed, he would scoot away from her.

The mornings were an entirely different story. Several times she woke up in his embrace, only to be pushed away the minute his eyes opened. His hands were always gloved. She sighed and looked back at Cuppins. Mouth gaping open and head lying across the table, he let out a large snore.

Knowing he wouldn't be much help to her in his sleep, she went to ready herself for dinner. Hunter had said it would be one of his last nights with them, and she had decided to make it special for him. Dominique still didn't know that his friend was leaving, but perhaps it was for the best. It would force them to get even closer than they had over the past week and a half.

Sighing, she left Cuppins to his snoring and went back to her rooms.

CHAPTER EIGHTEEN

The music was so important; I frequently didn't see things happening around me. Often times I would forget to eat meals because I was so obsessed. But one cannot be totally blind to everything. I saw the way she looked at him, the way he laughed with her, and it made me sick to think that I could have prevented what happened, had I just confronted her. But in the end, I doubt it would have worked. She was a stubborn woman and she was blinded by love. I refuse to suffer that same fate.

~The Diary of Dominique Maksylov

DOMINIQUE AWOKE TO LAUGHTER. The room was pitch black except for one tiny candle looming across the room on the table.

What happened? He felt sluggish and drugged. Thank goodness the storm was over. A smile crept across his face. Isabelle was full of surprises. Who knew the girl could play the piano? And so beautifully.

He shook the sleepiness from his head and made his way toward the door. Laughter echoed the halls again. Feminine laughter. Smiling to himself and wondering what was making Isabelle so happy, he followed in the direction of the noise, stopping in front of the dining room.

Sitting at the far end of the table were Hunter and Isabelle leaning toward one another. A single candle lit their end of the table. Blind rage poured through him as he stepped farther into the room and crossed his arms.

"Apologies, am I interrupting something?" he said roughly.

"Oh!" Isabelle rose from her chair. "You're awake! We were just—"

"Flirting? Yes, I know," he finished for her. "So my dear, it seems you've taken Hunter up on his offer. Tell me, how do his kisses compare?"

Isabelle flinched and stepped away from him, her face a mask of hurt and confusion. "We were just eating dinner. I allowed you to sleep, you were so exhausted and—"

"Do not tell me what I was! You—you tricked me into sleeping so that you could have time with him! Do not lie to me!"

"*I* tricked you!" Isabelle repeated, marching toward him with her finger pointed at his chest. "How the devil do you imagine I did so? Did I have sleeping oils on my hands when I touched you? Did I put you in some sort of trance and speak incantations over you? No. I merely helped!"

Dominique heard the words she was saying but refused to believe it, the pain he felt in his chest was too real, too raw. His own mother had betrayed his father and he was just like his father. In the end it made perfect sense. "You helped, selfishly, to get close to Hunter, is that it?"

A single tear slid down Isabelle's cheek. "After all this time? Our conversations? Our lessons? Is that what you think of me? That I would lie to you in order to obtain your best friend? Very well." Isabelle began to pace in front of him. "I'll give you the benefit that you do not know me as well as him. But to accuse your own best friend of such betrayal is ridiculous. You need not look any further than the mirror to see who the real liar is in this room."

"What the devil is that supposed to mean?" he yelled, grabbing her arm and yanking her toward him.

Her eyes narrowed. "You are the liar. You lie to yourself, which is worse than lying to others. The betrayer is you. You're a walking contradiction, projecting all your insecurities onto others until you push everyone who loves you away! I won't stand for it." Isabelle pulled away and walked over to Hunter. "It has been a pleasure knowing you, Hunter. And thank you."

"You are not leaving!" Dominique bellowed at Isabelle.

Her head turned just slightly, acknowledging him. "I'm quite aware that I'm stuck here, Dominique. Your friend, however, is not. If you would take a moment to think and stop acting like a fool, you'd realize that Hunter is the one leaving, on assignment."

She stormed out of the room leaving the scent of lavender in her wake.

Hunter groaned into his hands. "I swear to you, it's like breast feeding a small child. I give you all the nurturing and care you need and you still can't suck from the tit."

"What?" Dominique roared. "Did you just compare me to a—"

"Yes, yes I did. Now before you get angry and start throwing things, allow me…" Hunter rose, slowly from his seat and walked calmly toward Dominique.

It was the worst sort of waiting. Hunter was never one to mince words when he was well and truly angry. Dominique hated the silence; he much preferred when his friend acted the fool rather than the predator and killer he truly was.

Hunter lifted golden-flamed eyes toward Dominique and

smiled coldly before pulling his hand back and punching him in the face.

Falling to the floor in a thud, Dominique swore up and down as the throbbing intensified on his right eye. "What the—"

"Listen." Hunter grabbed the lapels of Dominique's coat and pulled him to his feet with one big swoop. "I swear by all that is holy, if you don't go fix the damage you just did, I will not only take her away from your bitter presence, I'll marry her myself. Anything would be better than being constantly vulnerable and then betrayed over and over again. As a gentleman, I refuse to stand by and watch. And as your friend, I cannot allow you to kill the one good thing in your life. Now go before I lose my temper."

Speechless, Dominique nodded his head and walked out of the room. What was happening to him? One minute he felt a slight moment of happiness and the next was filled with so much fear and anger he thought he might explode. And it all had to do with Isabelle. She made him feel things, she made him...

He stopped dead in his tracks.

She made him feel.

He didn't like it. Too unpredictable and terrifying. At least when he was a recluse he could pour himself into his music and cut himself off from the world. But now, now he found himself wanting things.

Silly things, like more light in the practice room.

A rose garden for Isabelle.

His past continued to pull him into the darkness, but Isabelle, she was his future. Her goodness pushed him into the light, but the light represented vulnerability. He wasn't so sure he would survive what she represented. For it was hope.

Isabelle threw her first vase, much like Dominique had demonstrated over the past few days.

It didn't help alleviate the pain in her chest, nor did it make her feel any better about her current situation. She felt hot and cold all at once, as if she couldn't make straight lines with her emotions. One minute she was blissfully happy just being near Dominique, the next she was so angry at him she could kick him in the shin.

Repeatedly.

She tried swearing, but all that did was sound silly on her lips. She never was good at cursing. Finally, she sat in the middle of the gallery and cried.

Quietly at first, and then her sobs grew louder. She missed her sisters, needed her mother even though something told her that her mother would never be the same, considering she had been having continual fits of illness and madness when Isabelle was given to Dominique.

At a total loss, she could only continue to cry and pray for strength. Each time she thought she was making progress with Dominique, he would shut her out, or worse, yell and accuse her of things she never entertained in the first place.

"She was beautiful," Dominique said behind her.

Isabelle lifted her eyes to the paintings on the wall, the gallery of his ancestors. She just so happened to be sitting near a picture of a woman with striking dark hair and blue eyes.

"Go away."

"Can't."

"Yes you can! Just move your feet back toward the door and close it."

Dominique sighed. "I do not lack the intelligence, just the will to do so."

"Then be silent," Isabelle sniffled.

"As you wish." Dominique took a seat next to her on the floor.

Tears continued to stream down her face. He handed her a handkerchief, and then pulled her tightly into his arms. Odd, that the same one who had hurt her would be the one to comfort her. The only one who could right the wrong.

"What do you want?" Her voice was muffled by his coat.

Dominique tilted her chin toward his face. "Are we speaking now?"

"That depends."

"On what?" His eyes held pain and remorse, a hint of a shadow was visible on his cheekbone.

"What you want to speak about." She shook in his arms, unable to stop herself from the emotional response she felt.

"I cannot bring myself to say everything that needs to be said, but I will say this…" He paused.

She waited, anxiety pricking her neck.

"I am sorry. For my temper, for my behavior, truly there is no excuse for it. I cannot even blame the circumstances of my upbringing, though I try to use it as a crutch. I imagine it is because it is much easier to justify one's actions when they are wrong than it is to be responsible for them."

Isabelle sniffled. "And…"

"And I apologize, for my own actions, for not taking the necessary steps to make you feel safe and secure, and finally for my race."

"Your race?" Isabelle blinked.

"Men in general. We are loathsome creatures. Those of us who embrace emotions are considered dandified fops. Those who refuse to acknowledge the presence of heart and soul are labeled rakes and cads of the first order. It's confusing, for I don't wish to be either."

At that, she felt herself smile even though she didn't want to give in. The pain was so fresh, still too deep.

"How do you plan on making amends for your sex?" Isabelle braved a glance into his piercing eyes.

"In every possible way. Starting with telling you how beautiful you are. From the tips of your fingers—" he held her hand lightly within his palm and drew circles in her wrist, "To your delicate arms—" he traced a line all the way to her elbow and continued upwards toward her shoulder. "To your collarbone..."

"My collarbone?"

"It's alluring, the first thing a man sees before looking lower, the vast expanse of a woman's gown is open, revealing just a tease of what treasures lay beneath. But I would be quite happy just to touch here." He traced her collar bone with his index finger. "And I would be delighted to ravish you just there." His fingers moved to hold her neck, his thumbs massaged down the front causing a shiver to run through her body. "And then your lips. Promises drip from your lips. Promises of pleasure, as well as pain." He tugged her bottom lip with his teeth, then dipped his tongue into her mouth. Pulling away, he whispered across her lips, "On behalf of men everywhere, but especially on behalf of the same cad who's lucky and selfish enough to keep your kisses, I do apologize."

"You're good at that…"

"Kissing?"

"No, apologizing."

"Funny, that was my first." He chuckled, then sobered. "Why do you stay?"

Isabelle wasn't prepared for his question, nor was her heart ready to answer. She had always been one to bring all kinds of stray animals to the manor. Not that he was a stray animal by any means. She looked up at his ruggedly handsome face. Perhaps he was a type of animal, and maybe a little lost.

She shrugged. Dare she say what she'd been feeling this whole time? That when he touched her, it was like experiencing life for the first time? Everything seemed brighter, but with his touch came his scorn and oftentimes his anger. And she was left wondering at night, if the benefits outweighed the costs, for she wanted nothing more than to love what he deemed unlovable. To save what he said could not be rescued, to redeem what was once damned.

She tried to think of a simpler answer. "I am your wife."

"So you stay because we had a ceremony aboard a ship, performed by a captain?" He brushed her hair away from her face, his touch searing her skin where his fingers had lingered. "We have not yet consummated the marriage, there is nothing keeping you here." His eyes were hopeful, rimmed with tears and pain.

"You keep me here. If I left today, my body would be in England, but my heart would be with you."

"I've done nothing to earn your affection, your compassion, nor even your kindness, yet you are loyal to an absolute fault."

"Love does not always make sense, Dominique. Sometimes it asks great tasks of us, asks us to sacrifice everything in hope of finding the one true thing in this life. Love makes us bleed; it makes us fight, for if we did none of those things, how would it ever be worth it? And how would we ever deserve its rewards?"

"A philosopher as well as a poet." Dominique brushed a kiss across her cheek. "I cannot give you love. You must know that."

Isabelle's heavy heart sank even further, not that she expected him to be capable of such a choice, such an emotion. "I only ask that you respect me, that you cease from talking down to me, that you try to control your temper instead of making snap judgments. I ask that you do as you promised."

"As I promised?" Dominique's eyes flickered with confusion.

"To honor and cherish… in sickness and in health… for

as long as we both shall live. But your punishment will be that I haunt you even if I die first, for you will honor and cherish me until your soul leaves the earth."

"I imagine I can do that." He looked down at his hands and sighed. "Tell me, has every man been as difficult as me?"

"There have been no other men."

His head snapped up.

Isabelle felt herself flush and was suddenly grateful that the gallery was shadowed in darkness.

"Not even one stolen kiss at a ball?" Dominique murmured into her hair.

"Not one."

"Perhaps a secret embrace?"

"Never."

"And any offers of marriage?"

"You were my first, that I know of."

Dominique's smile lit up the dark room, his white teeth against olive skin. Black hair fell over his blue eyes. "Good."

His mouth came crushing down across hers. A guttural moan erupted from deep within his chest, and the room began to spin as Isabelle felt herself being lifted into the air by strong arms.

"Where are we going?"

"I'm going to show you. I may not be able to give you what you need in every capacity, but I'm going to give you everything I know I have."

"Why?" She choked out as she told herself not to cry again.

"Because despite obvious reasons why you should leave…you don't."

CHAPTER NINETEEN

At times I hate my gift. If I had been born normal, then my life would not be as such. It seems with great gifts comes great opposition. A better man should have possessed the music, for a better man would have known what to do with the life he was given.

~The Diary of Dominique Maksylov

DOMINIQUE HAD ALWAYS WAITED until Isabelle was asleep, for if she was awake he would have to look into her eyes, and if he looked he was afraid he would see his own desire reflected back, and he hadn't the strength to be a gentleman.

Thinking back on the night's festivities, he had to laugh. Isabelle had been so distraught and tired, she fell asleep in his arms the minute he reached their bedroom. A maid had helped her ready for bed, only waking her when she needed to get Isabelle out of her dress.

Dominique had waited in the study. His control was at the point of snapping. Every kiss, every touch, made him crave her more and more. Until he could do nothing but think about what it would be like to be her first lover, the man who made her scream with pleasure, the man she looked at with passion-filled eyes.

He had nearly ruined everything. She gave and gave, until nothing was left, and he took, yet was never satisfied or content in his taking.

The quill on his desk seemed to be staring at him. He knew what he had to do. Somehow during the past few weeks in Isabelle's presence, he had found a semblance of honor as well as a conscience, which was quite inconvenient, all things considered.

With a curse, he grabbed a piece of fresh paper and addressed it: "To his Grace, The Duke of Montmouth."

Hours later, he was utterly exhausted; he pulled off his boots and shrugged out of his dinner jacket once he reached the bedroom. Going to bed late meant he had no use for his valet, not that he found much use for one in the first place. Trying to tip toe around the room, he finally found the softness of the bed and reached down to pull the blankets back.

Shock was an adequate word to describe his thoughts as his hand touched Isabelle's bare arm. Apparently she had fallen asleep sprawled across the bed in a diagonal manner. Her sleeping habits amused him; he'd thought he was the only person alive that slept so fitfully, but Isabelle tossed and turned just as badly, if not worse.

Biting back a smile, he pulled her into his arms and tried to set her on her back, but the blankets were tangled within her legs, making it near-impossible for her body to move comfortably without being twisted.

Letting out a frustrated sigh, Dominique reached down and gave the blankets a tug. Eventually they came free, but as they did so, they pulled up Isabelle's nightgown, giving him a view of her creamy legs. Even in the dark he could see their perfect outline, could almost taste their sweetness on his lips.

Without thinking he bent down and bestowed a kiss on her exposed thigh, but found his thirst—his hunger—was not quenched.

Cursing, mainly because his wife was sleeping through his assault, his lips met her leg again. This time his tongue drew circles around the tender flesh. Instantly aroused beyond all logic, he placed his hands on her hips in hopes to memorize their feel.

"Dominique?" Her feminine voice was thick with sleep and so blasted arousing, he had trouble thinking straight.

"Y-yes," he stammered.

He hadn't stammered since he was a lad.

"I had a terrible dream."

"What was it about, love?"

"A beast was attacking me..."

Dominique bit back a laugh. "Did he harm you?"

"Irrevocably." She sighed. "And then he stopped."

"Did you want him to continue?"

Her eyes flashed open. "That depends on the beast."

Dominique hovered over her, noting her face in the moonlight as her eyes blinked rapidly back at him. "Does it?"

She nodded and then stretched beneath him. The light cast from the moon revealed her perfect silhouette against the darkness of the room.

At the same time, as if planned, they reached for one another, and Dominique knew there was no going back this time. Because he had waited for this moment it seemed, his entire existence.

With great effort, that of a god no doubt, he pulled back to gaze upon her face. He didn't deserve any sort of affection, but how his body craved it, needed it. More than he could have ever imagined.

Her warm hand touched his chest, drawing circles with her fingers until finally trailing down to his hips and pulling him tighter against her. Sadly, her actions pushed the last rational thoughts from his mind.

And in their place…

Need. Hunger. Craving—like he had never before known.

With a guttural growl he slipped his hands beneath her nightgown and pulled it over her head. He tossed it to the floor.

Her nakedness made him lose his nerve. Too beautiful. She was too beautiful for his scars to touch. Thankfully she couldn't see his hands, but if she knew how his sins were touching her purity, she would hate him. And for once, he didn't want her to hate him.

With a smile, Isabelle reached out and grabbed his wrists, allowing his hands to press against her body. Her head flew back, her eyes closed, and she exhaled a feminine sigh at his touch.

He bent his head to her neck, his tongue reaching out to lick the softness behind her ear. To bite the tender flesh at her shoulder. Her hands gripped his shoulders as his teeth nipped.

Warmth spread across his body; he no longer felt chilled or alone. Rather, he felt a part of something bigger than his sins, bigger than his past.

As his lips pushed against hers, surely bruising her in the process, her hands scratched at his back and her legs wrapped around his body.

With haste he pulled back to remove the rest of his clothing, for he had always slept in his pants to keep the girl from scratching his eyes out.

His scarred hands fumbled and he cursed. Isabelle reached out just in time for him to pull his hands away so she couldn't feel the hard ridges of his burnt skin.

With ease, she helped remove the last barrier keeping them separate. Her eyes took him in, all of him, and instead of shying away as good virgins were taught to do, she reached up and wrapped her hands around his neck, pulling him on top of her in such an erotic embrace, he saw heaven.

He pulled her legs up so she could wrap them yet again around him, and plowed her mouth with his tongue. Her lips pushed equally against his; he didn't even have time to warn her, to tell her what to expect, his desire was such that his brain hadn't caught up to the act.

She cried out beneath his kiss. A single tear ran down her cheek. Dominique's heart nearly burst. She gave herself to him freely, without wanting anything in return. And by all that was great and good, he would die before she regretted it.

With aching slowness, he kissed her cheeks, allowing his tongue to lick away the tears as they rolled down her face, and then his lips met hers in reverence. They danced and pulled tenderly; he worshipped her face as if it was one of the most precious treasures.

She met his kiss with one of her own, moving beneath him; he both wanted her to stop and continue. With a moan he deepened the kiss as she whispered into his neck, "Dominique."

Isabelle tried to focus her thoughts, but it was nearly impossible. Not when she was feeling such foreign sensations all over her body. It had started as a dream. Warm hands had touched her flesh, and then she felt a bite and then a lick across her thigh. Thinking she was surely going mad, she opened her eyes and was shocked to see Dominique's dark hair spilling over his eyes, his lips carefully dancing across her skin, and she wanted much more than he was giving.

The attraction she had felt for him had been slowly growing into a blazing inferno. But she hadn't wanted to be the one to give in first. After all, she did have her pride. Yet, in this moment, she cursed her pride, cursed everything, for she wanted the man, broken as he may be, and her desire was that together they could become more than what they were apart.

Isabelle hadn't counted on feeling so vulnerable, but with Dominique lying across her, both of them in the aftermath of their love-making, slick with sweat and breathing heavily, she realized that she could not have given her heart to anyone else but him. And her hope soared that by doing so, he would finally open himself up completely to her. Finally trust her with everything, rather than shut her out of the darkness he surrounded himself with.

"I'm sorry." He rolled away from her and pushed away from the bed. Embarrassed, Isabelle began to pull at the blankets so she could hide her body. But within seconds Dominique had returned, and attended to her.

Surely she was blushing all the way to her toes! His strong hands lifted her with little effort as he placed her on the edge of the bed and with a damp towel washed the sweat from her body, and torturously alternated between kissing where he touched and washing.

She closed her eyes again as those same sensations made her desire so heavy that she nearly leaned back across the bed again in open invitation.

Dominique laughed. "Too soon, love. Believe me." When he was finished, he cradled her in his arms and tucked her into the bed, taking his place beside her.

The air was alive with tension. What was she to say? What was normal practice? Fighting the desire to ask the questions that burned in the back of her mind, she managed to bite her lip to keep from speaking. It was Dominique, after all. Having any sort of uncomfortable discussions was always on the bottom of his list.

"Are you well?" He sighed. The bed dipped with his weight as he moved closer to her and pulled her in the crook of his arm. "Did I…do you…?"

Isabelle burst out laughing. "Are you stuttering?"

Dominique cursed. "Perhaps, but it is only because I do not normally…That is to say, with virgins. This is…this is a first and I find myself worried for your welfare."

So he was insecure, was he? Never had she heard the man sound anything less than the arrogant fool that he was. Wanting him to suffer, she let out a long sigh, before dipping her head beneath his head to kiss his neck.

He stiffened and then moaned. "I take it that you are much recovered?"

"Much," she purred, wrapping her hands around his body and pulling him tighter against her.

Isabelle felt him swallow, and then he tensed. "We cannot do that again."

It was her turn to tense. A mixture of outrage, confusion, and rejection poured through her. "I don't understand? Are we not husband and wife? And you, you feel for me?"

Dominique pushed away. "What I feel has nothing to do with what we did. What we did was a natural thing, when put together so many nights on end. It was bound to happen. I'm merely saying it cannot happen again."

"But..."

"Do not argue with me on this, for I doubt I have the strength to deny you anything so soon after seeing you without clothing. I stand by my decision."

"Your decision?" she repeated, outraged. "And what about me? Am I to have a say in our relationship at all?"

"No." He didn't even blink.

Isabelle let out a curse word she often heard Dominique use and pushed away from him, ending up in the cold part of the bed. She began to shake uncontrollably. The man had taken everything from her! Everything she had and he treated it like it was the most horrendous of sins.

"Did I not please you?" Her voice was small, vulnerable.

Cursing, Dominique reached and pulled her firmly against his body. "Love, you would please any male who had the benefit of good sight and youth. Your pleasing me is not the issue."

"I don't understand." A warm tear ran down her cheek.

"Children," he spouted venomously. "We cannot have children."

"Is this a choice or an ailment?" she asked, hoping for the latter, because then at least the rejection of him wanting no part of her wouldn't destroy the beating of her heart.

"A choice."

"I see." She moved away though he tried to keep her pinned against him. Dominique reached for her again but she slapped his hand away. "We have nothing more to discuss."

Dominique's breath hitched. She knew she had upset him, but she would take upset and irritated any day rather than the heartache she presently had. Why did he constantly reject her? Why was he so set against her? Better to have left her in London even if she was to meet death, than be stuck with a man she could never have, but had to endure the rest of her life.

Again, Dominique reached for her, but as his gloved hand touched her shoulder, she tensed. Immediately, he pulled back and pushed away from the bed, leaving the room with a curse.

CHAPTER TWENTY

Music, I understand. Notes make sense to me. Women? Romance? Love? They elude me and I fear will continue to elude me until the day I die.

~The Diary of Dominique Maksylov

HE PROMISED HIMSELF HE wouldn't allow the girl to get to him, and here he was, drinking brandy in the last place he wanted to be. It was more than the idea of having children. For the note he had just written was to her brother-in-law. If he continued to sleep with his wife—and how he wanted it!—he wasn't sure he could execute perfect control, and if she became pregnant, there was no way for her to go back. She would be stuck with him. Forever. She had proved time and time again that she deserved a life better than he could give her. To trap her, without her consent, would be the worst thing he could ever do to her.

The haunted practice room, still littered with glass and remnants of death, seemed to groan in the candlelight. He figured, after around seven swallows of brandy, that it would make him feel loads better to be surrounded by more darkness. To remember the light he witnessed while making love to his wife, the goodness she brought, the way her heart, her soul seemed to reach out and meet his...

Well, it was fruitless.

Because he would never have children. The idea of passing an heir repulsed him. For it meant that his father would have been proud that he was finally being the leader he demanded Dominique be. And although his father was dead, by his own hands nonetheless, he refused to give him one more thing to boast about in Hades.

Though the idea that any son or daughter would possess his wife's goodness brought a smile to his face, the smile was quickly removed when he walked into this room.

If he tarried with such thoughts any longer, he would live to regret it. For if he touched his wife one more time, he would be lost forever, and even he knew there were consequences to loving someone too much, becoming obsessed with that very thing until it consumes you and forces you to go beyond all logic, all reason. He knew he had his mother in him, knew that if love ever got a hold of him, it would never relent.

Dominique took another swig of brandy and sat on the piano bench. The melody from his childhood haunted him, its minor notes floating into the air, almost visible in his drunken state.

Candlelight danced off the walls, and the room seemed enchanted. With an exasperated sigh, he placed his gloved hands on the piano. They slipped across the dust. Taking a look around the room, he slowly removed the gloves and poured brandy onto them and then wiped the keys.

He tossed the gloves to the floor and brought his scarred hands to the piano. It was always a magical thing, the way his warm skin used to feel against the cold keys. And then the music would dance into the air and it would consume everything about him. A trance would take over and he would imagine himself floating above, basking in the joy of the music.

Even the haunting song brought him respite. Perhaps being with Isabelle was better for him than he realized. For the first time in fifteen years he was able to play the song without crying.

Or cursing.

Or throwing things, which Miss Ward would truly appreciate.

Isabelle awoke with a start.

The room, once bathed in the afterglow of love-making, was cold and lonely. She reached out her hand and ran it across the empty side of the bed where Dominique had just slept. Memories of a few hours before bombarded her brain. A nervous tremble ran down her body as she closed her eyes in remembrance of his erotic touch.

The way his lips pressed against her neck.

His hot breath tickling her ear.

And then she heard it.

Classical music.

The notes reached deep into her soul. An urge, stronger than she had ever known, came over her as she reached for her dressing gown and walked to the door, toward the direction of the music.

It grew louder as she descended the stairs.

A light glowing from the practice room drew her attention. Dominique had told her never to go into the room. But surely after everything they had shared that night, he wouldn't mind if she listened?

The music stopped. Disappointed she walked to the door

and leaned against it. It creaked open, and her feet moved her forward on their own accord. Tingling awareness washed over her as she took a tentative step into the room.

Dominique's back was to her. His head hovered over the dusty piano. He began playing the same haunting song again, and she fought to keep her eyes open when all she wanted to do was close them and get lost in the beauty of the music. It was bittersweet, just when the melody began to climb, it would fall back down and drown within the sharp notes, making her want to weep.

As he continued to play, she watched as his muscles tensed in his back, stretching underneath his white shirt. His fingers moved so fast, so effortlessly. She could only see a blur of his hands, only the pinkish skin protruding from the cuffs of his shirt.

With a sigh, she looked around the room, only now noticing the disarray it was in. Glass covered the floor. Curtains fell haphazardly across the windows, pieces of material torn and filled with dust. The marble floor had lost its shine. Everywhere she looked there was dirt and debris. Why hadn't Dominique or at least the servants cleaned up the room? It was obviously still in use, so it made no sense whatsoever that they wouldn't at least try to tidy it up.

Lost in thought, she didn't even realize the music had stopped. She looked up and took a step closer to Dominique. A loud crunch was heard, followed by her scream as a piece of glass lodged itself into her foot.

Dominique turned around, a horrified look on his face. Concern washed over his features, softening them just a bit. The edges of his mouth turned downward into a frown, and his eyebrows lifted as he looked at her cut foot.

Isabelle let out a pitiful whimper as it began to throb with pain. Dominique walked carefully over to her and knelt, his hands reached out to pull her foot onto his bended knee so he could retract the piece of glass.

Isabelle's eyes fell on his hands. White and red scars pinched his skin all the way from his fingers up his forearms where the scars were hardly visible, just slightly discolored. Fascinated, she leaned forward just as Dominique, with a curse, stumbled back; expletives flew out of his mouth as he grabbed his gloves from the piano and put them on.

"So, you've come to get a look at the beast?"

Isabelle choked on her words as she tried to get them out as fast as possible. "No, no, I just heard the music, and it was so beautiful and—"

"Beautiful until you saw my scars, is that it?" Dominique roared.

"No!"

"Well, if you want to look, look!" he yelled, stripping off his gloves and throwing them at her feet. "Take in your fill! It wouldn't be the first time someone was curious. Surely it won't be the last! You should at least see what type of creature shares your bed, touches your body, and brings you pleasure."

Isabelle kept her hands firmly at her sides. She bit the inside of her cheek to keep from crying. The pain in her foot was intense, but the pain in her heart, the way it skipped a beat when she saw the visible hurt across Dominique's features, nearly killed her.

"Here! Feel!" His eyes held unshed tears as he gave a mocking grin and pulled her hands into his.

She pulled back, not out of repulsion, but out of fear. He was acting mad, yet after all they had been through the day before, she knew his tactics well.

Hobbling over to him on her aching foot, she took his hands within her own and kissed the jagged scars, allowing her tears to flow freely over the marred white skin.

Dominique shook; his eyes were fixated on her face in a mixture of awe and outrage.

"I kiss the beast, I kiss the man, I kiss my husband, whom I love. Look into my eyes, Dominique. This is not the look of disgust, it is the look of acceptance."

His eyes closed and a tear escaped his before he could reach up and stop it.

"I cannot keep you," he choked. "I cannot do this. I—" He jerked away. "This is my life, my burden, my darkness. Isabelle, you do not belong here. You belong in England, where men will fall at your feet and women will adore you. Eventually your flame will go out. Isn't that what fire does when exposed to the cold, damp, darkness of the world? I cannot be responsible for it."

"Am I not strong enough to help us both?"

"It isn't a matter of strength, love." Dominique cursed and ran his scarred hands through his hair. "It's a matter of choice. And I'm making the choice for both of us. I've already made arrangements—"

"You're getting rid of me?" Isabelle cried. "Why, why would you do this? After everything we've shared? I don't understand. After your pretty speech about me staying? Do you even know your own mind?"

"Understand this." Dominique grabbed her arms, pulling her flush against his body, and kissed her forehead. "You are perfection, but beauty and beast do not mix, they do not pair. The beast will eventually devour your beauty, and I refuse to let that happen. Now run along to bed."

Despite the throbbing in her foot, Isabelle felt numb. Nodding her head, she limped back to her rooms, but felt nothing at all, not even the pain in her foot. Sleep wouldn't come, so she changed into her riding habit and went down to the stables.

Hunter was already there, readying his horse.

"Take me with you?" Isabelle asked in a small voice.

Hunter cursed. "What did he do?"

"Nothing." Isabelle began crying all over again. "He's—he's giving me up!"

"To Napoleon?" Hunter asked with eyebrows lifted and an amused grin plastered across his handsome face.

Stupid man! Why did he have to jest at such a time! "No, you idiot! He's sending me back home! And we, that is to say, I mean, last night..."

"Blast! Did he…" Hunter's face turned a bright red as he cursed and kicked the cold ground with his boot. "Let me speak to him, just, please wait before you do anything…irresponsible."

Isabelle nodded and patted the horse already saddled and grazing near her.

CHAPTER TWENTY-ONE

I shouldn't drink. The music always blurs when I numb my mind with brandy. I promised myself I would never be the type to drink over a woman. Lovely, proving one's theory so horribly wrong.

~The Diary of Dominique Maksylov

"I AM NOT YOUR nursemaid!" Hunter yelled, pushing the door open to the practice room where Dominique had fallen asleep the night before.

"And aren't we all so grateful that you aren't." Dominique yawned. "What the devil are you doing up at this ungodly hour? There are no tavern wenches, nor do I see any French soldiers within my vicinity. Can you perhaps bellow elsewhere? My head aches."

"Does that hard head of yours remember any conversations from last night? Or have you chosen to forget that you told your wife you no longer needed her?" Hunter paced in front of Dominique, slapping his leather gloves against his thigh.

Dominique winced. "I did nothing of the sort. I merely

explained that I didn't want her to feel trapped. I want her to choose to be with me, not be here because she is married to me or feels there is no other option. I stole that choice from her; yes, I protected her from danger. But I'm sure things have righted themselves within her family."

"Interesting," Hunter murmured, pausing in his stomping.

"What?"

"Your stupidity. Such a horrid case of it that I'm more amazed than appalled." Hunter cursed and took a seat opposite Dominique. "When a woman is told she should scurry on home, she takes it literally. She thinks you do not want her."

"I slept with her last night, she knows I want her." If her screams and womanly sighs were any indication, she enjoyed herself as well as he did.

"There it is!" Hunter said sarcastically.

"There what is?"

"The stupidity. It was speaking again. Furthermore—" Hunter leaned forward, "when a man sleeps with a woman he does not follow the deed by telling her he no longer wants her to live with him. Sends the wrong signals, if you get my meaning."

"I am helping her!"

"You are a fool if you think that is what you are accomplishing. Now run off and grovel, get down on your hands and knees, confess your stupidity, then take your woman to the bedroom and pleasure her again and again until she forgets the stupidity that briefly took over your body."

Devil take it, Hunter would have been a good general.

"So the final words you leave me with are *pleasure her*? Sounds frighteningly normal." Dominique rose to his full height. "For what it's worth, Hunter, I do apologize for last night. You are truly the best friend a man could ask for."

"Yes, yes, I know. Now go find the girl."

"My lord?" Cuppins limped into the room. "I'm sorry to disturb that lovely speech on your intelligence—"

Hunter gave a hearty laugh.

Dominique scowled. "Yes?"

Cuppins clenched his hands and shook his head. "This just came for you. I imagine it is information regarding the French. The fighting has been getting closer and closer and although I find us to be quite safe, I think you better read it."

"Why, when you already have?" Dominique lifted an eyebrow toward his old, retired butler.

"It isn't safe for the lady to go riding alone anymore. The letter says the area is littered with French soldiers and she's as English as they come."

"Right, well, good thing I was just on my way to break fast to see her."

Hunter paled and grabbed Dominique by the arm. "She isn't breaking her fast."

"Of course she is. Isn't that where you two had your intimate chat?"

Hunter cursed and ran for the door. "She was dressed for riding and at the stables. I told her to wait, but..."

Dominique stopped listening when he heard *stables*. Fear pricked at his heart. If he lost her, he would die.

CHAPTER TWENTY-TWO

Helplessness is the worst feeling imaginable. It is akin to swimming through the dark waters of the ocean not knowing which way will give you air and which way will be your death. Most of my regrets are directly related to helplessness. I was helpless to save my mother, my father, my teacher, and in the end myself. Perhaps that is why when the music calls to me, when it says there is danger, I heed the call regardless of the repercussions for I refuse to allow myself to feel helpless again.

~The Diary of Dominique Maksylov

THE AIR WAS TOO quiet, eerie almost. After waiting five minutes, Isabelle decided to take the horse that Hunter had already saddled. After all, she was only going to for a quick ride to clear her head, and she couldn't imagine him being with Dominique for any less than an hour. She looked down at her skirts, obviously she was properly attired, but the saddle wasn't what she was accustomed to. She looked back in the direction Hunter had left and exhaled, her breath dancing in front of her face. The horse neighed, decision made, she managed to sit across the horse and gain her balance.

The horse was weighed down by some of Hunter's belongings but she didn't care. She had no desire to run, merely to wander to the clearing that Dominique had shown her. The only problem was, she couldn't remember the way. After the thunderstorm last night it had rained, melting the snow into tiny icicles that froze over all the trees.

She continued in the general direction of the forest. The white crystals strewn through the trees were breathtaking; the ground was hard but no longer covered in snow. Isabelle's thoughts went to the night before.

Of Dominique's hands on her thighs, of his lips nibbling her ear. The air should have chilled her, but the idea of their skin making contact threatened to make her sweat. Isabelle shook the sensual thoughts from her consciousness and looked around again. The trees all looked the same. Perplexed, she bit her lip and continued riding in the general direction she assumed the little ice sculptures were.

Now, deeper within the forest, she was able to see through the trees to the little clearing where she and Dominique had spent their time. Excited that she had found it, she kicked the horse into a slow trot. Once she reached the clearing, she let out a little laugh and slid off the horse. It was just as magical as she remembered it. Perhaps the rejection of her husband, the idea of him not wanting her after such a wonderful night, maybe it wouldn't be as hard to deal with in this place. She twirled around, once, twice, and finally stopped.

"What have we here?" A foreign voice penetrated her magical world.

Frozen in place, Isabelle didn't want to turn, or think, or even blink for fear of what would happen. Unmistakably, the man was speaking French.

Another man laughed, *"An English bird?"*

Isabelle's own understanding of the language wasn't what it should have been, in fact it was nearly impossible to translate, but she was convinced the man just asked if she was English. Either that, or a bird, not that it mattered.

Slowly, she turned, and couldn't help the gasp that escaped her lips as her eyes locked on five French soldiers, fully armed, looking her up and down as if she was on the menu for devouring.

"A very pretty English bird, most likely alone." The man who had been speaking stepped closer to her and held his hand up for the other men to back away. "I said…" his accent was thick, "You are alone, yes?"

"No." Isabelle stepped toward her horse; a few more feet and she could make an escape, that is, if she didn't get shot first. "I am with my husband."

At that, the men burst out laughing. The one in front of her spit on the ground. "What kind of husband leaves a beautiful woman alone in the forest?" He took another careful step toward her. "Your husband is an imbecile, no?"

Isabelle opened her mouth to say *no*, but movement in the trees stopped her. Heart pounding, she glanced out of the corner of her eye; something else moved and then she saw Dominique.

She had to think quickly, but she didn't know how to distract them. The Frenchman lifted his eyebrow in mockery. "He is not an imbecile, as you delicately put it. You see, we, um, we like to play games."

"Games?" he repeated. "Interesting. Are others invited?"

"Always." Isabelle managed a saucy smile. "In fact, he often uses me as bait, in order to make things more… interesting." She swallowed the bile in her throat as the man walked purposefully toward her. He was going to hurt her; his face was menacing, his eyes hard and cold.

"I think I would like to be the first to play, *oui*?" His gaze narrowed on her bosom. She pulled tightly at her cloak and crossed her arms.

"Ah, patience, my love, don't I always go first?" Dominique's voice was calm and reassuring as he stepped into the clearing. "After all, there is enough of you to go around, wouldn't you say?"

What was he doing? Her eyes widened in horror and then she saw it, he tilted his head just slightly; she looked in the direction he indicated and noticed Hunter pulling out a pistol.

"Yes, well, last time, that is to say, l-last time, I was so fatigued after just one round that I nearly fainted…" Isabelle stammered, thoroughly disgusted with their topic but knowing it was necessary.

"But dear, you're forgetting." Dominique walked to her side and pulled her into his embrace; it was then that she noticed how thick his accent was, as if he had reverted back to his Russian heritage. He didn't seem English at all, not that he was completely English. But at this moment, he seemed foreign if not more foreign than the soldiers. "I own you, remember? Won you fair and square from the idiot, Wellington."

All five Frenchmen spit on the ground at the mention of the Duke's name. No love was lost on the man fighting against their fearless leader.

"You won her, you say?" The Frenchman cursed. "I would have liked to see that man's face when you stole this piece from his arms."

"She's nothing but a whore." Dominique clenched his arm tighter around her. "So she meant nothing to him. I imagine it was his pride that was hurt, not the loss of a beautiful woman."

The men nodded their agreement as Dominique turned Isabelle to face him. Laughing, he tilted her chin up and kissed her hard across the mouth. He forced her onto the ground and pulled out a pistol.

Everything happened so fast. One minute she was in his arms and the next she was in the dirt watching him open fire on the men. Firing his weapon, Hunter jumped from the brush. The Frenchmen cursed and shot their own pistols.

Isabelle tried to close her eyes. Attempted to cover her ears, but she was paralyzed with shock and watching in utter horror as one of the last men standing opened fire on Dominique, sending him sailing to the cold hard ground.

Hunter knocked the assailant unconscious and was immediately at Dominique's side.

"Isabelle!" Hunter yelled.

She couldn't move.

"Isabelle! This is not the time to play the frightened woman. You may cry later; right now Dominique needs you."

Nodding, she jumped to her feet and rushed to Dominique's side. Blood poured from a gunshot wound in his shoulder. His gloved hands were covered in blood.

"Hold this tight, right here." Hunter ripped a piece of fabric from his shirt and placed her hands over the cloth covering the wound. "Listen to me, Isabelle. I need you to take Dominique back to the castle. You just get on the horse and it will take you back, do you understand? I need to know you understand!"

Isabelle felt her head jerk into a nod. "But where are you going?" Her voice sounded hollow, foreign to her own ears.

"Wellington. I need to be sure he knows that we've not only killed five French soldiers, but that they are this deep into the country. They were supposed to be near Brussels, not…" He looked down at his hands. "Not here, it isn't safe. I must go. It's my job to go. If I don't…" his voice trailed off. "I was already planning to leave, now it's of the essence."

"I'll take care of him," Isabelle swore.

"See that you do. I've never lost a soldier yet." Hunter

nodded and went to his horse. "Horse is just behind the brush. Help me lift Dominique onto her, and I'll send you on your way."

Her husband was heavy, not that she shouldn't have thought as much. The man was finely built, muscles protruded from every tight angle of his body. It was torture trying to do a man's work, lifting such dead weight, but together she and Hunter managed to lay Dominique across Horse. Fortunately for them, Dominique was still semi-conscious and able to move his body enough to help.

Isabelle launched herself onto Horse's back but nearly fell; it was impossible to sit like a lady ought to when she had the beast of a man in front of her.

"Apologies," Hunter muttered before he reached underneath her skirts and ripped the fabric. "Don't tell Dominique, he'd most likely shoot me in the head. Now, off you go."

"Off I go?" Isabelle, still shaking, grabbed the reins. "Do you mean for me to sit..."

Hunter cursed. "Wrap your legs around the horse, Isabelle, and hold the man we both know you love close to your chest. Do not let him go. Notify Cuppins of the wound. The nearest doctor is over a half-day's ride away. I'll notify him in the next town. Until then, stop the bleeding and cauterize the wound. Cuppins will know what to do." Hunter whistled and Horse took off in a slow trot back to the house. Dominique was conscious enough to hold his weight even, though she couldn't be sure, considering she was so terrified she was going to fly off Horse before they made it back to the castle.

Terror nipped in the corners of her mind. What would she do if she lost him? Even after everything they had been through, she couldn't bring herself to imagine a world without the beast. Surely, it would be a world devoid of beauty as well.

Fighting back tears, she leaned over Horse as they made their way out of the forest. The castle loomed in the distance.

"Please," Isabelle sobbed, allowing tears to flow freely down her face. "Please, please let him survive this."

Dominique moaned. After being shot it was evident that he had hit his head on the hard ground rendering him unstable. Not only did she need to worry about infection, but the trauma done to his head as well as his hands. They were soaked with blood and she wasn't sure if it was someone else's or his.

As Horse neared the house, Isabelle began to scream for help. Within seconds servants poured out. Cuppins limped toward Horse and began calling for the footman and any able-bodied man.

"He, h-he, was shot, and I was in the forest and the French…"

Cuppins cursed when he heard the word *French,* and his ruddy face went pale with worry as his eyes took in Dominique's wound and form. "How long has he been unconscious?"

Isabelle racked her mind. "Minutes, it's only been a few minutes. We came as fast as we could, and Hunter, he..." Her lip began to tremble. "He went to tell Wellington a-and, and..." She burst into heavy sobs as she watched the men carry Dominique into the house. Cuppins held out his arm. Old and unsteady as it was, she took comfort in his gesture and leaned against him as they hobbled back into the house.

CHAPTER TWENTY-THREE

I have tasted death twice in my life, both times at a young age. The taste of death is something one never forgets, it takes over every other sense in your body until you fear you may go mad. To return to those moments in my life or to face death of my own accord absolutely terrifies me. I imagine I will be the sort to walk into death blindly knowing that I will not be returning into the land of the living. I know what death tastes like, and when that taste returns, I'll welcome it with open arms. Through death, perhaps, I may find my redemption, I may find my light.

~The Diary of Dominique Maksylov

HAUNTING DREAMS OVERTOOK DOMINIQUE'S thoughts. Dreams of dragons and monsters, of his father and his tragically beautiful mother.

She reached out to him, but her hand was cold, frigid. His entire dream reeked of death. His mother's eyes turned black, she threw back her head and laughed, and then his father entered into the dream. His eyes a blazing fire of hatred, he lifted a torch into the air and burned Dominique's hands for the second time, laughing as he did so. Dominique tried to scream for him to stop. After all, he was a man now; he could kill his father, the right way this time, not by accident.

The sob, the scream—everything died in his throat. And then heat, so intense, overtook him. His limbs were on fire, everything ached. His father reached his hand to Dominique's shoulder and pushed.

A scream erupted from Dominique's lips as his father increased the pressure, taking pleasure in Dominique's pain. "May you never play again," he said, over and over again until Dominique's face was wet with tears. Suddenly he was a boy again, reliving the worst nightmare of his life. He wanted his mother, but more than that?

He wanted Isabelle.

Lost in darkness, all he wanted was her light, so he said her name, quietly at first and then louder until finally his own voice shattered the nightmare, broke through the pain. "Isabelle!"

His head shook back and forth, so hot, he was still too hot, but he felt peace as something cold touched his forehead. He struggled to open his eyes. When he finally managed the difficult feat, everything was blurry. His tongue was thick in his mouth. Speaking would be impossible, blinking seemed to hurt all the way down to his toes. One last desperate attempt toward clear vision ended in a brilliant reward.

"Isabelle," he croaked, his voice raspy.

Her smile lit up the room. Bending over him she placed a kiss upon his cheek. "Sleep, Dominique, you need to heal. Promise me you won't leave me."

Leave? Where would he go? He wanted to scream at her to take back everything he had said that morning, get down on his hands and knees, beg for her to stay and never leave him.

His inner dialogue was so good, he cursed the idea that she couldn't read his thoughts. "Please," his voice begged.

"Don't go."

Smiling, she patted his hand. "I haven't left your side yet."

Isabelle tried to put a brave smile across her face, but it was becoming increasingly difficult. It had been the first time in two days that Dominique had opened his eyes. His wound had worsened with infection, and the fever seemed to leave for a few hours only to come back stronger.

His body was blazing hot, despite the packed snow and water she brought to his bedside. Every time his fever spiked, he would either scream out her name or scream out his father's. Mostly, he would revert back to the language of his childhood making it impossible for Isabelle to know what he was murmuring about. Worse, Hunter had yet to send word, and the doctor hadn't shown up, which could only mean that he had trouble making it to Wellington, or he was injured in the process.

Her mind would not allow herself to linger on the simple fact that Hunter could have failed in his mission.

"How is he this morning, my lady?" Cuppins walked unsteadily into the room. His forehead perspiring from exertion up the stairs.

"He isn't worse." Isabelle reached for the cold compress and held it to Dominique's head once more. "He keeps saying my name, then he begins speaking in Russian, and screams at his father. He must have been a horrid man."

Cuppins snorted. "A horrid man? No, my lady. That would be an understatement. Horrid does not even begin to describe the type of man the late prince was. Selfish, arrogant, prideful, hateful, he was the worst sort of man. His hate destroyed his relationship with his wife, forcing her to seek love elsewhere, and his disdain for Dominique's accomplishments at such a young age made everything worse."

Dominique twitched, his eyes moving behind his eyelids at a rapid pace. And then his hand jerked out from the blankets and grabbed Isabelle's arm.

His eyes flew open. "I killed him."

Hatred dripped from Dominique's fevered voice as he repeated the sentiment over and over again until finally he laughed and closed his eyes. "Death will not keep me from killing him twice." His eyes fluttered closed again.

Shaking, Isabelle removed Dominique's hand from her arm, placing it gently back at his side and tucking the blanket around his shoulder. The scars seemed to scream for vengeance. What tragedy befell Dominique? What would cause such twisted scars to appear on one's hands? And were these the same hands that stole the life from another?

"Who is he speaking of?"

Cuppins had gone silent behind her. The only sounds in the room were the heavy breathing of the old man and the shallow breathing of her husband.

The elderly butler took a seat on the other side of Dominique near the bed and cursed. "I'm going to need this." He reached into his jacket pocket and pulled out a flask. Grimacing, he tipped back the entire container and wiped his mouth.

"Hunter made me swear I would allow Dominique to tell you his story, when he was ready, but I think now is as good of time as any."

Now meaning what, exactly? *That he was doing to die.* Fear pricked her heart again as she reached for Dominique's hand. For some reason, if she could touch him—it seemed to her that he could use her warmth, her strength, to pull through.

"As I said, his father was an evil man. On one particular

evening, much like the thunderous evening we experienced a few nights ago, Dominique went in search of his father. Predictably, his father was in one of the large practice rooms, drinking. Much like the dreaded practice room where he had, just two years previously, shot and killed not only Dominique's favorite teacher, but his mother. Dominique witnessed the murders."

Isabelle gasped. Of all the horrors for a little boy to see, that would have to be the worst.

"I will not explain the pain at having experienced such a nightmare, but I tell you this so you understand the grief and guilt the late prince was under. When Dominique approached him…" Cuppins cursed and rubbed his tired eyes. "His father tried to attack him. Dominique was quite small and fast; he moved out of the way but his father tripped and fell through the window to the ground. It wasn't such a high fall, but he had lost his balance so severely that he landed on his head. He died instantly."

Fresh tears ran down Isabelle's cheeks and onto Dominique's scarred hands. "What type of man tries to kill his own son?"

Cuppins looked away, his eyes filled with unshed tears. "The type of man who does this." He lifted Dominique's other hand.

Isabelle shook her head in confusion. "Surely, surely his own father did not—"

"His own father did this. When Dominique wakes up, and believe me, he has to wake up…I will allow him to tell you that part of his story. I have stolen enough from him already. But a favor, my lady?"

"Anything." Her heart pounded in her chest. Palms sweaty she reached out and touched Cuppins's hand trying to convey the emotion welling within her. Her desperation to help Dominique out of this darkness was her heart's greatest desire.

"Give him something to live for."

Cuppins rose slowly to his feet, a grimace crossing his weathered face. He took his time leaving, stopping twice to catch his breath before reaching the door. "Give him something to live for," he repeated again, and left her alone with her husband.

What could she possibly say? Or even do? To show him, to make him understand that she would be here for him, take care of him. Love the unlovely.

As another tear ran down her cheek and dropped onto her thumb, she gasped. It was the first time they had held hands. Ever.

The scars came alive on his hands. White and pink skin lined the inside of his palm as well as the top of his wrist. Oddly, it seemed beautiful to her, as if his scars were a representation of what he had overcome. Even more amazing was that he could still play the piano. He was a walking miracle and didn't even know it. Was he not aware that fate had somehow needed him to live for a purpose greater than his own imaginings?

She carefully threaded his fingers with hers as if they were the most delicate treasures she had ever seen. And slowly she began to massage them as well as his arms.

It was an honor, she realized. To be his servant, to wash the scars that made him the man he was, but no longer would she allow them to define his future.

"I love you," she whispered kissing his right hand. "I love you," She kissed his left hand, tears dripped onto the scars and slid down his arms.

"Live." Her lips grazed his.

Isabelle fell asleep holding his hand across her heart.

CHAPTER TWENTY-FOUR

I have a secret. I've never felt love. What I had for my parents was duty, what I have for my music is passion. Perhaps I am not made to love, maybe that is what God traded music for in my life. He gifted me with something extraordinary, but in return, took the one thing people will go to the ends of the earth for. It hardly seems fair, but my life has never been fair, nor was I ever promised it would be. Sometimes, I think I catch a glimpse of love when the music is perfect, but it never sustains me, or fulfills me. Would life be different, I wonder, had I been born out of love and not obligation? These are the things I muse about when I'm writing my music. Mayhap, that is the reason behind the music's sadness. People weep when they hear it, because love is not present. And where love is not present, people cannot experience joy. Only pain.

~The Diary of Dominique Maksylov

THE FIRE WAS FADING. He remembered the minute it began to decrease in its heat. Cold lips had pressed against his, and then his scarred hand had been placed across something warm. He wasn't sure how he knew it was warm, just that it was. And then he felt a rhythm. It was perfect.

He hadn't felt such a rhythm in his entire lifetime. He had searched for an eternity to feel such a steady and strong beat.

It wasn't until the heat began to leave his body that he realized what the rhythm was. A heart.

Moments passed, or perhaps days, even years. Dominique could not tell. All he knew was that he felt oddly at peace.

The smell of fresh biscuits made his eyes flutter open. Isabelle was sprawled next to him on the bed.

And she was holding his hand.

Without his gloves.

He thought she was sleeping, that is until her lips moved ever so slowly. Was she speaking to him? Praying?

Ears straining, he waited.

"Beautiful…" She sighed and kissed his hand. "So beautiful."

Shock radiated all the way down to his toes. If he could have roared or at least shouted, he would have. *Beautiful?* Surely she was dreaming! Impossible that she was holding his scar, his beastly scar, and commenting that it was beautiful. He opened his mouth to say so, but she sighed again and moved, this time releasing his hand and wrapping her arm around his chest.

It felt nice.

Perhaps he would pretend to sleep for a little while longer.

She pressed closer to him, her breath coming out in lazy movements against his neck.

Memories of the past few days, of Isabelle being in danger, almost losing her, and finally getting shot came flooding back. He should be panicked, outraged, irritated, and most likely dead, considering he must have been feverish.

Instead all he felt was contentment.

Isabelle let out a faint feminine sigh and tucked her face deeper into his neck.

Perhaps he did die, and this was Heaven.

Dominique fought to keep his lips from turning into a smug smile, he truly did, but in the end, he could not help himself.

"You're awake!" Cuppins announced from the door.

He should be fired for his insolence.

Men should have a sixth sense about such things, especially concerning women. Dominique narrowed his eyes, but Cuppins didn't seem the least bit affected.

Isabelle jerked away from Dominique, nearly tumbling off the bed. "I was, I mean. I was helping you..."

"Oh, believe me, love," Dominique winked. "You were helping. Care to help some more? Cuppins? Go away. My wife has it on her mind to be helpful. Who am I to deny her such a simple request?"

"Right away, my lord." Cuppins grinned and stepped back out into the hall, shutting the door behind him.

Isabelle flushed when Dominique gazed at her.

And then she did the oddest thing.

She burst into tears.

What sort of world did he wake up in? "Isabelle?" He tried to move but his body was so fatigued. The best he could do was pat the side of the bed where she had previously been sitting. "Is this how you mean to help me? Showering tears across my bed seems unnecessary, considering I've been a victim of my own sweat from fever, but won't you tell me what plagues you so?"

Isabelle uttered a sigh and tentatively sat on the bed, as gentle as a mouse. "I—" she started. "I thought you were gone."

"Sorry to disappoint," Dominique teased.

Poor timing on his part, considering Isabelle burst into

fresh tears. With a chuckle he reached for her hand, knowing that his scars were visible in the morning light. "It seems as much as the devil wanted me, an angel needed me to stay here. Soft lips touched mine in the most achingly beautiful kiss I'd ever experienced. Tell me, was it you? Or my imagination?"

Isabelle touched her lips with her hand. "It's silly really." Wet, tear-filled eyes answered his question. "I kept thinking that if I kissed you, you'd awaken from your fever."

"As in a true fairy tale, is that it? The prince is turned from a frog to a prince? The beast into a handsome man?"

Isabelle nodded, red creeping up her neck.

"Did it work?" Dominique asked. The room was still and silent except for their breathing.

Slowly, Isabelle craned her head tilting it this way and that as she leaned over his body and whispered against his lips, "Yes."

What he wouldn't give for a little bit of strength, anything to be able to pull her into his arms and prove to her how he would fight, how he would live, how he would die with her name on his lips. "Am I a prince or merely handsome then? Which fairy tale will I be? Hmm?" His lips found a delicate spot on her neck, just below her ear. Fascinated with that tender piece of skin, he flicked it with his tongue, waiting for her to answer.

"Both," she whispered. "You're both."

CHAPTER TWENTY-FIVE

I've seen the sun for the first time. Imagine seeing the sunrise without looking out the window. For a moment, can you feel how powerful it would be to see light after experiencing a lifetime of darkness? Of blindness? I can. It is so sweet that it aches, so powerful that for the first time in my life I want to weep with joy, yet…I wonder how long this light will last, how long will it fight against the dark? Will it one day resent the darkness? Resent the way the darkness seems to swallow everything whole? I wonder, I wonder if it is enough.

~The Diary of Dominique Maksylov

DOMINIQUE AWOKE WITH A start. It had been three days since he had been brought back from the land of the dead. His strength had yet to return full force, and if Isabelle came in one more time yelling at him to lie in bed he was going to go mad. Either that or ravish her, both options seeming quite promising this early in the morning if his arousal and irritation were any indicator.

Footsteps neared his door. He flinched and ducked

under the covers like some small lad waiting to get his ears boxed. The knob on the door turned. He began to sweat. Please, let it be anything other than what he thought it would be. If Cuppins brought in anymore tonic for him to drink he was going to go mad.

Hunter burst into the room a smile plastered across his face. "I have returned!"

"Alert the Regent, it seems we are to have a parade. Let me just lift my wounded arm so I can notify him by letter, oh wait…I was shot."

Hunter cursed. "Yes, and I rode for days into the middle of a battle. I imagine Isabelle has been nursing you to health quite well. Kissing all your bruises and brushing her breasts against your arm when she gets too close. Yes, it seems like you've suffered a terrible experience, while I had to be treated by a doxy who smelled of fresh meat and eggs. I shall never eat again, I fear."

Dominique burst out laughing. "What was the wench's name?"

"I do not wish to discuss it. I barely escaped with my honor intact." Hunter shuddered. "Have you ever been taken advantage of in your sleep? Drugged? Unable to move because the chit has poisoned your tea with opium? No?" Hunter lifted his coat tails and took a seat on the bed.

"You were able to deny her with opium in your system? Strong man!" Dominique cheerfully patted his friend on the back then bit back another grin as his friend cursed.

"I was unable to move."

"So she…" Dominique tilted his head, biting his lip in thought. "Good heavens, you were accosted by a woman!"

"She forced herself." Hunter shivered. "And do you know the worst of it?"

"I'm sure you'll tell me."

"She didn't even offer for my hand afterwards. No

apologies. I was compromised! And no trap of marriage! She slapped my b—"

Dominique lifted an eyebrow.

Hunter cleared his throat. "At any rate, I at least imagined some sort of thank you."

"I take it you were given nothing of the sort."

"Milk. She gave me milk and sent me on my way. I believe my nightmares will now consist of that woman instead of Napoleon."

"How sad for you," Dominique said dryly. "Now—" he clapped his hands together. "I need your help."

"You do realize every time you say that, something bad happens to me, right?"

Dominique shook his head. "Stop complaining. You've just spent the night in a woman's bed! You should be in a better mood!"

"Calling her a woman would be a large stretch, I imagine. Now, what do you need? You do realize I'm a spy, not your nurse maid, as we've discussed, so if you plan to trap me in this room with you then—"

"Gads, no. I wouldn't wish that on my worst enemy. Every time I hear someone approach the door, I begin to perspire. If I have to drink one more concoction that is said to make me strong as an ox, I believe I'll fake my own death."

"Brilliant, just take me with you so I don't have to drink the stuff." Hunter leaned back against the headboard, not at all flummoxed that both men were sitting in the bed like a gaggle of women gossiping about the rag sheets.

"So, your favor." Hunter inspected his nails. "What is it?"

"A ball."

"Absolutely not." Hunter shot up from the bed and began pacing. "You cannot ask me to do it. I will *not* do it. I refuse. I will end our friendship. I will jump from the window. I will—"

"For Isabelle?"

"Blasted nuisance." Hunter cursed. "Even if I could manage to plan a ball in her honor, and help you win her affection yet again…No Englishman is safe here, not even your pretty wife."

"I know," Dominique said smugly.

"Balls usually involve dancing, lots of dancing, and food, and something else. Oh yes, guests!" He fixed Dominique with a pointed stare.

"I am aware."

"Smug idiot. Wipe that smile off your face and tell me what you are about."

Dominique grinned. "I thought you'd never ask."

Isabelle sniffed the concoction that Cook had made for Dominique. She would have half a mind to pity him if he hadn't been such a difficult patient. The man was insufferable! Every time she neared the bed he would pull her into his arms; every minute she was in his room it was as if she was going to be seduced at any second.

Not that she minded all that much, but he had been so ill and the idea of losing him, even though he was doing so much better, nearly killed her.

Fighting back ridiculous tears, for she had been extremely emotional as of late, she straightened her shoulders and carried the tray upstairs to Dominique's bedroom. Oh, she knew a servant would be more than happy to do the job, but something about nursing him back to health on her own, without servants, held its appeal. They were often alone during the day. And in order to keep him from jumping out the window, she had agreed to read to him.

His interests, however, were not the typical books a young lady of gentle breeding read. They were vulgar, and, well, she had to admit, interesting. But Dominique would watch her when she read. His eyes would be trained on her lips as if they fascinated him, and then he would close his eyes and dip his hand into the air as if conducting some sort of invisible song.

After three days of this she finally came to the conclusion that he was either mad, or truly heard music where others could not. For every time she spoke, it seemed to calm him, to make him smile. So she read, even though it mortified her all the way down to her toes to speak about such things aloud.

Just yesterday he had asked her if she would be so kind as to demonstrate what the book was discussing.

It was from India.

And had more pictures than it did words.

She threw it at his head.

He laughed, a hearty laugh rich with amusement and full of his baritone timbre, but he never apologized.

She imagined he would come up with another way to embarrass her, or flirt with her, today. A small smile danced across her lips as she pushed open the door.

Only to find Hunter and Dominique in each other's arms, dancing.

Wonders never cease.

Quietly, she lifted an eyebrow as she set the tray down on the nearest table and crossed her arms. They paused in their dancing, jerking away from one another. "Oh please." She waved her hand in dismissal. "Do not stop on my account."

Hunter cleared his throat. "We were…" Words died as he squinted and closed his mouth.

"Making sure Hunter could dance at the masquerade in a few months. His leg hasn't yet fully healed. He was concerned he would clobber someone with his boot. Isn't that right, Hunter?" Dominique patted him on the back. "He's a dreadful dancer in the first place. Women scurry away in hopes he won't ask for their hand, tends to step on their new slippers and all that. Not to mention the fact that he cannot count…well."

"Cannot count." Hunter repeated through clenched teeth. "Right. I'm dumb as an ox. Been spending too much time with this one." He pointed at Dominique. "Say," he walked toward the table. "Dominique was just speaking to me about how lovely this certain concoction was! He is so diligent about taking his medication, aren't you, my friend?"

Dominique's glare turned murderous as his nostrils flared in response. "Yes, well. I seem to be quite full of…" His eyes greedily searched the room.

Hunter grinned. "Brilliant, seems you haven't yet had your tea, this should slide down quite easily. We don't want Isabelle to be disappointed, now do we?"

"No," Isabelle joined in. "We don't."

"I miss my seclusion." Dominique cursed and took the concoction. Isabelle's eyes trained on his grimace as he drank the medicine in a few gulps. "Delightful." He coughed and hit his chest. "Lovely how it burns there at the end, what is that again?"

"It's best I keep it a surprise." Isabelle reached for the biscuits and tea. "Now, shall I pour?"

"Please," both men said in unison.

"Care to explain the real reason I interrupted such a delightful lover's embrace?" Isabelle fought to keep a straight face as Hunter kicked Dominique in the shin.

To his credit Dominique didn't wince, just smiled as if the world was exactly as it should be. "In due time, love. Now, for now, I beg that you accompany me to the village. It will be a short visit. Hunter has inquired and discovered that many of the French soldiers are no longer in this certain territory."

Isabelle nodded. "When are we to leave?"

"As soon as you are ready, love."

Smiling, she rose from her chair. "Well then, I better see to it. Gentleman..." She curtsied and turned toward the door, pausing before she left. "And, Hunter?"

His head snapped up.

"While dancing, it is important that you hold your partner closer. I trust you'll work hard to remember those difficult numbers while dancing at the masquerade?"

"Yes, well, one, two, three, and four, are all such a mouthful. I have my doubts." He seethed.

"Try." Isabelle winked. "After all, we wouldn't want people thinking you were stupid, would we?"

Dominique choked on his tea, but otherwise kept an impassive face.

"Right." Hunter took a deep breath and leaned lazily back into his chair. "We wouldn't want any of those women getting the wrong impression."

Isabelle waved and made her exit, laughing all the way down the hall. Whatever those two boys—not men—were up to, it was amusing.

Try as she might, she could not push down the excitement that jumped her pulse when Dominique asked to take her into the village. She hadn't yet visited, but imagined it would be ideal.

With a squeal, she went to her room and called for her maid.

CHAPTER TWENTY-SIX

Lost... I am so hopelessly, joyfully, incomparably…Lost.
~The Diary of Dominique Maksylov

"SOMETIMES," HUNTER GROWLED ONCE Isabelle had left, "I wish I could wring your neck and throw *you* out the window. Perhaps you'll allow me to use you for target practice while you zigzag through the forest, hmm?"

"Of course, anything you say." Dominique had only partially heard what his friend nattered about. His focus, his only focus, was for his wife. The quirk of her lips, the lightness of her steps, her delicate hands. Blood surged to all the wrong places, making him uncomfortable. He wanted to possess her, to ravish her, but most of all, and he would never admit it aloud, he wanted to just touch her, breathe next to her in hopes that her air would mingle with his and he could savor her scent, taste her skin…

"And then I shall smite thee with my fist!" Hunter finished.

"What the devil?" Dominique turned to his friend who

was now wielding a pretend sword in the air.

"Caught my performance did you? I nearly stopped once I had been acting out scene one for an ungodly amount of time, then got quite caught up. Done wool gathering, are you? Run along, it seems I've a ball to prepare tonight!" Hunter clapped his hands. "Now, do you remember the steps from the dance?"

"I believe so." Dominique nodded his head. "I don't remember it being that difficult."

"It's a waltz," Hunter replied. "Not meant to be difficult, but sensual; it is the only dance you may dance in public where you can fully embrace a woman, feel her soft supple body against your—"

"Your eyes are closed. Tell me you're imagining that doxy who took advantage of you and not my wife."

"I wish it were anything but the doxy, but alas, she is the freshest in my mind. Blasted meat."

Dominique bit his lip to keep from smiling and slapped his friend on the back. "Thank you, I owe you so very much..."

Hunter grinned wolfishly. "Yes well, there will be a time when you will pay me back in full. Now off you go, it seems I am to discuss food with your kitchen help, amongst other things."

Dominique made his way toward the door. "Try not to scare the wits out of my staff, Hunter."

"The wolf will not bare his teeth, beast, now go!" Hunter laughed.

Dominique was happy to find his wife at the bottom of the stairs, covered in a tightly-fitted pelisse that brought his eye to the trim feminine figure. Lined with fur, it seemed to be worn for two purposes.

Warmth and seduction.

At the moment he was imagining both, which was why, when his foot slipped on the last stair, he went flying to the ground at alarming speed, almost not catching his face before it slapped against the cold marble floor.

"Dominique!" Isabelle gasped, kneeling next to him on the floor. "Is it the fever? Is it back? Are you ill?" She pulled his head against her chest and kissed him on the hair; his cheek brushed against something soft, supple, distinctly feminine.

He moaned.

"Oh no!" Isabelle then cursed quite soundly for a female. "I just knew an outing was a tragic idea."

Dominique nodded, allowing his cheek to rub against her chest. Bliss. Complete and utter bliss. If only she would move slightly to the right so he could…

Chuckling, because he truly could not help the mirth escaping through his mouth, he bent his head into the opening of her pelisse and kissed her exposed skin just below the neck.

"You cad!" With a thud she whacked him with her reticule and pushed away from the floor. "And to think I felt sorry for you!" A smile curved at her lips, but she looked to be desperately trying to keep it from showing.

"I was injured, truly out of my mind. No idea what came over me." As the lie tumbled out, he chuckled and rose to his feet. "Now that I've not only embarrassed myself beyond all reason by first falling and then being so uncomfortably aroused I fear I won't walk straight again, should we go to the village?"

Isabelle flushed and he could tell she was trying very hard not to peek at his afflicted area.

"Perhaps," conquering a grin he walked over to her and lifted a hand to rub the side of her neck with his thumb, "when we return we can read some more?"

"Read." Her lips quivered, a blush stained her cheek. "Is that what you are going to call it from now on?"

"Call what?"

"You know exactly what I'm talking about, you rake." Her eyes narrowed.

"Truthfully, I'm in no mood to read, that is unless you plan to read in hopes to advise me the best position for me to—"

She clamped a hand over his mouth.

He nipped at it then pulled her roughly across his chest, kissing her lips, stealing the breath straight from her lungs in hopes that she would have no other choice but to inhale all of him. "Don't bother ringing for your maid when we return, love."

Reluctantly, he released her and offered his arm. With a sigh and a dramatic eye roll, she took his arm as he led her outside to the waiting carriage.

Once they were seated comfortably, mind you, not seductively or sensually as he would have liked, but comfortably apart from one another. He began to put his little plan into action. It had taken not only a generous amount of blunt, but also seamstresses, who agreed to make alterations to one of the pre-made ball gowns in the village. It was supposed to be of the newest style, boasting a rich burgundy and an almost backless dip. Just hearing about it made Dominique think all sorts of improper thoughts.

"What are we to do in the village?" Isabelle asked, interrupting his vivid fantasy of what a chocolate-dipped female would taste like.

"Er…" Dominique stuttered then coughed. "I have a few matters to take care of, and you, my dear, need some new gloves, and slippers, and well, sadly, we never purchased your trousseau. I have decided to amend the situation immediately."

"For your own pleasure, no doubt." Isabelle lifted an eyebrow in his direction then used her hands to smooth out her skirts. "Now, what is Hunter to be doing all day? And do not lie to me, I can tell when you are trying to avoid the truth, you always bite the inside of your cheek."

"I have never lied to you!" Dominique tried to appear offended while racking his brain for instances of dishonesty.

"You said you enjoyed your morning tonic."

"I do. You bring it."

"Lie number one." Isabelle counted off on her fingers. "You also said you lack the patience to read."

"I find large words terribly troublesome." He feigned boredom and looked out the window.

Out of the corner of his eye, he watched Isabelle shake her head. "Right, which explains why Cuppins claims you've mastered six languages and hold an honorary degree in botany from Oxford."

"Can a man help that he enjoys roses?" Dominique countered.

"Tell me, do you lose often at the tables?" Isabelle leaned forward. Dominique wrenched his gaze from her pert décolletage and struggled to pull his mind away from the vision in front of him.

"I do not gamble."

An amused grin spread across her face. "You wouldn't."

"Whatever do you mean?" He leaned forward to meet her in the middle of the carriage.

"A man like you wouldn't gamble money. You do not take chances, or at least you do not enjoy the risk in doing so. Besides, as I said, you bite your cheek when you lie. You'd lose the entire estate in a manner of minutes."

Dominique leaned back and grumbled. "Fine, now, let us talk of other things. I find it uncomfortable when you examine me so closely."

He had just opened his mouth to steer the subject elsewhere when she asked in her soft voice the question he was hoping to avoid.

"Why?"

Time stood still. He looked out the window, noticing the way the snow melted and dripped off the trees. "Because, I fear you will find me lacking."

Only cowards made admissions and refused to look into the person's eyes when doing so, but he found his old insecurities crawl back full force. The weight of rejection heavy on his chest yet again. Would he never be rid of it?

Isabelle sighed, then pulled the drapes across the windows. In an instant she was straddling him. Lifting her skirts over his form it was truly something he would remember for his entire existence. Especially the way her legs braced either side of him. How pieces of hair fell out of her hat. The smell of berries from her breakfast warm on her breath. She bit her lip and cocked her head to one side.

His pulse pounded in his neck; no doubt she could see it. The whole blasted world would be able to view it. But he could not stop the blood roaring in his ears, or the distinct arousal emblazing his body. He wanted to stay there, in between her thighs forever. Even if she was clothed the entire time. Her warmth, her body, embraced his in such an intimate way that he wondered if he ever truly knew passion until this day.

Yet her lips hadn't touched his mouth.

Her hands hadn't reached for his breeches.

And he wasn't driving into her like a lust-filled madman.

They were merely sitting, staring, gazing. Like besotted fools.

He loved it. He loved *her*.

"I am the liar. For I have fought, very hard, not to show you how much I care, how much I feel, how I would die for another taste of your lips." Isabelle brushed her lips across his as she whispered, "Want to know a secret?"

"Tell me," he demanded.

Isabelle settled comfortably across his lap, her lips brushing his as she spoke, "When I lie, I hold my breath. I think it's because I am fearful."

"Are you holding your breath now?" he asked.

"No. Why would I? When all I want is to taste your skin." Her kiss both alarmed and invigorated him. Her tongue dipped out to trace the hollow of his neck. He didn't deserve such a perfect, bold female. But he was going to take her, and pleasure her and—

The carriage jolted to a stop.

Isabelle held her bottom lip captive between her teeth and grinned mischievously. "It seems our trip is finished. Shall we shop?"

Dominique closed his eyes. It really was the only way he could think to blast out her image without ravishing her completely and fully in view of the entire village.

"Right," he ground out, his voice raspy and thick. "Let us just shop." He cursed shopping the rest of the day, for it was the obstacle that kept him from doing the thing he wanted more than anything.

Making love to his wife.

CHAPTER TWENTY-SEVEN

I remember my first performance. It was for the Czar of Russia. I was terrified, but so excited. My palms perspired as I touched the keys of the piano and set out to impress my father's friend. It was the most terrifying time of my life. Yet, when I gaze into the eyes of my wife, a new terror takes hold, gripping my heart until it hurts to breathe. To lose her would be to lose myself. I cannot grasp, nor fathom the depths of my sorrow, if I were to no longer have her by my side. I would give up my music, my life, my very soul, to keep her.

~The Diary of Dominique Maksylov

BY THE TIME ISABELLE returned to the carriage with Dominique, the sun was going down. It had been a dreadfully long day, but she hadn't imagined it would be so fun. Dominique was showing a completely different side of himself. At one point she thought he was foxed. He was too carefree, he laughed often, and his smile was so beautiful it took her breath away. Surely there was some sort of explanation for his behavior? She wasn't naive enough to believe it had to do with being in her presence, though she ached for it to be true. Men despised shopping as well as socializing, at least men like Dominique, but he seemed to enjoy walking into the village, talking with the local butcher and even the modiste as he explained exactly what type of dress he needed to be made for Isabelle, stating that she was to never wear the colors of a debutante again.

The ladies of the village noticed his charisma as well. The women shared their smiles too freely and found any number of excuses to reach out and touch Dominique. One of the ladies at the shop had the audacity to even claim she was concerned there was a rip in his jacket. Jealousy poured out of Isabelle until, in one final act of a day of poor choices—for she had shamelessly attached herself to his person publically all day—she even went as far as to kiss him in the middle of the village square.

"Feeling possessive?" Dominique asked, his lips forming a mischievous grin.

"No." Isabelle brushed his hair out of his face. "Feeling happy." And it was true, she was happy, though it was entirely possible that her happiness was being overshadowed by a sort of jealous rage she had never before experienced.

"Even better." He winked.

As they sat across from one another and made their way home, Isabelle could not help the feeling of foreboding that took over. What if it was all a lie? Was Dominique truly reformed or would she put her heart even further out only to see it snatched away the minute he allowed the darkness that haunted him to seep back into his soul?

Dresses, gloves, hats—he did not even stop to ask if she wanted any of these things, rather he insisted that she add to her wardrobe. His way of repaying her, no doubt, for her kindness during his illness. But what she wanted, what she needed, was the very thing he hadn't once offered since his recovery.

His heart.

Dominique had made it clear that he desired her, but that he too feared rejection. How was she to continue on in the same fashion, knowing that fear kept both of them from proclaiming what needed to be said? If she took the first step, if she were to be bold and confess her love, then she put her heart and what felt like her soul out into the open. Oh she had said it before, but after he was shot, she wasn't even sure if he still remembered, or if he thought it was merely her emotions running high. If he did so, then he feared she would reject him and if her answer was less than perfect or if she paused in any way, would he begin to shout and act beastly, thinking she felt differently.

It was all too much. Her mind whirled with possibilities. She chewed her lip in thought, keeping her eyes downcast the entire way home. Clearly, Dominique was distracted, for he said nothing to her once they pulled up to the large estate. Instead, he jumped out of the carriage, offered his hand, and made some ridiculous excuse about seeing that Hunter hadn't jumped headfirst from the balcony.

Bewildered and quite tired from spending the last of her energy arguing with herself the entire way home, Isabelle walked blindly into the castle, not bothering to look any direction but at the stairs as she slowly ascended to her bedroom.

Perhaps a nap would set her to rights? She stifled a yawn. Yes, a nap would be just the thing. Maybe her imagination would be at rest and she could wake up refreshed, ready to find out why her husband was in such a hurry to find Hunter.

Dominique watched his wife slowly walk up the stairs. Always the lady, she covered her mouth with the back of her hand to hide her yawn. She must be utterly exhausted, for she hadn't said a word the entire ride home. Not that he could blame her, for the past few days had been anything but restful for the girl and he had gone and overwhelmed her with a shopping excursion. But it was necessary, for not only did he need her away from the estate, but he required her exact measurements to put final touches on the ball gown he had ordered for her.

Now, he just had to locate Hunter to make sure everything was set for that evening. Everything had to be perfect.

As expected, Hunter was indeed leaning over one of the balconies above the stairs; he was not, however, planning his own demise. Rather, he was helping one of the servants string up a slew of lanterns filled with candles.

"There you are." Dominique took a deep breath and looked around the transformed entry leading into the ballroom at the bottom of the stairs. "Do you think you can manage to hurry?"

Hunter glared, his eyes burning with indignation. "Why yes, why don't I just snap my fingers? Perhaps magical fairies will appear and decorate the entire house to your liking, considering what I'm doing isn't enough."

At that precise moment, one of the candles hit the corner of Hunter's jacket lighting him on fire. The outburst caused quite a commotion as the man turned in circles and cursed before a nearby maid finally doused him with a bucket of water.

Dominique desperately tried to hold in his laughter; truly he wasn't prone to laughing so much in one day. But the sight of his friend, drenched after a day of women's work and decorating was too much.

A chuckle broke free and then another, before Dominique bent over in pure merriment as his laughter echoed off the walls. Hunter joined in. The maids, however, looked shocked for Dominique knew better than any that it had been years since such laughter had danced through the house.

Surely it hadn't been as bad as all that, had it? His mind played tricks with him. Surely he had at least smiled! But as his gaze quickly darted to the shocked maids, he realized that yes, it had been that bad. If anything it had been worse. And he was to blame for all of it.

Perhaps if he would have visited this particular home, the country estate once in the last ten years, his smile wouldn't shock them so. But all they had to go on was rumors of the murders and Dominique's eccentric reputation. He hadn't been to this estate in years. And his staff still wasn't sure how to respond to him.

Gathering his wits, he managed to stop laughing as he nudged Hunter, who also stopped grinning like a fool. "Thank you," Dominique addressed the maid. "For all your hard work, as Hunter has, I'm sure, explained, we are to have a ball in honor of my wife for agreeing to be saddled with me the rest of her days. And, as a surprise, every single staff member is to bring their family and friends to the glorious event tonight."

At his announcement, the maid's eyes widened until he was certain they would roll back as she fainted dead away.

"Are you able to notify the staff, Miss…?" Truly, he hadn't even a clue what her name was. What type of man was he that he could not remember a person's name! It was as if the darkness he had lived in had destroyed his memory as well.

"Hopkins, Beth Hopkins, your highness." She curtsied, a flush rising to her cheeks.

"Miss Hopkins." Dominique said the name. "Do I pay you well?"

Hunter cleared his throat and nudged him. "Dominique, stop scaring the poor girl. I'm sure there is a better time or place to discuss such things. This is not it."

Dominique ignored him. It wasn't at all proper to discuss such things publicly in front of anyone, especially a titled guest such as Hunter, but his curiosity was piqued. The fact he had no idea of her name spurred him to think of other notions he hadn't considered. Had he been a better master than his father? Had he provided for his servants?

He nodded his head and crossed his arms. After a few minutes, in which Miss Hopkins looked to be thinking of a lie, she licked her lips and answered, "You pay me quite well, my lord, for I am able to feed my family and that is all I ask."

"And clothes, are you able to purchase clothes?"

She was silent.

"And coal for your fire?"

Still no answer. Tears pooled in her eyes.

"Wax for your candles?"

Her lip began to tremble. Hunter's hand braced Dominique's arm. Devil take it, he wasn't going to bite the woman's head off!

"Allow me to ask you again, Miss Hopkins, and pray do not insult my intelligence by being anything but honest, yes?"

She nodded and closed her eyes.

"Do I pay you well?"

"No, my lord. You do not pay me well."

"Thank you," Dominique answered.

Miss Hopkins eyes flashed open, darting from Hunter to Dominique before settling back onto Dominique with a quizzical look.

"I shall double your salary and that of every other staff member as of today. I imagine you can include that piece of information when you invite everyone to the ball tonight, yes?"

"Y-yes, my lord." A tear ran down her cheek as she curtsied, then reached for his hand, his gloved hand, and bestowed a kiss upon it. "God preserve you, my prince."

It was the first time any of his staff had ever called him "prince" since his father's death. In his bitterness, Dominique had always thought it was because of the horrid memories of his father, that they had no desire to remind him of his title, of the title he inherited after murdering his own father.

But now, the way that Miss Hopkins said "my prince", made him believe that perhaps, for the first time in his life he had earned his title. And all because he extended the one thing his father never had.

Mercy.

CHAPTER TWENTY-EIGHT

If I would have known that my music would become my cocoon, that I would turn a blind eye to the darkness of the world, using my own justification for my actions, then it is entirely possible I would have tried to stop what I became. After all, no man wakes up one day hoping to be a beast, praying he can turn into something that people will mock and hate. No, it is a slow fade into the very thing you promised you would never become. How could I have not seen my own father's reflection when I looked into the mirror? Had I known, I would have fought; I would have tried to be something—anything but him.

~The Diary of Dominique Maksylov

ISABELLE AWOKE WITH A start. The room was cast in evening shadows. With a yawn, she made her way to the window and noticed the bright white moon had begun to rise into depths of the blue sky. How long had she been asleep? Confused, she looked around her room. Was dinner to commence soon?

She walked to the door adjoining her room and Dominique's, the one where she so often shared his bed. Why was it, that as her hand touched the door, memories of his touch flooded her body until she was shivering with desire? It was ridiculous.

But wonderful all the same.

The sleep did nothing to alleviate her worries, for although she felt more rested than she had in the past week, she still could not help but concentrate on his sudden change in behavior. With a sigh she leaned her head against the door and allowed herself a few selfish tears. She was so hopelessly in love with him.

What was wrong with her? She was made of stronger stuff, and yet she couldn't help but have a heavy heart as she pushed open the door.

But the thing of it was…Well, it wouldn't budge.

She pushed harder, this time allowing her whole body to move against it.

Still, no movement.

Panic overwhelmed her. Had Dominique locked her in her room?

She banged her fist against the door, twice. Before a throat cleared.

"Miss? May I be of service?" Her maid, Amy, gave her a slightly bewildered look from the open door in the bedroom. Drat, why hadn't she thought of that? Clearly, sleep had done nothing to clear her muddled thoughts. If anything it had made it worse. How could she forget the actual door into the hallway?

"No, er, that is to say, I was just wondering where I might find my husband."

Amy grinned and looked down at the floor. "Pardon my firm hand in this, my lady. But the master of the house has left strict instructions as to dinner this evening. If we are to be on time, we must get you ready."

"But..." Isabelle put her hands on her hips and bit her lip.

"Surely, he isn't demanding I meet him for dinner? Are we truly back to the origin of how I arrived?"

Amy beamed. "Quite the opposite, my lady. Now, if you'll just have a seat here. The gown just arrived an hour ago and has been pressed. If you'll allow me, I'll help dress you before I fix your hair."

"Dress me?" Isabelle looked down. Indeed, her dress was quite wrinkled. Something fresh would be just the thing. But wait, hadn't Amy said the gown had just arrived? "Was my gown misplaced for it to just arrive?"

Amy began the tedious task of loosening the worn afternoon dress from Isabelle's body. "The dressmakers, my lady. They worked tirelessly through the day to finish it for you."

"For dinner?" Isabelle asked, still confused and a trifle muddled.

"Yes, and the ball," Amy said quietly.

"Ball?"

Amy nodded. "Now, that is all I am permitted to say, my lady. But may I just say, thank you again for the raises."

"Raises?" Truly, had Isabelle woken up in a different time and place? What was the girl blabbering about?

"Oh yes," Amy gushed. "Why the master said you were in full agreement that all the staff would receive a raise. I wasn't to say anything, but I hadn't a chance to express my thanks as of yet."

"Tell me," Isabelle tried to keep her voice knowledgeable as she bit her lip, "What did my dear husband decide on as adequate for a raise?"

Amy's hands stilled on Isabelle's back. "It isn't proper to discuss such things."

"I give you leave," Isabelle said, amused.

"Double," Amy mumbled.

"Double what?"

"Our salary. It was doubled. Did he not discuss the final number with you?"

"Oh he did," Isabelle lied through her teeth. "Forgive me, I am still waking up from my nap. Now, let us hurry along with the preparations. I would hate to keep my generous husband waiting."

Isabelle's heart warmed at the thought. Her husband, the lying little beast, had set her up to be a part of his gift, when it truly came from his heart, not her own. She stifled a gleeful laugh and turned around to face Amy, but her maid was busy pulling out the most beautiful gown Isabelle had ever seen.

Dark burgundy material flew out from an empire waist bodice. Lower than something she would have ever chosen for herself, it boasted of see-through material across the arms, floating lazily down to an open back with a black-laced train.

It was the exact dress he had picked out, not hours before. Only this time, she suspected, it would fit her perfectly.

"Do you like it?" Amy asked, her voice hinting at concern.

"No." Isabelle giggled. "I adore it."

Amy beamed. "Wait until you see the gloves."

Dominique paced at the bottom of the stairs. What the devil was taking her so long? He had specifically sent the maid in to help her get dressed over an hour ago. Surely changing gowns and fixing one's hair didn't take this long?

Not that he had any experience in the matter.

What with only recently deciding to cut his hair and groom himself.

With a groan, he leaned against the stairway and crossed his arms.

"Impatient?" A familiar and altogether unwelcome voice

said behind him.

"Hunter," Dominique said through clenched teeth. "Aren't you supposed to be making the final arrangements?"

"They've been made, thrice, now stop whining and let me have a look at you."

Dominique scowled and reluctantly pushed away from the railing to face his friend.

"Dominique, I don't think I've ever seen you look so cleaned up." Hunter's eyes held no amusement, strictly astonishment. Dominique wasn't sure if he should be offended or complimented.

"Are you to say that I normally look disheveled?" He fired back.

"Disheveled?"

Dominique nodded.

"Of course not."

He exhaled.

"That would be putting it mildly, I'm afraid. In the past you've always looked positively rugged, like a pirate lord ready to ravish the lady and take over another ship's treasure."

Dominique bit back a sharp retort. "And now? Do I still resemble the pirate?"

Hunter smirked. "No, I imagine a pirate will be the furthest thing from your young wife's mind. Though, I daresay she may mistake you for a rake if you don't get that smoldering look under control, and please direct it elsewhere. It's making me deuced uncomfortable."

"Apologies." Dominique felt himself flush with embarrassment.

"No need." Hunter slapped his back. "Just be sure to direct your gaze to your wife, and do not forget to please her tonight, lest I find myself on the other end of one of your lust-filled glances again and feel the need to punch you."

"Agreed." Dominique cleared his throat just as his gaze

swept upwards to the top of the stairs, where the most beautiful woman in the world was making her descent.

Mouth dry, Dominique continued to stare a hole straight through the woman. It was near impossible to drag his eyes away from her face. Lit with excitement, her eyes dazzled with mischief. Lush brown hair was partially held with pins, allowing silky tendrils to dance over her collarbone.

Reluctantly, he allowed his gaze to trail down her graceful neck, to the swell of her bosom as her dress, as if painted on, unapologetically clung to every feminine curve. Her skin seemed to glow, almost translucent through the thin fabric, and he could have sworn he was given glimpses of her long legs as she descended the stairs.

Pride swelled within him. She was his. That was his wife.

He looked to Hunter.

Whose mouth was also gaping open.

Dominique briefly contemplated shooting him.

But then again, he was his best friend.

"One night," Hunter whispered. "Just give me one night and I'll secure her affection…"

Where were the pistols? Dominique growled, and pushed Hunter toward the entrance to the dining room, all the while keeping his eyes trained on his friend for any sudden movement.

"It was merely a jest." Hunter argued, though his voice was husky and his face flushed.

"Do you hear me laughing?"

"No," Hunter bit out. "Though I could have sworn you growled."

Dominique smiled. "Yes, well. Beast trumps wolf, now, leave me and my wife a few moments of peace before we join you for dinner, and if you do not cease from making eyes at her I will gouge them out."

"Truly?" Hunter gave him a knowing look and crossed

his arms.

"Fine, I won't cause blindness, but I will be forced to wrap a blindfold around your head."

Hunter grinned. "Just makes things more amusing in the bedroom, don't you think?"

"Hunter..." Dominique warned. "Any more comments such as that and you will truly know what it is like to spend the night with a tavern wench. Don't make me locate the woman that near traumatized you for life just a few days ago. And don't you deny it, I still hear you screaming in your sleep."

"You wouldn't."

"I would, and I will. Don't tempt me. What did she do to you again?" Dominique had just recently heard the full story of how the woman—Hunter swore it was indeed a woman though Dominique now had his doubts—tortured him and forced him to eat from her large, hairy hands in order to sustain himself.

"Fine. I'll be just over there—" Hunter nodded to where the brandy was, "Attempting to drink myself into a stupor. Perhaps I'll be too foxed to remember the smell of sweaty meat. One can only hope." With a nod, he hastily made his way toward the liquor. "Cheers," he grumbled.

Dominique couldn't even muster the ability to feel guilty for his threat. Quickly he reentered the room. Isabelle was waiting at the bottom of the stairs, examining her gloves.

"Do you like them?" he asked once he was close enough to talk to her without shouting. Her eyes twinkled with delight as she held her hands out in front of her and squealed, "They do not even look real!"

Pleased, Dominique grinned and brought her hand to his face. "They are made of the softest silk. It was near impossible to sew the gloves together for the fabric had the tendency to tear."

"How did you manage it?"

"Magic," he whispered against her lips. And he believed it. For the first time in his life, he truly believed in the fairy tales. That a man's job was to chase after the princess, rescue her from the horrid beast, even if the person he was rescuing her from was himself.

Perhaps his mother was right. Hadn't she said that one day he would storm a castle in hopes to secure his own love? At the time the vision had been of him galloping into a large estate on his horse.

Now, older and hopefully wiser, he realized what his mother meant. Sometimes, it takes no great feat of physical strength, but that of emotions and will, for the walls one has to break, the ones that hold the greatest threat, are the ones around a person's heart.

He would secure her heart, once and for all, tonight.

Pulling away, he bent low before his wife, and kissed both of her hands before offering his arm. "After dinner, we will dance."

"I cannot believe you would throw a ball for two people."

Dominique grinned. "Love, who ever told you there would only be two?"

Isabelle opened her mouth to speak, but was interrupted by Dominique's clap. With a jerk and a gasp, she looked around the dining room table. Blanketed in a pool of light, the area looked like something that when future generations asked him how he had won the heart of the beauty, he would have trouble explaining just how breath-taking it had been.

Sconces lined the walls of the room, all lit, and blazing light into the otherwise dark, cold, dining area. The long table held candles of every shape and size, and in the middle, an ice sculpture of two people dancing.

Dominique and Isabelle.

Cuppins had outdone himself, if the smirk on his face

was any indication as he sat in the corner of the room.

Dominique was slightly worried the sculpture would melt with all the candles near it, but it seemed to be holding its own. Thankful, he led Isabelle to the table and pulled out her chair, shaking his head to the servant who had stepped forward to do so.

If anyone was going to touch his wife, it would be him.

Not a servant.

Certainly not Hunter.

And tonight, not even her lady's maid.

The thought brought a smile to his lips as he pushed her chair in and took a seat opposite.

"Dinner is served." Cook walked in, proud as a peacock. Dominique had requested that the servants involve themselves in the explaining of the dishes; it seemed Isabelle was always asking questions. To satisfy her curiosity about the local dishes, he asked Cook to explain each and every one of the foods that graced her plate.

Isabelle wasn't sure she could eat another bite. Not used to such rich food, she felt positively ready to burst. But ladies never said such things aloud, so she bit the inside of her cheek and declined Cook's invitation to have a bite of dessert.

Never had she seen Dominique look so carefree. The candlelight danced on his sculpted features, making his face appear like a live painting. She found herself shamelessly staring at him more often than her own food. The planes of his face were smooth with sharp angles. His full lips would part as he smiled seductively at her. More than once she felt herself overheat, and then tremble just by the mere sight of his smile! Merciful heavens, he was beautiful, and she could not gather the strength to look away. Her eyes, it seemed, had a mind of their own, as they stayed focused on the most beautiful man. Surely it did not go unnoticed by the staff, as well as Hunter, who every few minutes entered the dining room to pour himself more brandy and found the need to continuously roll his eyes at them in exaggeration.

His bad attitude gained him two swift kicks in the shin until finally he mumbled an apology and glared into his glass of brandy, looking as if he wished it to turn into a beautiful woman. Truly, the man needed to get a hold of his lust before Dominique did it for him. It wasn't natural for a man to look so interested in spirits or food as if gorging himself of those simple things would sate his desires.

She looked back to where Dominique was sitting and noticed he no longer occupied the seat. Glancing around the room, he was nowhere to be found. Panic seized her. What if he had seen her glance at Hunter? Truly it wasn't that she held a secret tender for him. If anything, she was concerned for his welfare. Bile rose in her throat, the last time she had talked with Hunter, Dominique had thrown a fit.

Rising quickly, she was just about ready to make her apologies, when a beautiful masterpiece reached her ears.

It was painfully obvious Dominique was gracing the piano with his presence, but the music, the song pouring forth, was magical. It reminded her of fairies dancing in the forest. Of sea nymphs swirling in the ocean. It held no hatred, no anger, no darkness.

Without excusing herself, she made her way into the large ballroom, where she was certain the music was coming from. It reached high into the ceilings, begging to be released into the night sky. The notes swirled and danced around her and she almost lifted her hands above her head in worship—for music had never truly been this beautiful.

As she entered the large ballroom, her eyes fixed on her husband's back, she could think of nothing except caressing those scarred hands, which brought forth so much beauty. Hands that played through haunting pain.

"Beautiful." She placed her hands on his broad shoulders and sighed as she felt the muscles flex beneath his dinner jacket. His head tilted back. Eyes closed, he continued to play with his head rested against her body, inky black hair falling over one eye.

A thrill shot through her at the intimate notion, as if her body was inspiring him, her love, her touch. Spellbound, she watched as his beautifully marked hands flew effortlessly over the keys of the piano, as if man and instrument were one and the same.

Without thinking, she placed both hands on either side of his face, and leaned forward, gasping at the feel of his lips against hers.

Desire made her lips quiver at the touch of his tongue as it parted her lips. Obviously more talented than she realized, he continued to play as his mouth sent delicious shivers down her spine. As his tongue flicked across hers and then withdrew, the music stopped. With a groan he turned around and pulled her across his lap.

His kiss was hot and urgent, reckless, but like his music, unique and beautiful. His lips beckoned her, called out to her, sung to her. She could not stop if her life depended on it.

Abruptly, he slowed the kiss, his lips dancing merrily across her chin as he grinned and then with his teeth tugged at her bottom lip, alternating between sucking and licking before he reached his hands into her hair and jerked her forward against his hard body.

"Ahem," a male voice said through the haze of passion. "As much as I enjoy watching you two engage in such… hobbies. Especially considering I am a young virile male without companionship, it seems the guests have all but arrived and are ready to enter into the ballroom. I have tried to keep them busy, poured wine, though I find it beneath me, told jokes, though nobody laughed... Alas, my only other option was to interrupt...this." Hunter's voice feigned indifference. Truly he would be a fabulous butler. Not that she would ever say as much to his face lest he give her another one of his infamous glares.

"No," Dominique answered roughly against her mouth. "Send them away." He reached his hand around to her bum, pulling her roughly against him.

"Blast it all, it's like watching a naughty play," Hunter complained. "Dominique, you invited them here. Devil take it! Now show your wife a good time."

Isabelle giggled. "Oh, I'm having a good—"

"Isabelle!" Hunter scolded.

With great effort she pried herself way from Dominique's arms, and nearly lost her nerve at the look of passion in his eyes, half-lidded with promises of seduction, and secrets of a night full of pleasure, if only she would take him up on the offer. Obviously lacking any sort of proper self-control, she leaned forward again, despite Hunter's curses, but Dominique stopped her.

"Hunter's right, love." He kissed her nose. "Besides, the ball is part of the surprise."

"And our guests?"

"The staff and their family, welcoming you to your home." He brushed his thumb across her bottom lip, dipping it slightly into her mouth and closing his eyes. "And Hunter did go to a lot of work to carry out my instructions with the decorations."

"Decorations?"

Dominique grinned. "Are you to tell me you haven't looked at your surroundings?"

Isabelle lifted her head slowly to the ceiling, and then to the walls of the ballroom. Tears welled behind her eyes.

"How did you—"

"Hush." He kissed her lightly across the lips. "You are deserving of far more."

Isabelle shook her head as she slowly rose to her wobbly legs. "It looks enchanted."

"Thanks to Hunter's skill of persuasion, manipulation, and apparently decoration, we have given you just that. An enchanted castle."

"Heard that," Hunter muttered as his footsteps echoed across the marble floors. People began filing in as he opened the doors, musicians, families, and servants with goblets of wine. *Why there must be at least a hundred or more people!*

Isabelle looked at the ceiling, draped in white billowy fabric. Lanterns of every shape and size fell from the tall ceiling, though she wasn't sure how it was managed for they were ridiculously high. The room was bathed in whites and golds, and the candlelight made things come alive.

Considering how old the castle was, it was no surprise to see the gargoyles that decorated the main ballroom. Bronze and gold plated, they glowed in the candlelight, almost giving them a life-like effect that both thrilled and scared her.

The servants and their families formed a sort of circle around her and Dominique. He winked, and bowed over her hand. "May I have the honor of this dance?"

Breathless, she nodded, and gave a low curtsy.

The entire room erupted into applause as he pulled her into his arms. Floating, she was floating across the room, with the beast turned prince. Her smile hurt, it was so wide. Perhaps it was worth all the pain, to arrive at this exact moment. A moment when a much traumatized little boy finally turned into a man.

After two dances in a row, they mingled with guests and made toasts to the families who had visited. Room abuzz with excitement, it felt that the night would go on forever.

Hours later, as Dominique gazed into her eyes, the true merriment expressed as they danced in front of the servants and their families, Dominique knew.

He had to tell her.

It was time to kill the beast.

To show her the man within.

And pray to God that she would accept him as he was.

For if she couldn't…If the beauty smiling at him with trusting eyes and a light-hearted laugh, if she rejected him, he wasn't sure he would ever be the same.

"Come," he whispered in her ear.

"But the guests?" Isabelle's voice was hushed. "What are we to say to them?"

"Believe me, love, they rejoice in our scandal. After all, it isn't at all improper for a husband to take his wife to bed when she is so utterly exhausted."

"I am nothing of the sort!" Isabelle exclaimed.

"Sure you are." Dominique put out his foot just as Isabelle walked over it, sending her sailing into his arms. "Apologies!" he said loud enough for a few guests nearby to hear. "It seems we've had enough excitement for one night. Please, stay as long as the music plays, drink and be merry. I have a wife to see to."

Cheers erupted in the ballroom. Dominique chuckled as he carried his irritated wife up the stairs.

"I cannot believe you did that!"

He looked down. With her cheeks flushed and lips in a firm line, Isabelle looked more likely to hit him than make love to him.

He sighed. Perhaps it was better this way. Better that she remained agitated while he spoke to her about his past, for if she was more amiable he may not get the words out. And he desperately needed to, for their marriage, and their future, truly depended on it.

CHAPTER TWENTY-NINE

There comes a time in a man's life when he has to question his own motives. Are they selfish? Purely self-seeking in their desire to gain without giving back? To take without asking questions? And to covet without any care for the person's feelings? I feel I have done this very thing. I have taken what was not mine hoping to keep it for myself, and as I watch my life unfold and experience what it truly is to love someone, I find that the only option is to let it go.

~The Diary of Dominique Maksylov

DOMINIQUE OPENED THE DOOR to his bedroom and placed Isabelle lightly onto her feet before walking over to the fire and sighing.

Not sure what was bothering him after such a night, Isabelle immediately felt ill at ease. Was this when the beast was to return? Was he going to reject her as she suspected he might? And why was it, after such a wonderful night, that she still felt fear every time he was quiet? Why was she holding her breath? Hands shaking, she smoothed out her dress and waited. Silence enveloped the room for minutes before

Dominique shifted on his feet and sighed.

He was facing the fire, his ungloved hands stretched out in front of the flames.

"Did you have a good time?" he asked, his voice raspy. He did not turn around but continued to stare into the fire; his hands did not move.

"Yes, quite. Thank you." Isabelle slowly approached him, curious as to what he was accomplishing. After such an eventful night, he should be resting, not attempting to burn his hands by standing so close to the orange flames. And surely not allowing himself to feel depressed over such a successful evening.

"I shouldn't feel anything," Dominique whispered. "For days I cried out for my mother. She was dead, but it didn't stop me from weeping her name."

Isabelle reached where he stood, her eyes falling on the pinkish white scars on his hands.

"He killed her." Dominique stated it so matter of factly that Isabelle had to shake her head to make sure she heard him right.

"Your father?" she asked in disbelief.

"Yes." Dominique walked over to his chair and took a seat. He poured himself a brandy and then poured another for her. Isabelle put up her hand—she was never one for strong spirits. "Believe me." Dominique took a large swallow. "You will need this by the time I am done."

Hands shaking, she reached for the amber-filled glass and took a seat opposite him, waiting for the dark tale to commence.

"I heard a commotion, and then the most haunting music of my life began to play in my mind. I thought I was either going mad, or I was finally dying. I had always been such a paranoid little boy. At any rate, it brought me down to the practice room. It wasn't at all odd for me to play into the early morning. It seemed to be the only time I could clear my mind." Dominique closed his eyes. "I found her." His voice was haunting as if he was reliving the moment again.

"Your mother?" Isabelle whispered.

"Yes, she had been shot in the head by my father. She was lying with her eyes open in a pool of her own blood. And my teacher, the one who had taught me how to use my gift, was dead on top of her. Both of their eyes were open as if their souls were screaming for vengeance for me to right the wrong that had been done them, but all I could do was stand there, in absolute horror." Voice raspy and thick with emotion, he cursed and took another swallow of brandy.

"And your father?" Isabelle found it hard to speak, for her voice felt shaky. She took a long sip of the brandy and barely kept herself from choking.

Dominique was silent for a few minutes, his eyes closed. "He laughed."

Isabelle felt her eyes pool with tears. Flames danced on the walls of the room, they cast shadows and light across Dominique's features. Such a beautiful man, so much talent and promise, utterly ruined as a boy. How could even the best of men come out of a similar situation without bearing scars?

Dominique smiled cynically and poured another glass of spirits. "He forced me to play one last song. It was as if I was playing the piano for my mother, only it was her funeral, not a birthday or a party or even a celebration. I still hear the song; it still haunts me. It has become a habit to write out the notes so I can sleep at night, but I burn what I write as if burning the memory of that night will purge it from me.

"I had no idea the depths of my father's own perversion. The pain was excruciating when he poured hot wax across my hands. I believe he meant to take away my gift, but hot wax does nothing more than burn you, it does not keep you from playing the same instrument he despised so much."

Feeling ill, Isabelle leaned forward; the smell of death seemed to permeate their room.

But Dominique continued, his voice hollow. "In the end, he threw my music into the fire, told me to follow it there. I was a silly child. I did not want to see my music, the music I had written for my mother, burn. So like a fool I reached into the flames to retrieve it."

"No more!" Isabelle sobbed into her hands. "Please." Her shoulders shook of their own accord as her sobs echoed in the silent room.

"I must, Isabelle. You must know." Dominique's hand was on her shoulder and then her neck. He had moved closer to her and was now kneeling in front of her, holding her hands within his own. His voice trembled as he continued. "He held my hands there until I passed out. I have no idea how long they were in the flames, all I know is Cuppins found me hours later. The trauma was enough for them to worry for my life. My father, who bore scars of his own, was never the same after that night."

Isabelle stopped crying and removed her hands from her eyes to gaze upon her husband. "Cuppins told me the rest, about how your father tried to kill you."

Dominique's eyes darkened. "Yes, though you should know it was I who achieved murder that night. Though accidental, there hasn't been a day that goes by that I don't wish I could kill him again, and do it without the immaturity that a boy possesses, make him suffer, make him suffer as I suffered, as my mother suffered being married to him…And now you know my darkness, what makes me so repulsive. For what man wakes up wishing to kill a man who is already dead?"

Isabelle sighed and reached her hand to his beautiful face. "A man who has been very wronged, Dominique."

"I have never spoken of it aloud." He cursed. "I am a

monster," he said underneath his breath. "I turned into what I hated, by focusing my hate so fully on the one man who destroyed my happiness, I succeeded in ruining my own."

Isabelle was silent for a moment. "You were but a boy, perhaps the hatred that you held is what sustained you, helped you get better. But with that hatred comes the responsibility to feed it, which you did quite well. I believe now—now you need to let it go." She held her breath, unsure if he would lash out at her, or simply never speak to her again or trust her with his innermost thoughts and demons.

"I did." Dominique sighed. "Let it go, that is, the moment I felt the beat of your heart against my hand. The steady rhythm pulled me back from the shadows when all I wanted to do was follow him into the depths of Hell."

Unable to speak lest she begin to sob all over again, Isabelle held his head between her hands and rained kisses on his eyelids, his cheeks, his forehead.

"Thank you for trusting me with this." Isabelle leaned forward and brushed a kiss across his lips. "Can you feel this?" She brought his scarred hands to her mouth and kissed across the pinkish white ridges.

With a deep breath, Dominique closed his eyes and sighed. "It feels wonderful. I should have lost sensation, and a whole lot more. Instead, it seems my senses are heightened on my hands." He laughed. "It was an actual blessing, if you can call it that, for I feel the keys of the piano much better now. It was why I kept playing. My final vengeance against my father, that even in all his hatred he did not keep me from being what my mother wanted most."

"And what was that?" Isabelle dipped her hands into his silky hair.

"To be a famous composer, a prodigy, something more than just heir to the royal line of princes."

"You are much more than that, my love." Isabelle smiled

at her husband, bestowing all the love in the world with one single glance, or at least she hoped so. "You are, brave, extraordinary, gifted, and I l—"

Why couldn't she say the words? He had given everything. Been vulnerable beyond all reason but the words stuck in her throat, the simple truth, which should be so easy, was now the most difficult feat imaginable.

"Shh." Dominique pressed his finger to her lips. "I'm going to undress you. I'm going to kiss you, make love to you, make you forget the nightmares I just told you…and if you say no, I may not possess the strength to listen."

Who could say no to such a good argument? Especially when his muscled body was so near hers that she could feel the heat radiating from him.

"Yes. Oh please, yes," she whispered as he jerked her against himself and pulled at her hair; pins fell at rapid speed to the ground as his hands massaged her scalp and freed her hair of its confinement.

Each of his fingers delicately dug into her head sending shuddering sensations all the way down her body. His hands pulled through her hair allowing the tresses to lay against her shoulders and arms, tickling the sensitive flesh that had suddenly become enflamed by his very presence. Dominique exhaled, his breath a hot sultry mix of brandy and desire. Eyes aflame, he moved his hands to her shoulders slowly turning her toward the fireplace. Her eyes closed, it was just as before on the ship as he nipped her neck with his teeth, only this time she wasn't afraid, just anxious to feel his heat against hers, pleading in her mind for him to touch her. Body aching, she would have fallen to the ground had he not roughly pulled her backside against him. His desire was obvious as he licked her earlobe, and the very tender spot on her neck just where her pulse roared.

Throwing her head back against his shoulder, she

shuddered as his hands, scars and all, grazed her arms. As if he was studying every exposed part of flesh. Endeavoring to engrain and memorize the feel of her body, the taste of her skin on his tongue. Her every response should have been mortifying, instead she felt empowered as he groaned in her ear and aggressively grabbed her hips, most likely imprinting his hands onto her person.

"You're so soft," his voice was raspy, almost impossible to hear as he whispered little bits of adoration in her ear. It was music, whispered music, and for the first time in her life she understood the power of words, when said by the very person you love, they can destroy you or set you free. "You are so smooth." His body shuddered behind hers as he held her firmly against himself, all the while continuing to kiss wherever he desired. She was, in a word, his prisoner.

Not that she cared.

He was going to die.

But oh, if death was this sweet, he would welcome it with arms open, smiling like the devil's own fool.

His mind tried to catch up with every sensation he was feeling, every touch, every gasp for breath, the erratic beating of her heart. Oh, how he loved her heart and how it brought him back from the darkness.

Being a besotted fool had never been high on his list of priorities; to be quite honest, it hadn't even been on a list. But now? Dear merciful heaven, he was drowning in it, lost in her, with no hope of being rescued.

So this was what it feels like to fall?

The exhilaration of the freefall was not terrifying as he had expected and always dreaded. No, in falling, he finally had freedom. Cynics would have liked him to believe that when he let go, he would lose his true self, but it was only when he finally allowed his heart to fall, that he found himself.

In a word, Dominique Maksylov had just been found.

Her heat scorched his body. With a gentle caress she shuddered, a quick nip on her neck and she moaned. Never had he fought so hard to keep himself in control.

And that was when he realized.

Control had been the very definition of his life.

And it was time to let his old life go.

With a smile that probably scared the blazes out of Isabelle, he turned her to face him. Her eyes were glowing, her skin so creamy, like satin. "I'm yours." His voice trembled as he watched the smile broaden across her face.

"Yours." He kissed one hand, then the other.

Lost in her gaze, he quickly, nimbly, removed all of his clothes standing before her once and for all, fully exposed within the light of the room, facing the very thing he feared the most in the entire world. Losing his heart, his very soul, to someone who had the power to destroy him.

With a coy bat of her lashes, she slowly, achingly, removed the top of her dress then turned. Devil take it, he was actually perspiring! No longer hindered by his gloves, for he had already decided to relish the feel of his bare hands on her skin forever, he quickly removed her dress and dropped it to the floor where it pooled by her feet.

Isabelle stepped out, and that was all it took. One look, one blasted look from the minx and with a savage growl he threw her onto the bed.

This lovemaking was not slow, it was not sweet as it should have been, nor did he spend any extra time preparing her. It was possession; it was lust; it was primal. His teeth pulled at her lower lip as his body covered hers. Her hands scratched across his back as he plundered her mouth. Breaths mingled as they gasped, both searching and eager to be closer to one another.

Passion-induced haze filled his line of vision until all he saw was her body, her soft curves, delectable smile, everything fit perfectly, and it was all his. Their gazes locked, in a paused embrace as he made love to her, his wife. For beauty had in fact, tamed the savage beast. Finally.

CHAPTER THIRTY

What have I done…?
~The Diary of Dominique Maksylov

DOMINIQUE LOOKED AT THE correspondence once again. Surely, it had to be wrong. How many weeks had it been since he had written the letter? In hindsight, he had been so concerned for Isabelle that day that he had forgotten that the letter was sent to the duke.

And now, the script mocked him, the letter itself sealing his wife's fate. He was coming for her. The letter said they would arrive as soon as possible. They, meaning the duke and his wife, along with Isabelle's sister who had been miraculously found a few days ago only a few miles away from Dominique's own estate.

It seemed one of England's own spies was to thank for the feat, though the only spy in the area Dominique knew of was Hunter. And he had a hard time believing Hunter would rescue a beautiful damsel in distress and not boast about it.

The letter was burning a hole in his hand, but when he set

it on the desk, his eyes wouldn't pull away. How was he to handle this? Was he to admit to Isabelle that he had stupidly written the duke to come fetch her?

Was it silly of him to want her to stay on her own accord because she loved him and would do anything for him? *Would she stay?* he wondered, when faced with returning to her old life, to her family that she loved more than life itself? How was it that even though she told him where her loyalty was, that he still doubted her affection? Was he truly that insecure?

With a growl he pushed the objects on his desk to the floor. A feat he hadn't done in weeks, ever since the night of the ball when he had spent the dark hours and early morning making love to Isabelle.

Magic.

And now it seemed the magic was crumbling.

He could only hope and pray that when the day came she would not see betrayal on his face, but that of selfless love, for he would never keep her from her true heart's desires. And though he loved her with every part of himself, she had yet to give him the words he so wanted to hear.

The thought struck a chord within him, for if he didn't own her heart, he had to wonder who did?

Isabelle went in search of Dominique. Usually he spent the morning hours in his study replying to invitations and looking over estate matters.

She whistled on her way to his study, enjoying the smell of the castle, the feel of home it brought to her. Once she reached the large mahogany doors, she pushed them open, for he was a changed man and didn't care that she barged in. Frankly, it seemed to delight him all the more.

Just yesterday he had laid her across his desk and kissed

her senseless until the maid came with their morning tea.

She flushed with the memory as she entered the room, fully expecting to see him behind the large desk.

Empty.

But the fire was roaring and steam made a wispy design in the air from the freshly poured cup.

Strange? Had there been an emergency? And then she noticed the floor was littered with all types of papers from his desk. Something surely must be wrong for him to be this agitated. She hadn't seen one of his dark moods in weeks. It still caused a shiver to run down her spine, but she trusted in the man he had become, in the promise he had made her to control his temper.

Kneeling in front of the scattered pieces of paper, she started to sort through them in order to return them to his desk.

Within minutes she had the papers cleaned up and returned to rights. She moved by the desk and her skirt caught the edge of one of the stacks. Muttering a curse she knelt down to pick up the few pieces that had fluttered off.

"The Duke of Montmouth?" she said aloud. What the devil would he want from Dominique?

Curiosity piqued, she picked up the letter and read it.

To his Royal Highness, Dominique Maksylov, Royal Prince of Russia, Earl of Hariss,

I have received your letter and will come at once. My wife and I are grateful for your kindness in the matter.

Please be advised that we will take Isabelle off your hands, as you so gently put it, and restore her into the bosom of Society. Her sister, Gwendolyn, has also been located and is awaiting us near your estate. She was found by one of England's own spies. Apparently trying to locate Isabelle, believing her to be in grave danger.

In such a difficult year, you have given us reason to hope that our family will once more be united.

Many thanks,

His Grace, Stefan Hudson, Duke of Montmouth

Isabelle dropped the paper as if it had burned her fingers. Take her off his hands? Like some... some common mistress!

The note would have had to be sent weeks ago, but that changed nothing! He still wanted to be rid of her! He still wrote it, and the pain was more than she could bear. Had everything been a lie to him? The vulnerability too much? And to think, today was the day she was going to tell him she loved him, couldn't live without him, and he wanted to be rid of her? The monster! The absolute beast!

The—

"My lady?" A knock came at the door.

Isabelle dropped the paper onto the desk and turned around.

"Some guests have arrived, they asked to speak with you." Brink's face was grave.

"Why not my husband?" she spat.

"I was unable to locate him, my lady."

Isabelle's chest clenched. So this is why he was angry then? Why he threw the contents of his desk to the ground. He was angry that she was still here, not gone as he wished? The pain was unbearable, like a knife slicing her in two.

Numbly, she walked to the door. "Please show them into the East Salon, I will be there momentarily."

"As you wish." Brinkss gave a curt bow and walked out of the room.

Isabelle took three deep breaths. She could do this—she could be the perfect hostess to her guests, whoever they were. Drat! Her hands were shaking!

The pain of his rejection, his betrayal made her knees weak. Ill, she barely made it in time to the potted plant before throwing up the contents of her stomach.

Perhaps now would not be the best time to tell her husband that his worst nightmare had come true. For she was carrying his heir. She had decided to hide it from him in hopes that he would learn to accept the truth, that he would never be the man his father was, he would be the best father, always laughing and joyful.

But now, now she wanted to throw the information in his face, to hurt him as he hurt her.

Gathering courage, she left the room and made the few short steps to the salon. Upon opening the doors, however, she felt her world begin to tilt, for sitting near the fire were her sisters, Rosalind and Gwendolyn, and Montmouth. The last thing she remembered seeing was the concern in Rosalind's eyes as her knees gave way and her eyes succumbed to the blackness.

CHAPTER THIRTY-ONE

Can a wrong be righted? Will truth truly set you free? Or will lies and mistakes threaten to overtake the happiness you once saw within your reach? I wonder this and so much more. Is it only when you've loved everything that you truly understand what it means to love? For I have nothing left, yet my heart still beats for her. It will beat always for her.

~The Diary of Dominique Maksylov

THE WALK AROUND THE castle hadn't done Dominique any good, he was just as agitated if not more by the time he returned to the front of the castle. Matters worsened when he noted the carriages out front and the blazing crest on every one of them.

Montmouth.

Dominique truly didn't have God on his side, for the one thing he wished would not happen had come true. Now, Isabelle would know, and she would hate him, for who would she believe? The beast he once was? Or the man he had become?

Muttering an oath, he took the steps two at a time and entered into the house, only to find Hunter pacing outside the salon as if someone had died.

"What the devil are you doing?" Dominique all but yelled.

Hunter did not still, nor did he respond, merely cursed and closed his eyes.

Dominique took that as an invitation to shake him.

Which he did.

Hunter just cursed again.

"Get a hold of yourself!" Dominique jerked his friend away from the door. "Now tell me what is going on?"

"If you don't mind," Hunter seethed, "I'd like to continue my pacing, it makes me feel deuced better about the fact that the chit I rescued is on the other side of that door and my cover could be completely blown at any second!"

Realization dawned. Despite his foul mood Dominique laughed. "The chit you are referring to, would it be Gwen? Isabelle sister?"

Hunter paled.

"You little liar." Dominique crossed his arms. "So when I was in bed from a gunshot wound and you flew into the room with stories of being accosted by a woman who smelled of eggs and meat—"

Hunter slapped his hand across Dominique's mouth. "Do not remind me of that particular woman. This is not she, believe me." His eyes took on a lusty haze. "This is not she," he all but whispered. "I discovered her on my way back through the village, to take care of your sorry a—" He stopped himself and shuddered. "At any rate, she was alone, can you believe it? An English miss alone in the countryside asking questions!"

"Yes well," Dominique removed Hunter's hand. "I do believe women tend to do that when they are lost and searching for answers."

"She was gaining too much attention," Hunter muttered. "So I rescued her."

"Did she see it as a rescue or a capture?" Dominique asked, intrigued.

"I saved her life!"

Truly, Dominique had to fight to keep his expression indifferent. "Are they erecting a statue in your honor? Or perhaps giving you some sort of medal?"

"She doesn't know who I am, only that I work for the crown." Hunter ignored Dominique's teasing barbs. "And she cannot tell her family of my help in the matter."

"Why ever not? I believe they would be thankful! Joyous! That is unless you took advantage of a single woman, all alone in the woods, with nothing but the dress on her back and—" Dominique stopped talking as Hunter lost color in his face. Quite a feat considering he looked like a ghost already.

"Do not speak of it."

Dominique blanched. "Did you compromise her?"

"I did it for God and Country?" Hunter said it as more of a question as he broke his gaze away and stared at the floor.

"Yes well, be sure to say that when the duke murders your sorry excuse for an a—"

The doors opened swiftly, interrupting Dominique's speech.

Montmouth stood, arms crossed, looking every inch the formidable foe Dominique had remembered him being. He suddenly had a distasteful vision of the man ripping his limbs off, laughing all the while Isabelle watched.

Well, he would always have those few weeks of happy memories before he met his demise. *And here we go.*

"Montmouth, didn't expect to see you here," he rasped, casting a quick nervous glance at Isabelle.

Anger rolled off her. Face pale and hands on hips, she

sent him a murderous glare.

Dominique cringed. She knew.

"Did you not send for me?" Montmouth asked, clearly agitated as he paced in front of him.

"I did, but that was over a month ago, before the *accident*." He hoped that his emphasis on the word clued Isabelle in. He dared not look at her, lest he break down in front of a room of strangers. The infamous beast, felt like a broken man, a wounded puppy, and once again full of fear.

"Yes well, you can imagine it took a while for word to reach us, though it just so happened that Gwen nearly beat us here, imagine that."

Hunter spoke up, "Yes imagine it."

The raven-haired beauty glared at Hunter but said nothing. Nor did her body language give away any sort of previous meeting.

Family reunions. Truly glorious, something to look forward to in the future, no doubt.

Dominique cleared his throat. "I will have rooms readied for you at once, your grace." He nodded to Brinks who was standing outside the room watching the exchange with an amused grin on his face.

He cleared his throat for the second time, and Brinks disappeared around the corner.

"Now," Dominique addressed the Duke. "I trust one of England's greatest spies has yet again helped us retrieve your sister-in-law?"

Montmouth nodded. "Yes, it seems Gwen sold as many of her possessions as she could in order to go searching for her lost sister. She imagined the great beast of Russia was set on killing her."

"Lovely bedtime story, do be sure to tell me that one someday, Dominique," Hunter interjected with amusement.

Montmouth glared. "At any rate, the man who rescued

her, though I use the term loosely considering her disheveled state, hasn't been seen since, nor do I know his identity. However, I'm not sure I wish to thank him. Murdering him sounds more likely, since Gwen has yet to explain where she obtained the marks on her neck and arms."

Hunter chose that opportune moment to have a fit of coughing. He bent over and grabbed at Dominique's coat.

With a resigned sigh, Dominique pushed his friend away and once again faced the duke. "Your grace, as you can see Isabelle is quite alive and healthy."

"I cannot see that," Montmouth clipped. "Perhaps you need to look closer, for my sister-in-law looks ready to burst into tears at any moment, and since you are the only one I can imagine who caused such pain, you will forgive me for not being more polite or well-mannered. I have half a mind to shoot you for buying her. What's worse is you brought her into a heavily French-occupied area!"

Domnique didn't think it would be wise to point out that the duke had done the same with his own wife.

"My mother-in-law is in Bedlam, and it seems Isabelle has traded one nightmare for another. Do you deny it?"

He couldn't. Dominique wanted to deny it, to fight, to explain the whole story, but the truth of the matter was, Isabelle had put up with the worst of nightmares, and he was to blame.

"I do not deny it."

"At least you have *some* honor."

Hunter took a step forward, but Dominique stopped him with his hand.

"Now," Montmouth spat. "We will stay as long as it takes to gather what belongings Isabelle has here, and we will be returning to London with her. Do I make myself clear?"

The man seemed ruthless. Especially standing up to one with Dominique's reputation. With an amused chuckle and most likely an insane wish to be shot, Dominique said, "No, you do not make yourself clear. Perhaps you should speak louder."

Montmouth's face turned red with rage, he reached into his jacket pocket. But Dominique was quicker. With little effort he rendered the giant harmless by cracking his wrist. The pistol dropped to the floor, and he kicked it to Hunter who immediately made quick work of unloading it of its contents.

"Now, you have barged into my home, put your wife and her two sisters in danger, as well as the life of my unborn child…" He knew it was possible, though quite unlikely that Isabelle carried his heir, but he hoped Montmouth didn't see the fib, nor the trembling of Dominique's own voice at the thought. "All based on a letter that should have never been sent to you in the first place." Dominique used all his strength to push Montmouth down into a nearby chair and loomed over him. "Now, allow me to take myself clear. I love Isabelle. I have been to Hell and back in order to have her, and will not let some self-righteous duke trounce into my home and demand that the only woman I have ever loved return with him. You will have to kill me to get to her, and if her choice is to go with you, I beg you to kill me anyway, for I cannot imagine taking a breath without her by my side."

The room fell silent.

Montmouth's breathing slowed and then a grin broke out on his face. "Good work, man! I knew you had it in you! See, Isabelle, I told you it was a misunderstanding. Women, you can't truly believe a word that comes out of their mouths." Rosalind slapped him playfully on the arm.

Hunter swore a string of expletives and kicked the wall with his boot.

Exhausted and in utter shock, Dominique merely stared at the duke, slack jawed.

"Come now!" Montmouth rose to his feet and pulled him

into a tight embrace. "It seems we have a wedding to celebrate!"

Dumbstruck, it took a few seconds for what had just transpired and when it hit him, he was ready to pummel the man. "You smug son of a—"

"Easy…" Montmouth paused and looked Dominique straight in the eyes. "I know when a man is tortured, the haunting look in his eyes when he thinks he's lost what's most important to him. It was like looking in a mirror." Montmouth shook his head. "Now, let us adjourn elsewhere so the ladies can catch up. It seems they've all had adventures to last a lifetime."

Dominique nodded slowly and turned to look at Isabelle, tears were streaming down her face. She gave him a weak smile and nodded. He took that as a good sign, the only sign she could give him amidst the chatter.

Hunter led the way, a scowl on his face. Montmouth turned to Dominique. "Speaking of a man haunted, what the devil is wrong with your friend? It looks as if he's seen a ghost."

"Not a ghost…a memory." Dominique left it at that and went into the study where he kept his best whiskey. There would be time enough to talk to Isabelle after dinner. And he would make certain she knew where his loyalty lay.

CHAPTER THIRTY-TWO

I refuse to be him, therefore I won't be. I make a choice to be better, stronger, more loving. To be a true father.

~The Diary of Dominique Maksylov

ONCE SHE HAD AWOKEN from fainting, Stefan had demanded she tell him what was wrong. Was she held here by her own free will? Had she been harmed? Where was her husband? Truly it had all been too much.

She lost all control.

And in true feminine fashion, burst into tears. Never before had she been such a watering pot. She told them everything. Nothing was sacred, well, except for the stolen moments with Dominique.

To his credit, Stefan listened intently while Rosalind patted her hand and Gwendolyn held her in her arms whispering into her hair.

She loved him, and she told them as much, but also explained that she had just discovered an incriminating letter.

Heartbroken, she continued to sob, until with a laugh

Stefan jumped to his feet. "Well, this is perfect!"

Rosalind glared.

Gwen gasped.

And Isabelle whimpered.

"Hear me out!" Stefan clapped his hands. "All men need is a little push, and it seems the earl is at the brink of insanity!"

"Please explain yourself, husband, before you find yourself sleeping in the stables." Rosalind seethed.

Stefan ignored her angry comment and continued, "I'll threaten to take the thing he values most in life."

"His music?" Isabelle offered.

Stefan knelt in front of her, "No, my dear. The other half of his soul. You."

Well, Isabelle hadn't known what to say then, not that it mattered because as soon as the words left Stefan's mouth, low voices were heard outside the doors to the salon.

Stefan marched right over to the doors and threw them open revealing a pale-looking Hunter and irritated Dominique.

She was unable to meet his gaze, ashamed for believing the worst of him, but most of all, still doubtful of his affection. Isabelle was so used to his rejection, to his excuses, his justifications that no matter how much attention he paid her these past few weeks, she still feared the worst.

Dominique began his speech, defending himself. She didn't want to listen, wanted to stay in her miserable state. That is, until she heard him say that he sent the letter before the accident.

Before he was bed-ridden.

Before he reached for her.

And before he promised to hold and keep her heart forever.

She meant to put a stop to all the nonsense. Stefan truly should have made a go of it with the theater. He was yelling and threatening as if he was truly intent on causing physical harm, and just when she thought Dominique would hang his head and allow her to go with them, he rallied.

And in that moment, stole her heart all over again.

He loved her.

She smiled at the memory and touched her hand to her chest, surely she was dreaming! She hadn't realized she had an audience until she looked up at both her sisters. Each of them had their heads tilted, merriment twinkling in her eyes.

Isabelle cleared her throat. Drat, they looked at her again, and again she gave back a blank stare. Had they asked her a question?

"My, my, it is worse than I expected," Gwen mused. "Our dear sister has fallen so hard she has forgotten her own name."

"That isn't true." Isabelle cheeks heated.

"Sure it is." Gwen winked. "I've been repeating your name trying to gain your attention for the past five minutes. And all I received was a sigh."

"Don't forget the fluttering of her eyelashes, too," Rosalind interjected helpfully.

Isabelle glared. "I assure you, I remember my name, I was merely…" Drat, why couldn't she think of a better excuse than daydreaming about her husband's hands on her body?

"Lusting."

"Sinning." Gwen coughed.

Isabelle narrowed her eyes at her two sisters and promptly changed the subject. "So, how is mother?"

Apparently that was the one thing that would cause both of her sisters to lose their merriment immediately. Rosalind was the first to answer. "Quite mad. Tried to kill me. It was all very exciting, but that's another story, dear. All that matters is Stefan and I are enormously happy, and so thankful to have found both of you again."

"And Gwen, why ever would you run after me alone!"

"Adventure?" she offered.

"Go to the park to find your adventure. Read a book. You do not go gallivanting around Belgium while we are at war!" Isabelle grabbed her sister's hand and kissed it. "What if something would have happened to you?"

Her sister looked up, her clear blue eyes boring through Isabelle. "And who's to say something didn't?"

"Gwen…" Isabelle said in warning.

A blank stare washed over Gwen's face; she shrugged and gave a tight smile. "I assure you, I am just fine!"

But Isabelle knew her sister better than she knew herself. Something was amiss, but Gwen was never one to offer information freely. Isabelle would just have to bide her time until her sister was ready to talk about whatever transpired over the past few months.

A few months? Had it only been that long? Truthfully, Isabelle felt as if she had been in this castle for years! So much had happened, and so much more was in store. She closed her eyes and placed a hand over her stomach. Truthfully, it hadn't been a white lie on Dominique's part when he was confronted by Montmouth. It was, in fact, the truth. She closed her eyes and took a deep breath. Tonight. She would tell him tonight.

CHAPTER THIRTY-THREE

Can a man be more than he was born to be? Or will he be constantly haunted by the past? By what he was born into? Are we simply copies of those who bore us? Or can we live past that, can we exceed expectations. Can I exceed the consequences of my birth?

~The Diary of Dominique Maksylov

DOMINIQUE SLOWLY TRUDGED UP the stairs to his rooms. Dinner had been quite the fiasco, what with all three women chattering at once. It was impossible to get a word in edgewise. Stefan, which was how he was now to address the duke, simply watched and drank his wine in large gulps, clearly using the alcohol as a way to numb the pounding in his ears at the volume of talking around the table.

Hunter, however, crossed his arms and scowled the entire time, as if the wine was too sour, the food cold, and the company lacking. Never before had he seen his friend in such a foul mood, and that included the time Dominique set his coat tails on fire.

He smiled at the memory.

Whatever the issue, Hunter would never come out and say it. No, Dominique needed to bide his time until his friend was ready to discuss what was plaguing him. And Dominique had a sneaking suspicion that it had everything to do with the raven-haired beauty who sent equally murderous glares toward Hunter the entire meal.

Life had certainly taken a drastic change over the past twenty-four hours, and he was eternally grateful that he still had a wife to hold tonight, or in his case, make love to until the wee hours of the morning.

He knocked quietly, alerting her of his presence, and swiftly let himself in the bedroom.

Isabelle stood facing the fire, her brown hair trickling down her back like a blanket of dark honey. He wanted her so badly it hurt.

Slowly, he joined her and put an arm around her shoulders, pulling her into the warmth of his body.

"I'm sorry," he said.

Isabelle said nothing.

"I should have told you that I wrote the letter, but after I was ill, I had forgotten doing so and then when I heard back, I panicked. I should have gone straight to you, explained to you that I would die before letting you go." He took a deep breath, his heart pounding in his chest, surely she could hear it. "I love you."

For a moment, she said nothing. Then finally Isabelle whispered, "Say it again."

"I love you, I love you, I love you." He ran his fingers through her hair; a shiver of delight slammed into his chest as she turned and kissed him hard across the mouth.

"Oh, Isabelle." His hands reached around to grab her waist, thrusting her against himself as his tongue plummeted into her mouth, searching, grasping, tirelessly winding with hers.

"Stop." Flushed, Isabelle pulled away. "Before we..." She motioned to the bed, little did she know that the activity he had in mind was much more adventurous.

"Before I strip you naked, you mean? Before I kiss every part of your body that's exposed and parts that are hidden. Before I gaze upon your feminine beauty, the lush curves of your hips, the way your skin feels against my palm. Before I possess you with every ounce of my—"

Laughing and blushing profusely, Isabelle placed a hand over his mouth. "Yes, before a-all that. I have something exciting to tell you."

Taking a seat, he pulled Isabelle into his lap and played with her hair as she seemed to be struggling for words. Whatever it was, it was important.

"I have reason to believe..."

Devil take him, she was gorgeous. Brown wavy hair taunted and teased him until he wanted nothing more than to plunge his hands into its endless length.

"...I am carrying your heir."

"Pardon?" His stomach lurched, his heart nearly stopped beating.

"I think I'm increasing. I missed my last courses and it seems that—"

"Stop." Dominique pulled his hands back from her hair. It was as if she had poured cold water over him., He gently pulled her off of his lap and rose to his feet. So many emotions were swirling within him that he could not, dare not, say a thing lest he ruin something that by all accounts should be good news.

"A-are you upset?" Isabelle's voice was weak. He closed his eyes and prayed for patience, for strength, and turned around.

Large blue eyes gazed back at him, vulnerability rolling off of her, but also protectiveness, a fierceness that he'd never seen her possess. A mama in the making, no doubt.

"I do not know what to say." Dominique looked down at the floor. "I need some time, I need… I need to think." With that, he left the room, not stopping once. Not even when he heard his wife break down into sobs, or the painful whisper of his name on her lips as glass hit the floor.

Pregnant? How was it possible! He paced the damaged practice room like a caged animal. What the devil was he to do?

He cursed aloud in every language he knew, which was quite a lot of cursing to be honest. He only stopped when his voice was hoarse from shouting.

"Impressive, tell me, do you know Finnish?" a male voice asked.

"Stefan, this is none of your concern."

"Oh, when a man shouts in that many languages you can believe it is my concern. My poor ears will never be the same. I also have it on good authority that your wife is ruining what would have been a nice sensual moment with my own wife upstairs in our bedroom. In short, I have been ousted." He cursed, though not as loud or fluently as Dominique had.

"So yes, when a man gets kicked out of his own room, it's his concern. Now, what the devil did you do this time?"

"She's carrying my child." There, he'd said it.

"Ah, congratulations are in order then."

"I don't know how it happened... I don't..." Dominique ran his fingers through his hair, cursing again.

"Blast. Didn't think I'd have to give a biology lesson. All right…" Stefan took a seat and propped his feet up on the sofa. "When a man and woman find each other attractive, or in some cases, available, they begin a mating ritual I like to call—"

"Please, no further. I don't imagine I'll ever recover if you explain to me your sordid view on sex."

"Yes well, there was once a time when an innkeeper felt

the need to have the talk with me. In a room full of patrons, no less. Imagine that, and you'll know just part of the traumatizing moments I've been exposed to."

A smile cracked through Dominique's tough exterior, though he made great pains to hide it from Stefan. "I know how it happened. I just…I took precautions so it wouldn't."

"Don't all young men?" Stefan said indifferently. "But, you are married, are you not? Why, with your own wife?"

"I cannot have children."

"Evidence proves otherwise—"

"I know," Dominique interrupted. "What evidence proves and such. I should word this differently. I am able to have children, I do not wish to bring any into the world, not into my world, not of my seed."

"Is your seed particularly bad? Does it not do the job?" Stefan asked.

Dominique poured whiskey into two cups and handed one to Stefan. "I cannot be my father."

Stefan threw back the contents and grimaced. "Of course you cannot, because you are not your father. Just because you are his son does not mean you must be his copy."

"What if…" Dominique could not even bring himself to say it.

Stefan leaned forward, hands folded. "Go on."

"What if I cannot help it?"

Stefan laughed.

Dominique wasn't sure if he should feel insulted or just stupid.

"Everyone has a choice. By saying you cannot help it, you are saying that you are choosing not to fight against it. I cannot help but have my hair color. I was born with it. But when it comes to actions and behavior, you can always help it, you can always choose to do good despite your upbringing."

Dominique wanted to believe him, truly wished that he

didn't feel so helpless and cynical about what Stefan was saying. "I wish I could believe that. But my past proves..."

"What? That of the weak line of men in your family? Did any of them possess backbone enough to go against their father? Did they have the strength you have? Did they even try?"

"No."

"Did you defy your father?"

Dominique gave a hollow laugh and shook his head. "At every turn. I even pushed him to his death."

"Yes, well…" Stefan reached for the whiskey, obviously in need of more to steel himself against this particular conversation. "I'm sure he deserved it."

Was it so terribly wrong to agree with him? To say out loud that his father was a monster? That he would do anything not to become him?

And then a thought occurred. So brilliant, so clear and truthful in his mind that he had no choice but to believe it. To test the theory by speaking it aloud.

"I will not be him."

"By Jove, I think you've got it," Stefan muttered. "Of course, you will not be him. It isn't possible to be the same person he was, because you were made differently. You have been given the same type of choices that every human being has been given. Yes, we cannot help who or what we are born to, but you can help how you respond to your environment."

"I can."

"Yes." Stefan moved away from the sofa and put a hand on Dominique's shoulder. "You truly can. Dominique, you're a good man. I've no doubt in my mind you can make Isabelle happy. But you must let it go, everything. Just like this room."

Stefan sighed and looked around. "Do you see the mess around you? It has been kept this way, as a trophy in honor of the violence of your upbringing. But, it is time, don't you think? To sweep the floors?"

"How do you even know of my pain? My past?"

Montmouth shrugged. "That Hunter fellow told me quite a lot. He thought I should at least know why you were so disagreeable."

Dominique smiled then looked around. A weight lifted from Dominique's shoulders as he looked down at the glass beneath his boots. The blood stains, just to the left of the piano, the tattered curtains and finally the dust particles amidst the furniture. Why had he left it this way? Truly, he had used it as a reminder of what he was capable of.

Everyone was capable of darkness, but why glorify it? Why preserve it as he had? Revenge was never truly his to bestow, and justification for his actions was merely another poor excuse to live in solitude, to keep himself protected.

Truthfully, he had lived as the most selfish of men. Keeping his heart safe from the world, his mind safe from the hauntings of his music, and in return a part of him had died.

Until her.

"I need to speak with her." Dominique hastily walked to the door.

"Wait," Stefan called out. "I may not have the best expertise with the fairer sex. After all, I do believe it took me at least twelve times before I got my proposal right, but perhaps you should wait until the morning. Allow her the comfort of her sisters, and speak to her when she has slept. Nothing good comes of two people discussing their feelings in the wee hours of the night."

"Hmm…" Dominique let out a laugh.

"You think my advice amusing?"

"No." Dominique turned and purposefully walked to the sofa where Stefan still stood. "I just cannot believe I went through an entire conversation being scolded by an Englishman without drawing my pistols."

Stefan smirked.

"You're right, you know, I should wait." Though he hated to do so, he saw wisdom in allowing Isabelle her rest. After all, if she was correct, then she needed to take care of their baby. At the thought his heart leapt with joy.

"And you're smiling like an idiot because…?" Stefan asked.

"I'm going to be a father."

Stefan hit him across the back. "A toast! To the best father my little nephew could have."

Scales fell from Dominique's eyes. The walls around his heart all but crumbled, and for the first time in fifteen years, he was able to celebrate in what he had always thought of as his mother's grave. Where life was taken, life was now restored.

So they raised their cups, drank of the fine whiskey and toasted, to life, to family, but most of all, to true love.

CHAPTER THIRTY-FOUR

When you have lost your way, when the world appears as if it is crumbling around you, perhaps, just maybe, you should close your eyes. By looking outward we forget the strength that is given inward. We can only see part of the picture with our eyes open. But, when they are closed, we see as a whole. We concentrate not on what we can see, but on the faith of what we know to be true.

~The Diary of Beauty and her ~~Beast~~ Prince

ISABELLE WASN'T ONE TO pout or cry, yet she sat in her room for the remainder of the night doing exactly that. Either she truly was increasing or she was mad. Eyes puffy and tired, she wanted nothing more than to throw a hairbrush at the mirror for reminding her why her heart felt like breaking all over again.

In all fairness, he hadn't rejected her. But, his behavior had been less than thrilled. All because she carried his heir, and yet, she couldn't find it in herself to be sorry or even guilty.

Instead she felt a fierce protectiveness, and a need to fight until she was the victor. So she sat in her chair as the sun rose over the horizon, and when the pink light began to shimmer into her room, she still did not move.

When the pink turned into a yellow, a knock came on her door. Again, she did not move, but waited as it opened a crack and then fully revealed her husband.

Would it be too much to ask for him to look at least partially as frightened as she was? His hair was perfect, his skin refreshed and rejuvenated as if he had the best night's sleep and was a different man.

And then, she saw it.

The light behind his eyes.

The glow in his skin.

The absolute joy in his smile as he slowly walked toward her.

But truly, she was never the patient type.

So, in true Isabelle fashion, she met him halfway, stumbling into his arms until he caught her and fell with her gently to the floor, both of them on their knees, embracing one another.

"I—" Dominique's voice trembled. Merciful heavens, she hardly recognized the man in front of her, it was as if he had been reborn.

His scarred hands tenderly caressed hers as he continued to struggle for words. His clear blue eyes shimmered with unshed tears.

He bit his lip and closed his eyes as if needing to regain his strength, and when he opened them, he stopped trying to talk.

But then again, Dominique was the type of man who didn't need words. Actions meant so much more to him.

Isabelle watched in unspeakable joy as his hands slowly dropped to her flat stomach. His head soon followed, and then his lips pressed against her belly as he whispered, "I love you."

Naturally, she thought he meant her, but his eyes, his focus, his artist's gaze was not on her, but the gift they had been given.

"I love you," he repeated again. "I hope you have your mother's heart."

"And your father's talent," Isabelle added, pressing a kiss against the top of his head as he held her.

"What if I'm wrong?" she said, suddenly frightened. After all, it was quite early.

Dominique slowly lifted them both to their feet. "Then we will just have to keep trying. In fact—" His eyes turned predatory. "To be sure, we should probably engage in some illicit activities now, don't you think? I for one, want to be certain that my child is growing within you."

Isabelle giggled. "And are you fearful that you were not doing a good job the first few times?"

"I wasn't," he said bluntly. "I was making love to you, but I wasn't possessing you. I wasn't drinking you in while simultaneously opening myself up. I wasn't giving you what you deserve, but with God as my witness, I'm going to do that now."

With a rip, her dress fell to the floor.

"Are you entirely sure you should mention God's name in the same sentence you are using to explain how you plan to ravish your wife?"

Dominique chuckled as his lips met hers with a hot blaze of fire. "I don't think he'll mind, love…"

His wicked hands cupped her bottom and thrust her across the bed as he lay out on top of her and plunged his hands into her bodice and continued ruining all the clothing she had so carefully put on earlier that morning when she had nothing more to do then carefully choose her dress and wait.

"No." Dominique growled when Isabelle grasped the

tattered clothing in her hands. "I'll buy you more. But for now, I'm going to lose myself in you. I'm going to ravish you. Lay claim to you, and most likely cause great scandal in this house."

"Scandal?" Oh heavens! How was she to concentrate when his hands were doing such wicked things?

"Yes." His hands moved higher, his kiss was deeper. And then he pulled back to look into her eyes. "For when you scream my name, over and over again—when you tell me how to please you, what feels good and what makes you go insane—it will be music to my ears. But I believe our guests may be utterly scandalized."

"To be fair…" Isabelle was near panting, she just didn't want him to stop. "They do know your reputation as a beast… so surely it won't come as a shock." His lips moved to her ear as he breathed into her neck and began nibbling on the sensitive part that drove her wild.

"So really," he whispered. "I have a reputation to live up to. Now, let us make music."

"Music?" Perhaps being married to a musician would be odd, but it would also be magical and… Isabelle never finished her thought. She was too busy screaming her husband's name.

EPILOGUE

"MY EARS ARE ACTUALLY bleeding," Hunter said dryly as he sat at the breakfast table wishing for the third time that morning that someone would have done him the favor of an early death. Anything so he wouldn't have to listen to Dominique's sexual prowess in the bedroom.

It wasn't doing anything for his appetite, and to be quite honest, it was deuced hard not to constantly think of enjoying the same blasted activity, what with *her* sitting across from him.

At yet another loud noise from the upstairs, Stefan cleared his throat. "Would someone please pass the sugar?"

Rosalind burst out laughing. "I believe it's been passed, and passed, and p—"

Stefan glared at his wife. "There are unmarried women at the table, cease from your vulgarity and—"

Rosalind stretched her arms above her head. "Do you know? I feel quite sleepy. I think I shall retire for an early morning nap."

"Yes." Stefan nodded seriously. "Wouldn't want you

getting fatigued. I'll just, er, join you then. After all, you look much too sleepy to climb those stairs on your own, wouldn't want you to take a tumble."

Tea spewed out of Hunter's mouth. "Apologies." He wasn't that sorry. After all, they did just say "tumble" and Stefan looked ready to ravish his wife on the table where Hunter was trying to break his fast. He needed to get away from this place before he challenged himself to a duel.

Stefan and Rosalind left in quite a hurry for being so tired.

Hunter yawned, because truly he was fatigued. His eyes honestly just happened to fall on Gwen.

"Don't even think about it." She glared.

"I have no idea what you mean." But he kind of did. Was it so wrong to want her writhing beneath him? After all, upon their first meeting they had—

"You know exactly what I mean," she all but yelled, interrupting his glorious memory of her pale skin. "Eat your food, and wipe that ridiculous grin off your face."

Never one to say no to a lady, Hunter did exactly as he was told, though he did pay special attention to the way he held his goblet in his hand, and how he closed his eyes in ecstasy when he took a bite of eggs.

Truthfully, he was having a devil of a time not jumping across the table. He couldn't remember a time when he'd felt this tempted.

Gwen cleared her throat. He looked up.

She dropped a piece of jam on her chest. Purposefully. Her eyes, innocent and wide, looked shocked. And then she grinned, took her ungloved hand and wiped the jam with her finger, slowly dipping it into her mouth. A moan escaped her lips as she closed her eyes.

Lust pounded through Hunter. With a jolt he stood up, with every intention on demanding she stop teasing him, though to be fair, he had deserved it.

But she beat him to the task, meeting him in the middle of the room. She sidestepped him and left.

Hunter swore and glared at her empty seat, as well as the jam that sat next to her plate.

He would never look at jam the same way again. Ever.

Dominique exhaled as Isabelle giggled beneath him. Their limbs were tangled.

"I believe we've scandalized the entire countryside." Isabelle sighed.

"To the devil with them all," Dominique growled. "I love you, my beauty."

"And I you," she answered.

They lay in silence for a few minutes before Isabelle asked, "What do you hear now?"

Dominique chuckled. "The most beautiful music I've ever heard in my existence."

"Can you sing it to me?"

Dominique kissed her cheek. "I'll do better. I'll show you."

They quickly dressed and tiptoed down to the music room.

Dominique walked to the piano, the instrument that had been a part of him his entire life, took a seat at the ivory keys, and began to play.

It was a slow melody at first that turned into a ferocious blend of the most beautiful song he had ever played. The music was no longer haunting but life-altering, so beautiful that he knew it had to be a representation of the completeness he felt.

When he was finished, he turned to his wife.

Apparently, all he was good for was making people cry when he played. A little defeated, he walked to her side and pulled her into his arms. "I'm sorry it made you sad." Could he do nothing right?

"I'm not sad." Isabelle sniffled. "I've just never heard anything so beautiful! What's it called?"

"Isabelle."

He didn't think it possible, but she cried harder.

He kissed her hair. "It is what I hear with every breath you take, every sigh that escapes your lips, every little moment I share with you."

"It's perfect."

He smiled. Yes. It was perfect.

ABOUT THE AUTHOR

Rachel Van Dyken is the *New York Times, Wall Street Journal,* and *USA Today* bestselling author of over 29 books. She is obsessed with all things Starbucks and makes her home in Idaho with her husband and two snoring boxers.

OTHER BOOKS BY RACHEL VAN DYKEN

The Bet Series

The Bet (Forever Romance)
The Wager (Forever Romance)
The Dare

Eagle Elite

Elite (Forever Romance)
Elect (Forever Romance)
Entice
Elicit

Seaside Series

Tear
Pull
Shatter
Forever
Fall
Strung

Wallflower Trilogy

Waltzing with the Wallflower
Beguiling Bridget
Taming Wilde

London Fairy Tales

Upon a Midnight Dream
Whispered Music
The Wolf's Pursuit

Renwick House

The Ugly Duckling Debutante
The Seduction of Sebastian St. James

The Redemption of Lord Rawlings
An Unlikely Alliance
The Devil Duke Takes a Bride

Ruin Series

Ruin
Toxic
Fearless
Shame (October 6, 2014)

Other Titles

The Parting Gift
Compromising Kessen
Savage Winter
Divine Uprising
Every Girl Does It

BLUE TULIP
PUBLISHING

41043844R00155

Made in the USA
Middletown, DE
02 March 2017